Being together is too dangerous... But they just can't stay apart...

There's almost nothing Alessandra Sinclair wouldn't do for Hudson Chase. He was her first love, and she's determined that he'll be her last. But when the terrible truth Hudson has been hiding comes to light, Allie finds herself caught in a deadly game of cat and mouse with a man from her past who's determined to use what he knows to ruin Hudson. Now, the only way to save the man she loves may be to lose him forever...

Hudson has always known that the secrets he keeps could be his downfall, but he never expected them to put Allie's life in danger as well. It's time for him to come clean--before everything he's ever wanted is destroyed...

"Walker and Rogers have raised the stakes in their Chasing Fire trilogy, and this conclusion may be the most thrilling of all."

~ RT Book Reviews **Magazine on RECLAIM ME**

D1522550

PRAISE FOR RECLAIM ME

"No one beats #HudsonChase when it comes to both the sweet and steam."

~Bookaholics Not So Anonymous

"Suggest that every romance reader out there get this series on their TBR list!"

~FMR Book Grind

"Sexy, captivating & thrilling conclusion to a trilogy that captured me from the start!"

~Dirty Girl Romance

"Absolutely spectacular ending to the Chasing Fire series...the perfect balance of mystery, intrigue and romance."

~The Book Enthusiast

"On my list of all time favorite series."

~Bookish Temptations

"WOW! This series is one I will definitely keep on my re-read list."

~Southern Yankee Book Reviews

RECLAIM ME

ANN MARIE WALKER
AMY K. ROGERS

After —
Happy Reading!
Ann Marie Walker

Reclaim Me

Trade Paperback ISBN: 978-1091035720

InterMix/Penguin eBook ISBN: 978-0-698-19478-6 (out of print)

Cover design by Simone Renou/In My Dreams Design

First Edition

A picture might be worth a thousand words,
but a shot of David Gandy is worth an entire novel.
Or three.

Thank you, David. You will always be our favorite distraction.

Happy goddamn New Year, Hudson thought as the slick, black Mercedes S65 took the corner at slingshot speed. With Max piloting the luxury rental, he was free to flip through page after page of the dossier his head of security had put together in less than an hour. The only thing he didn't have was Madame Bernadette Beauchene's medical records. Those would've probably taken Max the two hours he'd originally been given, and knowing her cholesterol level wasn't going to alter the current set of circumstances. Hudson wasn't even certain Beauchene was going to lead him anywhere besides a dead end, but it was the only thread he had, and damn straight he was going to yank on the son of a bitch.

Back at the train station he'd paced nearly the full length of the platform, checked his watch, turned on his heel and strode back, then checked his watch again. The more time that passed, the faster his heart had pounded, and when he'd realized Allie was going to be a no-show, he'd felt like his skin was being ripped off. He'd taken his cell phone out and dialed the George V to question the hotel staff on the whereabouts of their driver, then Max to hit the information highway. Based on the current intel, the only logical conclusion was that Allie had left him. What he didn't know was why. Now he was on full- blown autopilot with a single mission, and with every tick of the second hand he was losing ground.

Hudson swallowed his impatience, then tossed yet another press photo onto the leather seat. By all accounts the woman Allie had referred to as one of her mother's closest friends was nothing more than a wealthy European with a gift for graceful social maneuvering. And the copious events she was photographed at were giving him nothing but a crash course on the difference between Valentino and Chanel. The entire dossier was full of useless information, from the details of her marital marathon to her extended family tree, yet he continued to pore over it, trying to find something, anything, that might explain what the fuck was going on.

Was visiting Beauchene just an excuse? Had the past few days been an act, waiting for the perfect out? Or had it been a final good-bye, fucking each other senseless just to purge it out of her system? Had she realized that no matter what his zip code, he still wasn't good enough? Hudson gripped the document in his hand to avoid punching his fist through the tinted glass. He hadn't even had a fighting fucking chance to talk her out of it.

"Mr. Chase." Max's voice cut through the rhetoricals and Hudson's laser-sharp eyes darted to the rearview mirror. "The plane is on standby and the crew is ready to depart as soon as we arrive. ETA, eight minutes."

Hudson checked his watch. "Thank you." He took a deep breath in an attempt to downshift his nervous energy into focused calm, but his need to find Allie overrode all logic. If she thought she was walking without hearing him out. . . . Well, news flash, she was wrong. So fucking wrong.

After going through the airport's private security entrance, the Mercedes shot down the tarmac and around the fat turn that lead to the hanger housing the Chase Industries plane. The car came to an abrupt stop inside, its tires squeaking against the highly polished concrete floor. Hudson exploded out of the vehicle. He didn't give a shit if he had to fly halfway around the world to do it; he was going after her. Winning Allie back was a necessity, and if this was the way she wanted to play it, he was all fucking in.

Allie paced the Aubusson rug in front of the hearth in Julian's study. Her eyes were glued to the clock resting atop the intricately carved mantel. The ticking of the hands seemed to grow louder the longer she watched it, and her heart raced to keep time. Ten more strokes and it would chime, just as it had the past four hours, in yet another shrill reminder that she'd stood up the man she loved.

Her chest tightened at the thought of him waiting for her at the Paris train station. At first he might have assumed she was merely running late. It wouldn't have come as much of a surprise. But Hudson knew she would have called or texted if that had been the case. Eventually he would have realized something was wrong.

When she closed her eyes she could picture him standing on the platform, running a hand through his hair when he wasn't checking his watch, his brow furrowed and his jaw tight. How long had he waited? Had he called the police? They probably wouldn't consider her officially missing after only a few hours. Either way she was sure he'd interrogated the hotel about the limo they'd provided. Knowing firsthand what it was like to face a determined Hudson Chase, Allie had no doubt they'd given him whatever information they had. Which meant he knew the driver didn't take her to tea with an old family friend but rather to de Gaulle airport. *Oh God.* Did he assume she'd left him? Was he already on his way back to Chicago?

The clock chimed, and Allie's eyes flew open. She had to get out of there. She needed to find Hudson, to tell him she loved him and that she would never leave him. Ever.

Where the hell was Julian? He'd had her on a race against time since the moment he'd called, demanding she personally deliver his ring before an unreasonably short deadline. But she'd no sooner walked through the door when a rather imposing gentleman approached him with a message. Allie had seen enough over the past few weeks to recognize a bodyguard when she saw one. Ex-military, if she had to guess. After reading the note, Julian had excused himself, asking the man to escort Allie to his study. She didn't think much of it until he confiscated her cell phone and locked the door behind him.

She'd been pacing the rug ever since.

Her impatience was its own cruel irony since she'd hoped to never lay eyes on Julian Laurent again. She would have hung up on him when he called—scratch that, she would have told him to go to hell, *then* hung up on him—but he'd played the one card that guaranteed her cooperation. Hudson. Allie had no idea what had happened to the man whose lifeless body lay at Nick's feet in the surveillance video Julian sent her, or what Hudson's involvement had been. But it didn't matter. She trusted Hudson completely and would do anything to protect him. Which is why she'd had no choice but to follow Julian's instructions to the letter. She'd done everything he'd asked, and in return he'd trapped her in his study for hours. Enough was enough. Julian couldn't hold her hostage.

Allie crossed the cavernous room and tried the handles of the double doors, only to find them still locked. And when she pounded on the wood she once again heard nothing but an echoing silence in return. Why the hell was he doing this? A shiver of awareness trickled down Allie's spine. He was playing mind games with her, breaking down her defenses. But why? She had no intention of sticking around long enough to find out. She needed to get out of there, to find Hudson and tell him everything. Together they could figure out a way to deal with Julian.

Her eyes darted around the room, coming to rest on the arched casement window on the opposite wall. She hurried around Julian's desk and frantically cranked the handle on the stone sill. The drop wasn't too bad, if she lowered herself carefully . . .

A hinge squeaked behind her and then a door slammed shut. "Have a seat, Alessandra," Julian said, his accent thick and his voice low. "You're not going anywhere."

2

udson hit the stairs two at a time, eating up the distance in a matter of seconds. As he stepped inside his private jet he heard the captain radio the tower. The flight attendant greeted him almost immediately.

"Good evening, Mr. Chase." The woman looked over Hudson's shoulder. "Will Miss Sinclair be joining us?"

"There's been a change to the manifest." Hudson unbuttoned his wool coat and dropped it onto the cream couch opposite twin leather seats. "Only one passenger." He didn't need to elaborate and he wasn't going to.

Without missing a beat the flight attendant simply responded, "Yes, sir."

Hudson parked his ass in the chair that faced the door and ran a hand through his hair. Call it wishful thinking, but with his eyes focused on the door, he hoped—hell, he fucking prayed—that Allie would suddenly appear in the archway. But instead, a guy on the ground crew bounded up the stairs to close the hatch.

Hudson dipped his head and pinched the bridge of his nose as if that would stave off the pounder threatening to take over his frontal lobe.

"Sir." A soft voice pushed through the sound of the jet's engines warming up. "Might I offer you ibuprofen or aspirin, perhaps?"

"I'm fine, thank you. Just a glass of wat—"

His phone rang in his hand.

"Mr. Chase, we're preparing for takeoff, you will need to turn your phone off or set it to airplane mode."

Hudson held up a single finger as he glanced at the screen. His stomach took a nosedive when he realized it wasn't Allie, but rather an unknown number. "Chase," he clipped into the phone.

"Bonsoir, Monsieur Chase. C'est Claudette de la George V."

Hudson took the chilled glass of water from his flight attendant. "Procéder," he responded in near- perfect French. Outside the window, landscape began to pass by.

"Bien sûr, monsieur. Mlle Sinclair a rencontré un passager de Chicago, une jeune femme rousse selon le pilote. Il l'a emmenée à l'hôtel Ritz Carlton."

Sweet hell, she was rapid-firing at him. "Ralentissez, Anglais, s'il vous plaît."

"Désolé . . . uh, my apologies, Mr. Chase. You are a valued client of the George V, and as a courtesy we wanted to follow up on your inquiry regarding Miss Sinclair." The casual tone of her voice grated against his nerve endings. And for fuck's sake, the pause just about pitched him into thermonuclear status. "Miss Sinclair was taken to the arrivals terminal."

"Arrivals? You're certain?"

"Oui. She met a flight arriving from the United States."

"The US has fifty states, narrow it down." The aircraft eased over a bump on its way to the runway, and the water in the glass in front of him rippled.

"Chicago, sir. The driver said he picked up a redhead with . . . uh . . . colorful luggage, then proceeded to take her to the Ritz Carlton."

"Did Miss Sinclair go with her to the hotel?" And why the hell wasn't she taking her to a different one?

"No, sir."

Christ, this was like pulling teeth. "Did the driver take Miss Sinclair to another location?"

"No, Mr. Chase, he returned alone."

"Merci." Hudson ended the call. Why would Allie fly back to the states while her self-proclaimed B-fucking-F was in Paris? The pieces of the puzzle were beginning to shake out of different boxes with none of them matching. He shifted back into his seat, and at the same time the pilot throttled the engine. The engines roared and the plane began to pick up speed.

Fuck.

Hudson yanked back on his seat belt, the metal clanking against the armrests, and ordered the plane to stop.

Allie startled at the sound of the slamming door. She turned to find Julian standing in the doorway. His green eyes were glassy as they cast a leering glance over her body, causing alarm bells to ring loud and strong in her head. The last time she'd been in the same room with Julian, he'd tried to rape her. The cuts and bruises she'd suffered at his hands that night had healed, but the mere sight of him awakened a panic that lingered just below the surface.

"I believe I told you to sit." He stepped into the room and closed the door behind him.

"You can't keep me here," she said, her mouth suddenly dry. "This is kidnapping."

His lips twitched into a mocking smile. "You came here of your own free will, Alessandra."

It took every ounce of strength to hold her ground. "You blackmailed me into coming here."

"I simply provided an incentive for you to pay me a visit." He smirked. "As my guest." He sauntered toward the fireplace, stopping in front of a small table that held an arrangement of crystal decanters. "Drink?"

Allie shook her head. "Do you lock all your guests in the study?"

"You would have preferred the tower?"

To her horror Allie realized he might not have been joking. Either way he didn't wait for an answer to the absurd question. Instead he continued on as if the past few hours had been nothing more than a minor inconvenience.

"I had matters to attend to." Julian filled a squat glass with ice, then lifted the top from one of the decanters and poured himself a hefty glass of vodka. "But I'm here now, so let's, as you Americans are so fond of saying, get down to it, shall we?" His expression darkened when she didn't comply. "Sit, Alessandra. Don't make me say it again."

Allie sank into one of the chairs in front of Julian's desk. He passed by her in a cloud of sweet cologne mixed with the lingering stench of cigarette smoke. The combination made her stomach roll. When he reached his desk he fixed her with a hard stare. "I believe you have something of mine?"

She dug the leather ring box out of her purse and set it on the desk between them. He regarded her a moment, watching her over the rim of his glass as he sipped the vodka. Refusing to give him the satisfaction of knowing how he affected her, Allie fought the urge to look away.

After what seemed like an eternity, Julian finally reached for the box, holding it in one hand and pressing the lid open with his thumb. The late afternoon sun streaming in from the window behind him caught the facets of the stone, reflecting a brilliant white and blue. Despite what that ring had come to represent, Allie had to admit it was stunning. Twelve flawless carats, the diamond was truly one of a kind. A gift from Louis XIV to the first Marquis Laurent, the ring had been in Julian's family for centuries and was one of his most prized possessions. Yet as he stared at his precious heirloom nestled in black satin, he remained impassive and quiet. Too quiet.

For several excruciating moments, the ticking from the clock on the mantel was the only sound in the room. Allie stole a glance at it, but Julian either didn't notice or didn't care. He sat motionless, his gaze trained on the box in his hand, focused but somehow unseeing at the same time. It was like he was a million miles away.

When he finally spoke, Allie let out a breath she hadn't realized she'd been holding. "America's royal wedding," he mumbled before taking another sip from his glass. His voice was so low she wasn't sure she'd heard him correctly.

"Excuse me?"

"That's what the press was calling it." Julian snapped the box closed and set it back on the desk. The distant look in his eyes was gone, and in its place was a venom so tangible Allie could almost feel it crawl across her skin. "You were too busy spreading your legs all over Chicago to notice, but our impending merger made headlines."

Allie couldn't help but cringe at his word choice. Merger, not marriage. And certainly not love. To him their entire relationship had been nothing more than a business transaction, one her parents had shrewdly and callously negotiated to save Ingram Media from bankruptcy. Julian was chosen because he was the most desirable bidder in her father's eyes, not because he loved her. All of it had been a fraud. From the day they first met until the night he proposed, everything about their courtship had been a carefully orchestrated charade.

"I should be at the helm of Ingram right now. Not you and that stray who followed you home from the beach ten years later." He took another sip of vodka and slowly licked his lower lip.

"You must have been quite the fuck back then, because I certainly never experienced anything quite so . . . inspiring."

Allie had heard enough. "You've got what you wanted, Julian. I brought the ring back. Just give me the memory card and we never have to see each other again."

"Promises were made, Alessandra. Contracts signed. Money exchanged."

"I had my lawyer return everything you paid my father." Her voice was small. The fact that her father had taken money from Julian made her feel like the whore he'd once called her, bought and paid for.

Allie flinched at the sound of Julian's fist pounding the desk.

"You think that makes this right?" he shouted. His face was red and a muscle ticked in his jaw.

A beat of tense silence passed between them.

"Look around you," he ground out between clenched teeth. "I don't need your money. What I need is a high-level entry into the American market. A conglomerate to add to the Laurent holdings. What I need," he snarled, "is Ingram Media."

Allie took deep breaths through her nose in an effort to slow her racing heart. Julian's hair-trigger temper was amplified by the alcohol he was slugging back like water. She needed to remain calm, sympathize with him if that's what it took. Anything to get the hell out of there. "I understand your frustration, Julian. But I don't know what you expect me to do about any of this."

Julian composed himself almost as quickly as he'd lost it. With a final gulp he finished off the vodka. Slowly and methodically, he set the glass on the desk and leaned back in the chair, resting his elbows on the arms and steepling his fingers in front of his mouth. "It's quite simple, Alessandra. You're going to become my wife."

3

*H*udson's fist landed against the door like a sledgehammer. He was way past giving some dainty wake- up call, providing the jet lag had wiped out the redhead. And based on the number of times he'd knocked on the door, it had. As he stood there waiting . . . and waiting, he glanced up and down the hallway of the pricey establishment. A couple of silver trays were parked outside the room next to Harper's, and a housekeeper was making her way toward him carrying a fresh load of towels. He waited for her to pass before pounding the wood again.

The door finally swung open and the light from the hall sliced into the room. Harper's lids squeezed shut against the blinding intrusion. Her hair was sticking up in every direction possible, and the second her eyes got with the waking up program, they widened. Goddamn, he thought they were going to pop out of her skull and roll across the carpet.

"What are you doing here?" She tightened the belt on her white terry cloth robe as he pushed past her into the room.

"I was about to ask you the same thing."

"By all means," she mumbled. "Come in."

"Where's Allie?"

"I thought she was with you." She shut the door and finger-combed her hair. "I mean, aren't you two in the middle of some over-the-top getaway?"

"We should be having cocktails in London by now."

"Have you tried her cell?" Harper was doing her damnedest to avoid his direct line of questioning. He wasn't surprised she was covering for Allie, but it was getting him good and pissed off.

"Repeatedly. When did you last hear from her?"

"She called me . . ." She rubbed her eyes, then paused and let her hand flop to her side, the cuff of her robe swallowing her hand. "Wait, what day is it?"

"It's the first of January," he bit out.

"She called me yesterday morning."

"What time?"

Harper frowned. "Early. Well, here it was early. Like six, I think."

Hudson ran a hand through his hair while his mind recalibrated. He thought back to the previous morning on the train. Breakfast had been the first order of business after a night of unadulterated fucking on every surface of their cabin—against the cool window, his body pressed in behind her as they sped through the French countryside; on the floor, out of breath, but the thought of stopping a foreign concept wiped clean from their vocabulary; even those godforsaken bunk beds hadn't been off-limits. On that train there'd been nothing but the two of them, even in a packed dining car. Or so he'd thought.

"What did she say?" Hudson waited impatiently for Harper to fill in the blanks. Her eyes darted around the room as if the desk or chair, or maybe even the curtains, could help her out. Jesus Christ, she needed to cut the avoidance crap and start giving him information. "I know you think you're protecting your friend, but she was supposed to meet me three hours ago and she never showed."

"Oh fuck," Harper muttered as she sank down onto the navy-blue couch.

"My sentiments. Talk."

"She wanted my help."

"With?"

"She needed me to go to the brownstone and get something for her, said she'd have a ticket waiting for me at O'Hare and that she'd meet me at de Gaulle when I landed."

"What else?"

"That was about it. The call was pretty short."

"And at the airport?"

"Same thing. We only spoke for a few minutes."

Hudson knew she was telling the truth about the call at least; he hadn't been out of the cabin for very long. But he also knew that once the two of them got going, it was as if they were setting a new record for most words crammed into a solitary sentence. She had to know more. But the redhead had gone from clammed-up to shell-shocked. "What did she say," he prompted. "Walk me through the conversation."

"She was mostly thanking me and telling me about the reservations she'd made. Then she put me in a car and had the driver take me here. I should have called to check on her but I was so whacked, I passed out the minute I got to the room. Oh! Maybe she tried to call . . ." She shot up, snatched her cell off the table, and slid her thumb across the screen.

"Back up. What did she want you to get?"

Harper looked up and locked eyes with him. "Her engagement ring."

"Why the hell would she want that?"

"She didn't. Julian did."

"Come again?" How typical, Hudson thought, for Harper to leave out the biggest fucking detail.

"He called her that morning, said he wanted it back and gave her some sort of ultimatum."

15

With a quick surge, Hudson strode to the window in an attempt to throw off his aggression. Every cell in his body screamed for him to pick up the chair, the lamp—hell, even the couch—and go all rock star on the room.

"I told her this wasn't a good idea and that you needed to know what was going on, but she said she could handle it and—"

Hudson spun around. "Handle it?"

"—that it would all be over in a few hours and then she could get on with her life and she'd never have to see that bastard again." Harper's words came out rapid-fire. "I'm so sorry. I should have never agreed to help her. I knew better than to trust that asshole."

He had his phone out before she'd even motored through her last sentence.

Max answered the call on the first ring.

"Bring the car around," Hudson barked into the phone. "And I'll need an address for Julian Laurent." He started for the door at the same time Harper began flinging clothes out of her suitcase.

"Just give me a minute to get dressed."

"I got this."

"You're crazy if you think I'm letting you walk out that door without me." Harper's brows were raised in a hard stare, her hands white-knuckling some colorful montage of clothing.

He blew out a resigned breath. "Then get the lead out."

4

*A*llie was sure she'd heard him wrong. Julian couldn't have possibly been serious. After everything that had transpired between them, there was no way he could have deluded himself into thinking she would actually marry him.

"I want what was promised me," he said, leaning forward in his chair. "What I'm owed. It would have all been mine, everything: the cable network, the newspapers, the magazines. Merged with my Asian and European holdings, Ingram would have been a global leader."

"There are other media conglomerates, Julian."

He shook his head. "Not like Ingram. Their assets are unique." His bloodshot eyes roamed over her. Even in the dim afternoon light she could see his pupils dilate. "And while it's hardly a pedigree, the Ingram name is as close to royalty as Americans get."

"I don't love you, Julian. And you've made it clear you don't love me either."

"Love is for fairy tales, Alessandra. It has no place in the real world. I would have thought your mother taught you that by example if nothing else."

Allie stiffened. "I'm nothing like my mother."

Julian's head fell back on a harsh laugh. "Are you really so blind as to not see it? You're exactly like your mother. And I'm not referring to your looks, although I guess I should be grateful the trophy glitters." He ran a hand through his light brown hair, which fell perfectly back into place. "If it helps you sleep at night, consider our marriage a chance for you to carry on her legacy."

"This isn't the Dark Ages. You can't force me to marry you."

"That is correct." He stroked his lip with his index finger. "The decision is ultimately yours. Although if you defy me, that video will find its way to the proper authorities."

So this had been his plan all along. The race to return his ring was just the excuse to get her there so he could reveal his true end game.

Twisted amusement lit his eyes. "Don't look so shocked, Alessandra. You didn't really think I'd give up so easily, did you?"

"You don't have to do this," she said as if there were some way to reason with him.

"That is where you're wrong, ma cherie. You left me with no other option."

"Me?" The high pitch of her voice betrayed the raw emotions she struggled to control.

"Oui." His gaze turned impassive. "After all, you are to blame for the deal falling apart in the first place. All of this—" he waved his hand through the air "—is your fault. You brought it on yourself when you broke our engagement."

Allie looked down at her hands, balled into fists in her lap. "You attacked me."

Julian snorted. "How did you think I would react when I discovered my fiancée had been whoring her way through the city in my absence? You should have been grateful I was willing to look past your indiscretions, but instead you chose a man who quite literally had been your servant. Another lesson your dear mother should have imparted: the staff is for fucking in the shadows, Alessandra, not parading through the lobby of the symphony." He rattled the cubes inside the empty crystal tumbler. "Shame, really. If you had just left well enough alone, none of this unpleasantness would have been necessary. You'd be living here as the new Marquise Laurent, quite literally the queen of the castle; your precious Mr. Chase and his deadbeat brother wouldn't be on the proverbial chopping block; and your parents would still be alive."

Allie's head snapped up. "What does my parents' death have to do with any of this?"

"Your parents wanted Ingram to remain in the family. Your father would have withdrawn his support once you called off the wedding, and without the blessing of the almighty Richard Sinclair, I didn't stand a chance at convincing the rest of the board." He leaned back in the leather chair and crossed his ankle over the opposite knee. "I needed someone in power who was a bit easier to control."

A cold sweat misted Allie's skin. "What did you do?" she whispered.

Julian leveled his beady stare. "Whatever it took."

No, no, no . . .

"Once I ensured the Ingram-Sinclair holdings would be transferred to their sole heir, I simply turned to the seemingly illustrious Mr. Chase for a bit of leverage. I didn't even need to dig too far. Covering up a murder?" The corner of Julian's mouth twisted in a hideous grin. "It's as if he handed you over on a silver platter."

Allie struggled to catch her breath while Julian gloated about orchestrating her parents' murder as if it was a victory in a polo match. "Everything fell into place so easily it was almost boring, really. Other than the imbecile taking your mother's ring as a souvenir." He tsked. "As a professional, he should have known I couldn't leave that type of loose end. Then again, having the ring in his possession when his body was discovered did a nice job of setting him up to take the fall. From what I hear, the police have all but closed the case."

The taste of bile rose in Allie's throat, and for a moment she thought she might be sick.

"Are you sure you wouldn't like that drink now, Alessandra? You look a little pale."

Her mind spun as she struggled to process everything she'd learned, but one thing was certain: Julian had killed her parents in cold blood. Threatening to incriminate Hudson in a murder was only the tip of the iceberg. There was no telling the lengths he would go to force her to do his bidding. She was willing to do whatever it took to keep Hudson safe, but it wasn't in her power to give Julian what he wanted. "The shares from the estate aren't enough to give you control of the company," she told him. "Hudson owns a considerable amount."

"I'm well aware of his holdings. And I'm also aware of his weakness for you. You're his Achilles heel, Alessandra. It shouldn't be too difficult for you to get him to sign over his interest in the company."

"How exactly do you expect me to do that?'

"By ending your relationship."

"He won't believe me." There was no way Hudson would believe she was leaving him, that she didn't love him. Or would he? She'd been so horrible to him when she'd discovered he was the one secretly buying up shares of Ingram Media in a hostile takeover attempt. And now if he thought she had left the country without him . . .

"Convince him. Tell him you've had a change of heart, that you can't forgive him after all, or that you've simply grown tired of him. I don't care. But end it."

"He'll fight for me."

Julian sneered. "I'm counting on that. Let him grovel like he did before, then you can give him the ultimatum. Make him prove his love by signing the stock over to you. It's the decent thing to do seeing as how you're Jonathan Ingram's only surviving heir. Then, of course, you'll deliver the final blow to his ego by joining my side in wedded bliss." His words were a direct contrast to the bitter contempt in his tone. "And since you've already proven you can't control yourself around the dog, let me make one thing perfectly clear. Manipulate him, Alessandra, but don't fuck him. That's a service reserved for your future husband."

"If you think I'll sleep with you, you're crazy."

"Contrary to what that mongrel may have told you, you're not the lay of the century. Far from it, in fact. I have plenty of resources at my disposal to better meet those needs. You'll sleep in my bed by invitation. The frequency will depend on how fertile you are." He smirked. "And my mood, of course."

Allie gaped at him. "You expect me to have your child?"

He rose from his chair. "Two. An heir and a spare, as the Brits love to say."

Allie shrank back as he rounded the desk. "Relax," he said, his laugh mocking her fear. "No one shall call a Laurent a bastard. I won't be taking you again until after the wedding." He strolled past her to the row of crystal decanters and refilled his glass with a hefty pour. "Which brings me to the time frame. The annual shareholder's meeting is in April, and my sources tell me the board is set to vote on a permanent CEO when they convene in March.

His sources? Allie barely had time to consider who at Ingram was funneling high-level information to Julian when he dropped another bomb on her.

"We'll need the ceremony to take place well before that meeting. Mid-February at the latest." He cocked an eyebrow. "St. Valentine's Day? Perhaps more fitting for the massacre than a diaper-wearing cherub, but apropos nonetheless."

"You want to get married next month?" she asked. Her voice was hoarse.

"Oui. The arrangements won't be a problem given that the plans were already in place. Most of them can be adjusted to the February date. At least enough to capitalize on the PR . . . I'm thinking something along the lines of 'Dashing Prince Rescues Orphaned Heiress.'" Has a nice ring to it, don't you think?"

Clearly he had lost his mind. But she had to play along. It was the only hope she had of buying the time she needed to figure a way out of this mess. "Why so fast . . . I mean, we have our whole lives, what's the rush?"

"We need to allow adequate time for the blushing bride to realize how much the company has suffered at the hands of a corporate raider and replace him with her new husband."

"The co-CEO idea was just for the interim, Julian. I don't think anyone expects it to continue permanently, regardless of whom is sitting in that chair."

"Don't be ridiculous. I have no intention of working along-side you." He took a sip from the crystal glass. "Once we return from our honeymoon, you will have a change of heart, decide you have no place in the boardroom after all, and use your considerable stock percentage to vote your new husband into the position."

"And what am I supposed to do?"

He shrugged. "Fill your days with charity work and tennis matches like your mother did."

"So after everything I've done, I'm just supposed to suddenly change my mind about running my grandfather's company and hand it all over to you?" Allie straightened in her chair. She was proud of the work she'd been doing at Ingram. Her victories in the boardroom might have been small, but she was slowly earning their respect. Walking away at this point wouldn't make any sense. "No one will believe that."

"How you sell the story isn't my concern, Alessandra. But I

suggest you work on your poker face." He closed the distance between them until he was standing beside her chair. "I'll expect you to play the loving wife when we're in public."

His fingers traced the wildly pulsing vein in her neck. Allie squeezed her eyes closed, fighting the urge to jerk away from his touch. "I'm not that good of an actor."

"I felt the same way, but if I can pull it off, so can you. With enough practice you'll get it right, and if not, I will be happy to introduce certain methods of motivation." His hand tightened around her neck. "A training of sorts could be quite interesting."

"That won't be necessary," she murmured, trying to control her fear.

"Convince me." He pulled her cell phone out of his hip pocket and tossed it on the desk in front of her. "I believe there is a heart in need of crushing."

"You want me to do it now?"

"No time like the present. Consider it a good faith gesture on your part. Although now that I think about it, extra incentive never hurts." Julian drained the rest of the vodka from his glass as he moved to the other side of his desk. "My sources at Chicago PD are very thorough." He reached into the top drawer and pulled out a manila envelope. Allie knew what it contained even before he opened it. She tried to steel herself against the onslaught of emotion that welled inside her, but nothing could prepare her for what she was about to see. "Visual aides are always so helpful. Wouldn't you agree, Alessandra?"

With a flourish Julian fanned the eight by ten glossies out across his desk. Picture after picture, each one more gruesome than the next. Her father slumped over his desk, blood pooling around him on the leather top. Her mother on the dining room floor, her vacant stare reflected in the shattered mirrors that dangled from the wall. In that moment Allie realized this was no longer just a matter of protecting Hudson and Nick from possible prosecution. It was a matter of life and death. She hadn't been able to protect her parents, but she could keep the man she loved safe from the fate displayed in graphic detail in front of her.

"Enough." She reached for the phone and powered it on. Almost immediately it began to ping and vibrate with incoming texts, missed calls, and voice mails. As she watched them light up the screen, her vision began to blur. Damn it. She hated that she was crying in front of Julian, hated knowing the satisfaction it brought him. But the realization of what had happened to her parents combined with the reality of what she was about to do was too much, and tears streamed unbidden down her cheeks.

"Second thoughts already? Perhaps I need to come up with a more effective motivation."

"No," she snapped. "I've got this." It would kill her to end her relationship with Hudson, but she had no choice. She had to go along with Julian's charade, at least for the time being. It was the only way to ensure Hudson's safety.

She wiped her face with the back of her hand and pressed the speed dial for Hudson's cell phone. He answered on the first ring.

"Allie." The desperation in his voice broke her heart. "Where are you?"

"I'm fine," she assured him rather than answer his question.

"Why the hell did you agree to meet that asshole?"

He knew about Julian. But how?

"Tell me where you are and I'll come get you."

"Absolutely not," she blurted out. She hadn't meant the words to come out so harshly, but she needed to keep Hudson safe, and to do that she had to keep him as far away from Julian as possible. "I mean, that's not necessary. I'm flying back to Chicago tonight. Alone."

"What the fuck is going on?"

She took a deep breath in an attempt to steady her nerves. "I thought I could look past everything that happened, but I can't. It guess it took getting away to realize that." Pain lanced her heart as she prepared to deliver the final blow. "It's over."

"The hell it is." His frustration was palpable, but she knew beneath the anger he was hurting.

"Please don't make this harder than it has to be, Hudson."

"You expect me to accept this bullshit without a fight? You know me better than that. I'll trace your phone if I have to," he threatened. "Now tell me where you are."

Fuck. She needed to end the call and power off her cell.

"Let me talk to her," a woman said.

"Is Harper there?"

"Yes, she's with me. Were you just going to leave her here too?"

How the hell had he found Harper? "Put her on the phone, please."

Hudson blew out an exasperated breath, but a moment later Harper was on the line, asking one question after another.

"What's going on? Where have you been all day? Why haven't you been answering your cell? Did that French sleazebag threaten you?" If Harper only knew how on-target she was.

"No, I just needed some time to think this afternoon, that's all."

"And *this* is what you came up with?"

"I don't want to get into it right now."

"Look, I don't know what the hell is going through that head of yours, but you two need to work this out." Harper wasn't just Allie's best friend, she was practically a sister. Convincing her that she'd had a change of heart was going to be almost as difficult as convincing Hudson.

"There's nothing to discuss. I'm flying home."

There was a long pause. Allie could picture the two of them, Harper chewing on her bottom lip, Hudson running a frustrated hand through his hair. "Fine," she finally said. "I'll meet you at the airport."

"No, stay. Enjoy Paris; you just got here."

"Are you kidding me? I'm flying home with you. Text me the flight info when we hang up."

The look of smug satisfaction on Julian's face when Allie ended the call was almost more than she could bear. Somehow Allie had to find a way out of this mess. And she only had a few weeks to do it.

5

*A*llie settled into the leather seat and pulled the shade closed on the small window. She couldn't wait to get out of France. The sooner she put some distance between her and Julian, the better. If she was honest, the same applied to Hudson Chase as well. Clearly he wasn't buying what she'd told him on the phone. And if history was any indication, it was only a matter of time before he cornered her, demanding answers. After everything she'd been through already that day, she was nowhere near ready for a face- to-face confrontation with the man who knew her like no other.

"Would you like something to drink before takeoff?" the flight attendant asked. "A glass of champagne, perhaps?" A preflight cocktail was no doubt one of the many perks of traveling first class, but Allie didn't feel much like celebrating. At the moment she should have been dancing with Hudson aboard a yacht on the River Thames, not flying home without him after being forced to break his heart.

"No, thank you. But a blanket and pillow would be nice." With any luck she could manage to sleep the whole flight home, postponing the inevitable Harper Hayes inquisition until she'd had some time to get her story straight.

And speaking of her best friend, where the hell was she? The cabin was filling quickly and yet the seat next to her remained unoccupied. She glanced at her watch. Only a few more minutes until the flight was due to depart. Was Harper stuck in traffic? Or maybe customs?

Allie reached for her phone. If Harper was going to miss the flight, maybe she could at least help her rebook before they began to taxi. The call went straight to voice mail. She was about to leave her a message when a disembodied voice came over the plane's PA system.

"Ladies and gentleman, welcome aboard flight two twelve with nonstop service to Chicago's O'Hare International Airport. At this time please be sure your seat backs are in their full and upright positions and that your seat belt is securely fastened. All laptops must be stowed and all personal electronic devices should be switched to airplane mode."

Shit. She didn't even have time to fire off a quick text before the flight attendant reappeared.

"I'm afraid I'm going to have to ask you to turn off your cell phone," she said as she handed Allie a neatly folded blanket with a small pillow perched on top. "We're about to push back from the gate."

There was a commotion at the front of the plane just as the next announcement began. This time it was the pilot's voice over the loudspeaker. "Flight attendants, prepare for departure. Doors on automatic. Cross check and report."

Allie bent to tuck her phone into the carry-on stowed beneath the seat in front of her. A shiver of awareness swept over her skin and she stilled. *Hudson.* She felt his presence just as surely as if he'd touched her. But despite the brief moment she took to prepare herself, the sight of him still took her breath away. He was standing in the aisle, the muscles of his chest and arms flexing as he shrugged out of his wool coat and handed it to the flight attendant. His hair was damp, no doubt from the snow falling outside, and when he reached up to run his hand through the unruly mane, his sweater rode up, affording her a glimpse of his honed washboard abs and the trail of dark hair that disappeared beneath his belt.

He glanced down and caught her staring. "See something you like?"

She ignored his obvious innuendo, choosing instead to address the much bigger issue. "What are you doing here?"

"Going after what's mine." He slid into the seat beside her. His eyes never left hers as he efficiently fastened his seat belt. The intensity of his stare was overwhelming and she had to bite the inside of her cheek to keep from blurting out everything that had happened over the past two days. The urge to throw herself into his arms was almost more than she could bear. What she wouldn't give to have him hold her, to feel his hands stroking her hair, to hear his voice whispering in her ear, telling her they could face anything as long as they were together. But Julian had insured that was no longer an option, and in order to keep Hudson safe she had to do as she'd been instructed. So instead of telling him how relieved she was to see him, she laid into him for poaching her friend's ticket.

"Where is Harper?" she asked as the plane pushed back from the gate.

"I imagine right about now she's somewhere over the Atlantic, enjoying a lovely meal on a leather sofa, which is more than I can say for our current accommodations."

Thinking the best defense was a good offense, she shot back, "No one asked you to take this flight."

"Did you expect that I would return to Chicago without finding out what the hell is going on? You know me better than that, Alessandra."

"I told you on the phone—"

"Save it. You didn't tell me shit on the phone."

"I told you it's over, Hudson." Her throat tightened as she forced out the words. "And I mean it this time."

"Everything was going fine, better than fine." He paused and a muscle in his jaw flexed. "Until that asshole called."

The plane surged forward, hurtling down the runway. Allie's stomach sank as the wheels lifted from the ground, but the sensation had little to do with gravity and everything to do with the pained expression on Hudson's face.

"In fact, I can pin down the day and time that he did. Because that was the moment I felt you start to slip through my fingers."

Of course he had sensed the change. And he was right. Everything had been absolutely perfect until the morning Julian texted her that grainy black-and-white photo. Somehow she had to convince Hudson there was no connection. "Julian only called because he wanted his ring back."

"Yes, Harper filled me in on the details that brought her to Paris. But it wasn't about a goddamn ring, was it?"

"Two separate issues, Hudson. My decision to end things is based on us. It has nothing to do with Julian."

"Bullshit," he practically shouted.

Allie glanced around. The lights in the cabin had been dimmed in dereference to the passengers sleeping or watching in-flight movies on the monitors installed in the seat backs in front of them. A few were engrossed in e-readers or magazines and the woman across the aisle was playing solitaire on her tablet. Yet nearly all of them looked up at the sound of Hudson's outburst. "Keep your voice down, please," she whispered.

Hudson rested his elbow on the console between their two seats and leaned closer. When he spoke his voice was low and rough, and held the hard edge of unmistakable determination. "Julian is a man who is always working the sidelines. And I know there are no circumstances under which you would take that fucker's call, much less agree to meet with him, unless your hand was forced. What stings the most is that you lied to me. You didn't even give me the opportunity to help you handle the matter. So cut the shit and tell me what in the hell is going on."

He held her gaze but she held her ground. With a heavy exhale he sat back against the leather seat. "Fine. I'll wait. We have nine hours until we land in Chicago, so at some point you're going to start talking. And Allie, there's not an 'if' anywhere in that damn sentence."

"Ladies and gentlemen, our pilot has turned off the fasten seat belts sign. You are free to move about the cabin."

Thank God. Allie unbuckled her seat belt and bolted for the cluster of bathrooms in the middle of the plane. But when she tried to close the door an arm shot out to block it. Hudson stepped into the small lavatory, locking the door behind him. The space was tight and cramped, with barely a few inches between them.

"You can't come in here."

He smirked. "I believe I just did."

"What if someone saw you?"

"Half the plane heard us arguing, Alessandra. They'll assume we're seeking privacy to have the requisite makeup sex."

"That's exactly what I'm afraid of."

"No, it's not." He loomed over her in the tight quarters, enveloping her in his rich, masculine scent. She could feel the heat radiating off his body, see the dark desire that burned in his blue eyes.

Allie stepped back, bumping against the small sink. There was nowhere to go. No escape from the man who at the moment was both her temptation and torment. "Excuse me?"

"It's not what the people out there are thinking that has you worried. It's what you're thinking that has your pulse racing." His voice lowered to a husky drawl. "Because despite all the bullshit you're attempting to feed me, right now you'd like nothing more than to have my cock buried deep inside you."

His crude words had her sucking in a sharp breath but there was no denying their effect. Heat pulsed through her core and her nipples tightened against the rough lace of her bra. "Don't."

"A poker face was never your strong suit." His eyes roamed over her. "I can read you like an open book, Alessandra, and right now you've got that fuck-me look. Say it. Tell me you want my cock claiming you."

"Hudson . . ."

His lips hovered inches from hers. "Let me have you, Allie. Tell me you want me."

"Yes," she breathed.

In a heartbeat his mouth slanted over hers. The feel of his lips moving strong and insistent against hers was all it took to break through her last defense. In a rush of dizzying relief she moaned her surrender. He took full advantage, deepening their kiss with lush sweeps of his tongue.

"Are you ready for me? Because I can't wait. I have to feel you around my cock. Now."

His untamed need sent a surge of pure lust coursing through her veins. She reached between them and began unbuckling his belt. "People might hear us," she panted, her protest lacking the conviction of her frantic fingers.

"There is no one else, Allie. Just us."

And in that moment, it was true. There weren't hundreds of people just outside the door or even threats looming over their heads. Nothing existed but the two of them and a driving hunger to be joined on the most intimate level.

His hands skimmed down her hips to the hem of her skirt, pushing the fabric up as his palms glided over her skin. In one swift move he lifted her onto the edge of the small sink, positioning her at the perfect angle. He spread her legs, his hands smoothing along the inside of her thighs, until his fingertips found the soaked satin of her panties. His breath hissed and his grip tightened around the edge of the delicate fabric. Allie felt a sharp tug as his fingers shredded the material and then a rush of cool air against her core.

She reached for him, pushing his pants just low enough to free him from his boxer briefs. He groaned as he fell hot and heavy into her hand then he closed the distance between them, grinding his mouth against hers and wrapping her legs around his hips. "Put me inside you."

She guided him to where she was wet and aching, and with a hard, deep thrust he buried himself to the hilt. Her head fell back against the mirror, and though she knew they needed to be quiet, she couldn't help the low moan that escaped her lips. He pulled back and thrust again, quickly finding the rhythm they both craved as he moved inside her with slick, relentless drives.

The hum of the engines seemed to grow louder as Hudson's thrusts grew sharper and more desperate. "We'll never be over," he growled, his ragged breath warm against her skin. "Never." One hand slipped between their bodies to where they were joined, stroking her in that knowing way that never failed to make her come.

Allie's fingers raked into his hair, clutching him tight as a white-hot rush consumed her. The plane dipped into an air pocket and the momentary sense of weightlessness only added to the sensation that she was falling, spiraling over the edge into a mind shattering release. Hudson drove high and hard one last time, then stilled, his body shuddering as he came inside her.

Once the tremors subsided, Hudson lowered her carefully back to her feet. His arm banded around her waist and his hand slipped under her chin, forcing her to meet his gaze. The haunted look she saw reflected in his eyes broke her heart. It was too much. The emotion of the past two days came crashing down around her and she choked on a strangled sob.

"What happened? What did he threaten you with?"

"I can't."

"Don't start that again."

She shook her head. "I mean not here. When we get home." There was no sense in fighting the inevitable. She was crazy to think she could push him away, even if it was for his own protection. Their bond was too strong.

Hudson gave a tight nod. "Fine. But I want you to tell me everything." His expression was somber, but his touch was gentle as he brushed the pad of his thumb over her swollen lips. "Whatever it is, I can protect you."

She looked up at him through tear-filled eyes. "No, you don't understand. I'm the one who's protecting you."

---

6

*T*he plane pivoted, sending a shaft of artificial light through the window. The bright beam traveled around the first class cabin and settled on their entwined hands as the aircraft came to a stop at the gate. After fucking out some steam, they'd hardly spoken a word for the duration of the nine-hour flight.

That was not how Hudson had expected things to go down in that matchbox of a bathroom. He'd anticipated having one hell of a fight on his hands, same as the last time Allie had tried to walk out of his life. He thought she'd run when he pushed her, but instead she took everything he gave and wanted more. A certified come-to-her-senses moment that ended with her tight around his cock.

Hudson watched Allie look out the window as if she'd just noticed they had landed. Call it a knee-jerk reaction, but he half expected her to pull away as she comprehended that they were now back in Chicago. He waited to feel that emptiness, but her hand remained firmly in his grasp.

As if in a coordinated sequence, overhead bins popped open, carry-on handles jacked up, and the single-lane shuffle began.

Using his free hand, Hudson flipped the silver buckle on the seat belt and Allie did the same, still holding onto him. In fact, as he stood up she clutched his hand tighter in a squeeze that shot straight to his heart. Not a fucking chance in hell he was letting her go. Ever. He needed the feel of Allie's slender hand in his, the weight of it, and the connection of their touching palms.

With a solid grip he led her off the plane, across the standard-issue industrial blue carpet, and up the slow incline of the gateway. Passengers funneled through the door, flanking alongside them and then disbursing in various directions. Hudson and Allie bypassed baggage claim and headed straight to the sidewalk where Max waited by the black-on-black limo. He opened the door as they approached, but Allie stopped short at the curb.

"Harper?" she asked.

"A town car dropped Miss Hayes at her apartment about thirty minutes ago, Miss Sinclair." He cleared his throat. "She would like you to call her at your earliest convenience."

Hudson had to hand it to Max for his polite translation. Undoubtedly the message wasn't quite so eloquently worded, but rather along the lines of something out of a sailor's mouth. Harper had been almost as pissed at Allie as he'd been for what she put them through in Paris. Those frantic hours had thrown them into an unlikely alliance that dare he say might actually have been the start of an even more unlikely friendship. But at the moment, the redhead wasn't his concern. The blonde slipping into the back of his limo was the only thing on Hudson's mind.

He ducked in beside her as soon as Max shut the door. "All right, we're alone. Tell me what's going on."

In the split second Allie's mouth opened, her phone rang, cutting a path through the tension. Hudson glanced down at the screen to see a private caller interrupting his pending Q&A. "Answer it," he said.

Allie's hand shook with a subtle tremor as she accepted the

call. She'd barely said hello when her eyes flared in a wild panic. "What? I know . . . You're spying on me?"

Hudson's jaw clenched. It was taking every shred of control he had left to keep from ripping the phone from her hand and delivering a death threat to whoever was on the other end of that line.

The blood drained from Allie's face and a cool sweat misted her brow. "You don't have to keep reminding me . . . I'm taking care of it." She was quiet for long beats, the steady hum of the engine providing white noise to the otherwise silent interior of the car. As the stretch accelerated, then slowed, then redoubled with the rest of the late-night traffic, Allie finally ended the call.

Hudson angled his body toward her. "Level with me. Who's spying on you? What are you trying to protect me from?"

"Julian." Allie's voice came out as light as a breath, and the trembling in her hands was so bad she nearly dropped the phone.

Goddamn it.

Hudson wrapped his arms around her and pulled her close. When he did, her body went lax against him. "Talk to me, Allie." His voice was a rough plea. "I can't help you if you keep shutting me out."

"I'm so sorry I lied to you. It was killing me. I thought I could bring him his stupid ring and the whole thing would be over in a couple hours."

"Why on earth would you agree to meet with him? The last time you were in the same room with him . . ."

Hudson had bounded up the stairs two at a time, and when he'd kicked the door open the scene was instantly ingrained in his mind: Allie bent over the couch, her legs shaking and her fingers clawing at the cushions; Julian looming over her, one hand holding her down, the other working his fly. And fuck him, so much blood—from her lip, her head—and her eye beginning to blacken. He'd flung that French cocksucker across the room like a Frisbee. The memory had his fingers flexing against the heavy fabric covering Allie's arms. He wanted to hit something, wanted to go round-for-round with Julian until he was tapping out, pleading for his life. Even if it was until his own goddamn eyes were swollen shut, his ribs ached, and his head felt like the size of a melon.

"I know. But he was threatening to hurt you." Allie sat up and met his gaze with tear-filled eyes. "And Nick."

Hudson brushed the hair away from her face. "I can take care of myself, Allie. So can Nick." The corner of his mouth quirked into a reassuring grin. "For the most part."

"He has a video, Hudson, some sort of security footage from a bar." A tear trickled down her cheek.

Shit. This situation was taking him off the rails and into hard-core fuck me territory. The POS barkeep had assured him there weren't any cameras and he'd been well compensated to keep his mouth shut. Fucking hell . . . a headache slammed into his skull.

"He said he'd take the file to the police if I didn't follow his instructions." She took a moment to strengthen her voice. "I don't really understand what's on it, but the part I saw looked really incriminating."

Hudson quieted and his blood pressure dropped. The sound of his own breathing was like nails on a chalkboard.

When no explanation was offered, Allie asked the inevitable. "What happened to the man in the video?"

"I don't want to involve you." Christ, just the opposite. He wanted to talk to her, to clear the air, leaving no secrets between them. But he didn't want to pull her deeper into the clusterfuck of his own creation. And he wasn't going to drag Allie and Nick down into what might very well be his own demise.

"It's a little too late for that now, wouldn't you say? I'm already involved, Hudson. And even if I weren't, what happens to you affects me too." Allie laced her fingers with his. "You want to be in this together, that goes both ways."

Hudson exhaled all the air from his lungs. "It was an accident. Nick reacted in self-defense and I took care of it." He scrubbed a hand down his face. The nine hours of growth on his jaw scratched his palm. "A couple months ago, I got a phone call from the bartender at one of Nick's regular hangouts, a real dive. I hadn't heard from Nick for days, so any sign of life was a relief."

"The weekend we went to Lake Geneva," she murmured.

He gave a tight nod. "When I got there, Nick was pacing like a caged animal in the back room. His face was beat to hell—bleeding and swelling by the second—and the guy on the floor was dead. I asked who he was and Nick, true to form, tried to sell me some bullshit story about it being a random degenerate, but finally came clean. It was his dealer. Nick owed him money and when he didn't pay, the guy proved his point with a chair to Nick's face."

A small gasp escaped Allie's lips.

"It was a freak accident. When Nicky pushed him away the guy stumbled and fell, and in the process cracked his head on the table." Hudson met Allie's concerned gaze with a grave stare. "I had to protect my brother. It was all I could do."

"Which is exactly why I agreed to meet with Julian. Not just to protect you, but Nick too."

"What I don't understand is how returning his ring made you decide that breaking off our relationship and flying home alone was the best course of action."

"The ring was just an excuse. What Julian really wants is Ingram, and according to him it's my fault he doesn't have it."

"He's lucky all you did was force him out of the company. You should have had him arrested."

"Julian has it in his head that he's owed everything my father promised him, including me."

His hold on her tightened. "What are his demands?"

"In a few weeks I'm supposed to tell you that I'll take you back if you sign over your shares of the company." Combining their considerable holdings would allow Allie near total control, which is why what she said next came as no surprise. "Once that's done, Julian wants me to name him as CEO." Her voice dropped to barely a whisper as she threw him a last-second curve. "And marry him."

Hudson ground down on his molars. "Not an option. I'll turn myself in and hire a team of lawyers to keep my brother and me out of prison."

Allie shook her head. "You can't do that."

"It will neutralize any power that fucking sociopath thinks he has."

"He'll just find another way. He already . . ." Allie choked back a sob.

"What is it?" His voice softened despite how violent he felt at the moment. "Did he touch you?"

"He killed my parents, Hudson." The tears flowed steadily now. "Julian is the one who hired the hit man."

Hudson felt as though the wind had been knocked out of him. He knew Julian was a sick fucker, but a cold-blooded murderer? Even he hadn't thought him capable of that. And now Julian had set his sights not only on Ingram, but Allie, with Hudson and Nick as collateral damage.

"All the more reason for me to turn myself in. You can tell the police he's blackmailing you. Let them handle this." Some might have considered what Hudson was proposing suicidal, but there was nothing he wouldn't risk for Allie or his brother.

"No. I've already lost my parents; I won't let Julian take you and Nick away from me too."

"You won't lose us. I'll take care of it. And the police will take care of Julian."

"It's not that simple. You don't know what the DA will charge you with. And as for Julian, I don't have any proof. It would be my word against his."

"It will point the police in the right direction and remove any leverage he has over you."

Allie shook her head. "If I turn Julian in to the police, he'll take you and Nick with him."

"What's the alternative?"

"I don't know." She frowned. "We need something to hold over Julian's head. He will be here in a couple weeks. Maybe if I go along with him for a bit, spend some time with him––"

"No fucking way."

"I might be able to find something that incriminates him."

"I don't want you anywhere near that cocksucker." Hudson took a beat to reign in his temper. He gazed unseeingly at the dark lake for several minutes as his brain worked the options like a spreadsheet. "I'll have Max start looking into this. Quietly. He can have his team assembled in a matter of hours."

"The police have been investigating my parents' murder for over two months. The last time Detective Green called she said they were running out of leads."

"We have information the police don't have," he reminded her. "And they are required to operate within the confines of the law."

"You really think his men can find what we need?"

"You'd be surprised what money can buy."

Max curbed the limo in front of the Palmolive building. Allie looked out the window. "I can't stay here, Hudson."

"Why not?"

"We supposedly broke up tonight."

"Supposedly being the operative word."

"Julian has people watching me. He'll know if I don't go home alone. You showing up on my flight, he said he half expected, but if I stay the night . . ." She swallowed hard. "He has to think this limo ride was good-bye."

Hudson wasn't happy about it, but Allie was right. At least for the time being they had to go along with this ridiculous charade and play the estranged couple. So instead of having his hands all over her, his mouth sealed between her legs, and the moans of his name filling every square foot of his penthouse, he'd have to settle for a hot shower and a glass of scotch to burn off his edge.

Poor fucking substitute.

Hudson hit the intercom and instructed Max to head to Astor Place. When the limo eased away from the curb, the ticking clock became almost palpable. Allie pressed into him, as if to absorb every last minute they had together during the short drive to her brownstone. His lips brushed her temple and her hands slid inside his jacket, but there wasn't any amount of contact that would make it easier to let her step out of that car. Sending Allie into her apartment alone with a blackmailing lunatic on the loose went against everything his heart wanted, but precision strategy was going to be key in outsmarting Julian. Hudson had to take emotion out of the equation and let his instincts be the driving force in protecting his brother and the love of his life.

When they arrived at her place, Hudson watched helplessly as Allie slid out of his limo. No words were exchanged, which was just as well since none could have come close to what they were feeling. The ride back to his penthouse was just as silent—Max knew when to give him his space—and he was all set for a quiet evening in the company of a bottle of Blue Label. But as he stepped off the elevator, that plan went into the shitter.

"Dude, what the hell is going on?" Nick said the moment Hudson's feet hit the hardwood. "Harper took off for Paris and—"

"How did you know I was on my way up?"

"Me and the new door guy are tight now, rocking the whole bat signal thing." Nick's eyes zeroed in on him. "Don't change the subject."

"How do you know Harper went to Paris?"

"We hung out once or twice while everyone else we knew was with their families or jetting off to Europe for some ooh-la-la romantic love fest."

Hudson raised a brow at his little brother. "Your sponsor said no relationships until you're six months sober."

"Shit, you getting all big brother on me?"

"I'm always your big brother."

Nick chuckled. "Age before beauty, respect my elders and all that?"

"I mean it, Nick, not for a year." Hudson started to move deeper into his place, then did a double take at his brother's appearance. Nick was wearing his standard-issue jeans and a black tee, but they were clean and hole-free. And goddamn, had he had a haircut? Hudson shook his head as he made his way into the kitchen with Nick tight on his heels.

"Wait, I thought it was six months?"

Hudson wasn't in the mood to go round for round on the subject. "Call your sponsor."

"Ah, shit," Nick snorted. "You know I'm not the relationship type. Love 'em and leave 'em."

"Don't be an ass." Hudson tossed his coat over a barstool and began popping the top three buttons on his shirt. "You better not be pulling that 'love 'em and leave 'em' shit with Allie's best friend, you feel me?" Fuck, not how he should have played that. Pretending to be split from Allie was going to take an effort he had no desire to make.

"It's not like that. She's cool, but just a friend."

"Besides, Allie and I are through," he said, amending his previous objection. "Better you not get involved."

"What?" Nick stared at him for a beat. "What happened? You okay?"

"No, and I don't want to discuss it. I'm exhausted." Hudson finished unbuttoning his shirt as he walked toward his room. "I'm going to take a hot shower and go to bed." So much for the Blue Label. Just as well. He really wasn't up to slam dunking his mood further into the toilet.

"Mind if I crash here?"

"*Now* you're asking me?" Hudson stopped before turning the corner. "Haven't you been living here since Christmas?"

"Someone had to enjoy the amenities while you were gone. Can't let all that mortgage you shell out go to waste."

"It's not a hotel."

"Hey." Nick's voice dropped an octave. "I'm here if you need me."

"I don't need a babysitter." God, he sounded like a dick when his brother was just concerned. Hudson wanted to tell him what was going on, but if he did, it would stress Nick out to the nth degree and back, and might force him into using his two favorite coping mechanisms—drugs and booze. Though Nick did have new skills, relapse was always a threat. Playing it off like he and Allie were broken up was the best maneuver for the time being. And when he'd been dumped, Hudson shut down; he didn't go all chatty-Kathy-let's-paint-each-other's-nails.

"Hudson, I'm serious."

"I know, Nicky, thanks. You're always welcome to crash here," Hudson called out over his shoulder as he continued down the hall. With that, he shut the door to his bedroom and leaned against it. Closing his eyes, he took a deep breath.

There had to be another way.

7

*A*llie expected to find the thirtieth floor empty. Even if the combination of jet lag and stress had kept Hudson awake the same as it had her, he'd no doubt be across the river at Chase Industries. And at six in the morning it was unlikely any of the support staff would have arrived. Which was why she was so surprised to see Colin already at his desk.

A to-go tray of coffee that she was sure included an extra hot, two pump, light froth skinny vanilla latte sat in front of him. Her mouth would have watered at the sight of the much-needed caffeine if it weren't for the rest of the scene in front of her: Harper with her chair pulled up in front of Colin's desk, a box full of croissants open between them.

Colin greeted her as she approached. "Morning, Boss Lady. I thought you'd be early, time change and all." He lifted one of the cups out of the cardboard holder. "And Harper here delivered croissants straight from Paris." His lips curved into a smile but the question in his eyes was impossible to miss. Allie couldn't blame him for his curiosity. Colin was the only one at Ingram who was aware of her personal involvement with Hudson Chase. And while he knew very little about the relationship between the co-CEOs, he knew enough to question why Allie's best friend would have joined them on a romantic trip through Europe.

"I didn't have time to shop for souvenirs," Harper said. Although she left out the words "because we left Paris like a bat out of hell," Allie still heard them loud and clear. "But I figured these would do."

"I'll say." Colin flashed Harper a dazzling grin. "Not every day a beautiful woman bearing French pastries stops by to say hello."

Harper looked at Allie and laughed. "Quite the charmer, this one."

Allie had to agree. With his easy laugh and quick wit, Colin James was charm personified. Not to mention the cover model looks and the boy band hair that fell in a perfectly disheveled mess over his green eyes. But while Allie could certainly appreciate all those attributes, it was his razor-sharp mind and his degree from the nation's number-one journalism school that had pushed his résumé to the top of the pile.

"And a proper introduction was long overdue," Harper said. "At least in my opinion." It was true she'd wanted to meet the man she chatted with far too long whenever she called the office, but Allie knew that wasn't her real motivation for the crack-of-dawn delivery. Harper had questions and she wanted answers that Allie wasn't prepared or able to give her. Not now and maybe not ever.

"Well, you two enjoy your picnic," Allie said, attempting a quick getaway. "I've got a week's worth of e-mails to catch up on."

Harper stood in a rush, affording Allie her first full look at her friend's Friday morning ensemble. The black-and-white dress she wore made her look more like Don Draper's assistant than a twenty-four- year-old from the twenty-first century, but on her it worked. The rotary phone imprint on the skirt complemented the vintage look while the red patent leather flats sent more of a

Dorothy vibe. The whole look was wacky and whimsical and totally Harper Hayes. Her tone however, was all business. "Not so fast," she said. "We need to talk."

It was worth a shot, Allie thought as she made her way into her office with Harper close behind.

"Okay, cut the crap and level with me," Harper said the minute Allie had closed the door.

"It wasn't crap. I haven't so much as looked at an e-mail in days." Allie hung her coat in a closet concealed behind a wood panel. Like everything else in her father's office, it had a rich mahogany finish. Before the holidays Ben Weiss had suggested bringing in a designer to redecorate the decidedly masculine space. At the time she'd had bigger concerns than color swatches, and had agreed to do so only if her position was confirmed. Now both topics seemed trivial. Keeping the people she loved safe was the only thing that mattered. Not her title, and certainly not her office. But she had to keep up appearances.

"I wasn't referring to the e-mails and you know it."

"Well I am. And I'll be lucky to come up for air by dinner."

"Then you better start talking." Harper dropped her purse and coat in one of the leather wingback chairs facing Allie's desk, then plopped down in the other. "Because I'm not leaving until you tell me what the hell happened in France."

Allie rounded her desk and took a seat across from her friend. "Nothing happened. I went to Julian's chateau and gave him his precious ring. End of story."

"You were gone for *hours*."

"Because in true Julian form he left me waiting in his office while he went to attend to other matters," she said, accenting the last word with finger quotes. At least that part was true. Allie met Harper's gaze, hoping she'd take the tiny sliver of truth at face value and drop her interrogation.

No such luck.

Harper shook her head. "Sorry, not buying it."

"Why not? You know how he is." Allie woke her computer and launched the e-mail app. Her inbox contained numerous Google alerts with Hudson's name. Against her better judgment she opened one . . . and there it was. She and Hudson were officially over, at least according to TMZ. *How the hell?* Not that it mattered. Whoever leaked the news, for once, was actually helping them.

"Julian being an asshole and making you wait?" Harper snorted her disdain. "Sure, that I buy. But the rest of this? No way. You can't seriously expect me to believe that while you were cooling your heels in the Haunted Mansion you had this great epiphany that Prince Prissy Pants is your soul mate?"

"I never said that." And she never would.

"Well then how the hell do you explain your sudden change of heart?" There was a moment of unexpected silence followed by Harper's sharp intake of air. "Did he threaten you?"

Allie's hands stilled.

"Because if he did, you need to go to the police and—"

"This has nothing to do with Julian," she interrupted. It wasn't a total lie. Julian's threats weren't Allie's motivation; protecting Hudson and Nick was. And unless she wanted to add Harper to the list of those at risk, she had to somehow convince her to stand down. "Things were off between Hudson and me before I even saw Julian."

"But not before he called." Harper met Allie's surprised reaction with a smirk. "Don't bother denying it; me and your man had a meeting of the minds in my hotel room."

"Yeah, about that—some secret agent you are," Allie teased. "How long did it take before you spilled the whole story?"

"Hey, don't look at me like that. You were the one not answering your phone. We were worried about you. And besides, Hudson is . . ." She shook her head but said nothing. Apparently even Harper Hayes was at a loss for words when it came to Hudson Chase. "Well, you know how he is."

Did she ever. There was no deterring Hudson when he wanted something. A fact he kept proving to Allie time and time again. Only this time she was done fighting him. This time they would fight together, as a team, even if no one else knew it but them.

"I'm sorry I scared you," Allie said. "Honestly, I lost track of time when I was at Julian's, but everything is fine."

"Then why did you break things off with Hudson? I saw the way the two of you were at Christmas. Despite everything else that has happened, you were happy."

Allie shrugged. "I'm not denying he got me through a rough time. I'd been dreading the holidays and he was a welcome distraction."

"Distraction?" Harper squeaked. "No, no, no. A tub of chocolate-chocolate chip is a distraction. What you two had was real. I could feel it every time you looked at each other." Harper's expression softened and her voice grew uncharacteristically quiet. "You love him."

Allie took a deep breath, willing her voice to remain level. "No, I was caught up with the idea of him. The teen romance, recapturing a more innocent time. None of it was real. This . . ." She waved her hand around the office. "This is real. My family's legacy, the one Hudson tried to steal out from under me, is real. I was too distracted by grief and sex to remember that, but hearing Julian's voice on the train that morning brought it all back into focus. My father brokered that deal with Julian because Chase Industries was breathing down his neck. And no matter how hard I try, I can't separate that man from the one you saw on Christmas Eve."

A beat of silence passed as Allie's words hung in the air. Harper had just opened her mouth to speak when there was a knock at the door.

"Come in," Allie called.

Colin poked his head around the door. "Sorry to interrupt.

Seems word has spread that you're back in the office. The phone hasn't stopped ringing."

Allie waved him into the room. "Hit me."

He began reading items off the tablet in his hand. "There's an issue with this morning's cover story—liability seems limited but legal wants to brief you on the potential fallout; the web designers want you to sign off on the cable news layout; that editor from *Chicago* magazine called again; and the union rep wants five minutes today or there won't be a tomorrow." He glanced up. "His words, not mine."

"Have legal run the issue past Ben's office; refer Shaw to the PR department, but give them a heads-up and tell them I won't be granting any interviews at this time; and add the union guy to today's calendar, a ten-minute block, but put him in just before lunch so ten doesn't dissolve into thirty."

"Got it." Colin nodded as he tapped the screen. "And web?"

"Take a look at the design; if it's in line with what we discussed, then go ahead and sign off on it."

His head snapped up. "You want me to sign off on the new look?"

"You're the one who came up with the idea. I trust you can determine if they followed through."

"Will do." Colin's wide grin was almost enough to brighten what was already shaping up to be a shit day, even without factoring in the lack of Hudson time. Allie respected the fact that Colin had chosen to gain practical experience while earning the money he needed for grad school. And while there were certain mundane duties he'd need to perform as her assistant, he was also a valuable asset she had no desire to squander.

She thanked him before he left, then turned her attention back to Harper. "I know you mean well, but—"

"But you have an empire to run. Yeah, yeah, I get it." Harper grinned. "I need to get work too. But don't think this is over."

Allie was quite sure it wasn't. "How about we meet for a run tomorrow?" she offered as a compromise, secretly hoping the exertion would distract from the inquisition.

Harper groaned. "How about I meet you for coffee after your run?"

"Fine. Text me where and when." Allie made a mental note to hit the gym after work as well. All those rich European meals were starting to bite her in the ass. Literally. And it wasn't like she was going to have anything better to do with her Friday night. Might as well work off a few calories along with her sexual frustration.

"I can never repay you for everything you've done for me," she said as she walked her friend to the door. "And not just this week—"

Harper cut her off with a wave of her hand. "You really need to stop thanking me. That's what friends are for. Especially when one of the friends has access to a private jet. How the hell am I ever supposed to fly Southwest again?" she asked, laughing to herself as she pushed through the glass doors that led to the elevator bank.

Allie turned to find Colin waiting for her with a small white envelope. "What's this?" she asked.

"No clue. Found it when I came back to my desk. It's marked *Personal and Confidential*, so I didn't open it."

Allie's breath caught when she saw the handwriting. "Thank you, Colin. Hold my calls." She hurried back into her office and closed the door. Inside the envelope was a note scratched in the same handwriting.

25th Floor, 353B. Now.

Her heart raced as she yanked open the door.

"Everything all right?" Colin asked as she rushed past his desk.

"Yes. Be back in a few," she told him. But the truth was she had no idea how long she'd be gone.

The elevator seemed to move even slower than usual,

although in all likelihood it was just her impatience that made the five-floor ride seem like it took an eternity. The pulleys yanked to a stop twice as she descended the nearly hundred-year-old building, the doors jerking open slowly with each ping, though she scarcely heard them over the sound of her own blood rushing in her ears. What could have prompted such a summons? And so early in the morning. Dozens of scenarios raced through her mind as she made her way down the hallway of the twenty-fifth floor, checking the engraved plaques until she found the one with the number she sought. But as she opened the door, all thoughts left her but one.

Hudson.

He stood with his back to her, his phone pressed to his ear as he stared out across the river to the lake, barely visible through the gray January fog. His tall, muscular frame filled the window of the small office, dominating the space just as he did the world below them. Nearly all of Chicago seemed his for the taking, and yet he'd made it clear that the only thing he wanted was her. And the attraction was more than just physical. It was an inexplicable pull they'd both felt from the very start, a yearning so strong it not only defied the odds, but logic and reason as well. With everything that hung in the balance, the two of them needed to keep their distance. Yet no matter what new development had brought him there, and what risk he was taking, there was no denying the thrill that shot through her just from being in the same room with him.

He turned, his gaze darkening at the sight of her, and all at once she realized the purpose of the visit. He wanted her, needed to be with her as badly as she needed him. Leaving him in the limo the night before had felt like leaving a piece of her heart behind. She craved him, needed him desperately, especially after everything she'd been through that last day in Paris. Julian's threats and the revelation that he'd orchestrated her parents' murder had left her reeling. Now more than ever she needed the strength she drew from their connection. When they were together, all was right in her world. She'd been a fool to ever think otherwise.

"I'll be in my office in an hour. Meet me there." He was speaking into the phone, but his focus was solely on her. She could feel the heat of his stare as though it were his hands exploring her fevered skin. She returned his hungry gaze with one of her own, drinking in the sight of him. The way the hard planes of his body moved beneath his designer suit, the way his dark, unruly hair framed his beautiful face, the way his blue eyes raked her from head to toe. Everything about him had her body trembling with a desire only he could satisfy.

Hudson ended the call and slid his phone onto the empty desk.

"Whose office is this?" she asked. Under normal circumstances she wouldn't have been comfortable having a tryst in a random office. And yet she couldn't deny the desire she felt coursing through her veins. She wanted him too. Wanted his arms around her, his warm skin against hers, renewing their connection and bringing the soothing reassurance only he could provide. If it had been up to her they would have spent a leisurely jet-lagged morning together, making love as the sun came up over Chicago. But since neither time nor location were on their side, she'd take what she could get. And if that meant a fast fuck in a random office, then so be it. The thought alone had her pressing her thighs together in an effort to find relief.

"Mine." He smirked. "When I need one."

Allie glanced around the nearly bare office. A desk, a phone, a couch. Nothing to indicate one of the world's most powerful businessmen used the room as a satellite command center. "Doesn't look like you use it very often."

"I don't." He moved toward her with a slow, predatory stride. "When I'm here it's usually for meetings in the boardroom." His tongue darted out to lick his lips. "Nothing requiring . . . privacy."

"And now?" she asked. Her voice was breathy and needy.

"Now . . ." He stretched his arm out and her heart pounded in anticipation. But instead of touching her, he merely reached behind her. She heard a lock engage with a faint click. "Now I need this." In a heartbeat he took her mouth in a bruising kiss, his fingers threading into her hair as he pushed her up against the door. She moaned when she felt the urgent press of his erection straining against her core, and her lips parted, allowing his tongue to slide fast and hot over hers.

Groaning, Hudson pulled away just long enough to speak. "It fucking killed me to be without you last night." His lips moved with hers again and his hands slid down the column of her throat, across her shoulders, and to her breasts, pausing to brush his thumbs across her taut nipples before smoothing over her waist and the curve of her hips. "I can't keep my hands off you. I need to feel you." He flexed against her and a warm rush of desire flooded her core. "I need to be inside you."

A whimper escaped her lips. "Yes," she said, breathing hard and trembling with need. "Please . . ."

With that he bent low and lifted her, hooking her legs around his waist. He carried her to the couch, where he laid her out lengthwise along the cushions, then lowered himself so his body loomed over hers. Allie wasted no time reaching for his fly, her eager fingers jerking his belt loose before yanking his zipper down to free his throbbing erection.

Hudson reared back, pulling her panties down and over her stilettos. "Definitely leaving these on." Curling his fingers around one ankle, he spread her open, placing her foot on his shoulder. His eyes darkened as his gaze dropped to where she was wet and aching for him. With one finger he traced her quivering entrance. "You're soaked for me, baby. So swollen and slick."

The pad of his thumb stroked over the top of her sex as his

middle finger slipped inside her. Allie's back arched off the coach as he eased out, then back in with a second finger, preparing her for what would no doubt be a fast and furious ride.

"Don't make me wait, Hudson," she panted. "I'm ready."

He claimed her mouth again, his tongue filling her with a deep, searing stroke as he pushed into her on a single thrust. The dual assault was overwhelming. She moaned and her hips lifted, trying to get more of him inside her.

"That's it, take me. Take all of me." Hudson's neck chorded with strain as he pulled back and thrust again, forcing his way deeper as her body clenched around him.

Instinct took over and she began to move with him, her hands clawing at his hair and down his back.

"Christ, Allie, you feel so good." His voice was rough, carnal, and as desperate as the moment between them. "It's like you were made to fuck me."

"You. Only you." And it was true. No one had ever affected her the way Hudson did. Her reaction to him was more than physical; it was raw and primal and as essential as the air she breathed. He was what she needed, what she craved.

The couch thumped against the wall as Hudson powered into her with slick, relentless drives. Over and over he took her—harder, faster, deeper—fucking her like a man possessed until her core began to spasm.

"Come for me," he growled. "Give me what's mine."

"I love you," she gasped as the sweet release of her orgasm rolled through her.

Hudson's head dropped on a groan and his body jerked, driving to the hilt one last time as he came deep inside her. "I love you, too," he said, his breath gusting harsh against her ear. His broad palm smoothed down her thigh and carefully lowered her leg.

Allie wrapped her arms around him and her eyes drifted shut. They lay like that for long moments, their hearts beating in time as their collective breathing slowed and reality seeped back into their consciousness. When Hudson finally lifted his head, he did his best to offer a reassuring smile, but the haunted look in his eyes was like a knife to Allie's soul. He lowered his head to rest it on her chest and her arms around him tightened, too afraid to let go.

8

In the tight confines of the elevator at Chase Industries, Hudson could still smell Allie on his skin. He could feel the lingering sensation of her gripping him, and he could hear the noises she made when she came. God, the thought of her was making his cock go Sear's Tower behind his fly. After their early morning quickie, he should've been relaxed and ready to roll through the rest of the day like a well- satisfied man. Instead he was wired, and now had a hard-on.

For fuck's sake.

The elevator glided to a stop and Hudson shot out like a horse at the gate. His assistant was waiting for him just outside the doors. Hudson glanced over at him and caught sight of a hyper-pink bow tie. Jesus fucking Christ, hadn't that trend worn itself out by now?

"Afternoon, Mr. Chase." Darren took a couple quick steps to catch up, then fell into stride alongside him. "Ben Weiss called; so did that woman from the Ingram board, and Laurie from the press department. Three times," he added, continuing to scroll through his iPad. Darren preferred modern technology to scraps of paper, which Hudson appreciated. He had enough paper cluttering his desk. He didn't need a million color-coordinated Post-its stuck to every damn surface. "Oh, and Sophia requested that you call her as soon as you get her message."

"Of course," Hudson muttered. "Anyone else?"

"About a half-dozen more." Darren grinned. "Your harem awakens."

The news that he and Allie had split must have hit the news-stands and gossip rags, which would explain the ghosts of girl-friends past along with why his PR department was blowing up his call list. He could already picture the headlines, and just like that, the impulse to safeguard Allie's heart, in addition to her well-being, kicked in. The implication that they had broken up grated against his nerves. He wanted to buy every newspaper, magazine or blog that had reported the story, then fire them all for splashing that horseshit across their pages. They needed the world to believe their relationship was over, but that didn't mean he had to like it.

"Darren, normally I appreciate your sense of humor along with your efficiency, but not today." Hudson's jaw tightened.

"My apologies, sir. The numbers, times, and messages have been uploaded to your call list. The contracts needing your signa-ture are arranged in order of priority on your desk. The one on top is time sensitive." Darren was back to business as they closed in on his office. "And your first meeting is all set up in the confer-ence room, as requested."

"How long have they been waiting?"

Darren pushed his horn-rimmed glasses up his nose. "Five minutes at the most."

"Hold all my calls until I say otherwise." Hudson strode past his office and into the adjoining conference room. Max was seated at the table along with two men and a woman, all strategi-cally facing the door. Hudson's gaze drifted from one to the next. Without a doubt each of them were skilled observers, protectors, and when shit hit the fan, killers, if need be. He gave them a quick nod as he shut the door. "Good morning."

"Mr. Chase." Max stood up, and in perfect unison, the other three did as well. There was an elegance to the way they moved, efficient and smooth. These were not rent-a-cops. Max only worked with the best, and these individuals were deadly weapons in the guise of civilians.

"Please sit." Hudson unbuttoned his suit jacket and took a seat at the head of the table. The group followed his lead, lowering their bodies with the same efficiency. "I appreciate you all coming on such short notice. Before we discuss why you're here, I like to know who I'm talking to."

Max nodded to his left. "This is Ivan," he said, offering no last name. The man was built like a tank, and when he shifted his massive body into a more comfortable position, the cuff of his shirt rode up, revealing tattoos that undoubtedly covered his arm in a full sleeve. "Former US Special Forces and high precision marksman." So in other words, a sniper. As if confirming Hudson's train of thought, Max added, "Ivan has extensive training in observation, surveillance, and target acquisition, as well as unconventional warfare."

"Unconventional warfare?" Hudson lifted a brow.

"Hybrid tactics combining protocol with unorthodox methods," Ivan answered.

Military tactics weren't Hudson's forte, but dollars to shit piles he'd just been fed a diplomatic explanation of guerilla warfare. His gaze shifted to the guy with the military-grade haircut. His suit was perfectly tailored, his white shirt high on the starch, and judging by the sharp, clean edges, his hair was freshly trimmed. This was a guy you'd pass on the street a hundred times without noticing.

"Jim," he said. "CIA."

Well, that explained his John Doe look—he wasn't in the

market to be noticed or draw attention. No further description of Jim's training was given, nor was more needed.

Next was the only woman on Max's team. With her slight build and long blond hair, she could have passed for Allie at a distance. Hudson wondered if that was merely coincidental or part of a contingency plan. Either way, he thought, the similarity could prove useful in the future.

"Jessica, former Israeli intelligence, computer science and communications expert." There was no artifice to her introduction; it was clear and concise.

"Pleasure to meet you, Jessica, Ivan, Jim." Hudson said their names, though he doubted they were the ones bestowed upon them at birth. "I'm sure you're as anxious as I am to get started, so I'll dive right in. Victoria and Richard Sinclair were murdered in cold blood at their Lake Forest home. Shot to death—Richard in his study and Victoria in the dining room."

Max hit a button on a remote, and in unison a screen lowered and the lights dimmed. With another push of a button images from the crime scene flashed in full color: Richard slumped over his desk, Victoria on the dining room floor. Hudson had seen the images before, but knowing Julian was responsible, and that he had his sights set on Allie, spun them in an even darker light.

"The police labeled it a home invasion," Hudson continued, "until a cataloging of the home's contents revealed nothing was missing with the exception of Mrs. Sinclair's engagement ring." A large sapphire surrounded by a ring of diamonds filled the screen. "A few weeks later, a known assassin was found dead with that ring in his possession."

Max hit the remote and pictures of the murdered gun-for-hire flashed onscreen, one after the other. Hudson had no idea how his head of security had gotten his hands on them, and he had no intention of asking. When it came to this assignment, the less he knew, the better.

"The Sinclair murders were sloppy for a professional hit," Ivan said. "Especially the wife."

"The police believe that was intentional," Hudson said. "To make it look more like a break-in gone bad."

"Then why take out the shooter?" Jessica asked.

"Loose end." Jim casually crossed his leg at the knee. "Is there a money trail?"

"None that the authorities have been able to find. But I've recently learned that the man responsible for orchestrating their deaths is Julian Laurent." A picture from the Laurent website popped up, and in spite of the gravity, Hudson nearly laughed. The fucker looked more like Miss Clairol than the head of a global conglomerate.

"Is he on Chicago PD's radar?" Ivan asked.

"No. And his alibi is rock solid, placing him in France at the time of the murders."

Ivan frowned. "Wait, isn't he engaged to their daughter?"

"Was." Hudson's voice was clipped. Hearing Julian referred to as Allie's fiancé, regardless of his current status, didn't set well, and seeing the two of them together was even worse. He bit down on his molars as their official engagement photo flashed onto the screen.

The sound of Jim's voice was a welcome distraction from the sight of Julian's hand curled possessively around Allie's shoulder. "Are you sure your information is reliable?"

"From the man himself," Hudson said. "Alessandra Sinclair is being blackmailed by Laurent into marrying him for the sole purpose of gaining control of Ingram Media. He incarcerated her at his château in Paris for several hours yesterday after luring her there under the pretense of returning his engagement ring."

"Tacky of him to ask her to return it," Jessica said, completely unfazed by the mention of blackmail or kidnapping.

"It is a family heirloom gifted down from one French fuck to another." Hudson dragged in a breath and made an effort to sound more politically correct. "I'm sure there are decent individuals in the Laurent family, but right now I'd like to annihilate their entire bloodline." Okay, not entirely PC, but he was way past playing nice.

"Appropriate given the origin of the piece," Ivan said dryly.

Back to business. "Over the course of his conversation with Miss Sinclair, Laurent admitted to murdering her parents. But we have no proof, no money tied to the hit, and an assassin whose talking days are over. That's where you come in." Hudson's options were limited to the confines of the law, but this group could push the boundaries and end this nightmare by any means necessary. "If you're as good as Max says you are, then I'm certain with your combined expertise you can nail the son of a bitch."

Ivan leaned forward in his chair. "If I may, what's your stake in all this?"

"I have a vested interest as a significant shareholder of Ingram Media."

"And your relationship to Miss Sinclair?" he asked.

Hudson pushed to his feet and walked over to the floor-to-ceiling windows. In the distance he could see the river cutting the city in half, and Ingram Media on the opposite bank. Somewhere in that building was the woman who owned every corner of his heart and his entire soul; the woman he'd sacrifice himself to protect. He glanced over his shoulder at the team of intelligence experts he'd assembled to quite literally save her life. "Business associates."

"No offense, Mr. Chase," Jessica said. "But a man doesn't go to all this trouble for a business associate." He noted the sardonic tone in her voice. "Especially one that just broke his heart. Again."

Hudson turned away from the window and his eyes clashed with Jessica's. "I didn't take you for the type to gather intel from gossip sites."

"Video paparazzi can provide valuable surveillance footage." She smiled. "Unknowingly, of course."

Hudson narrowed his gaze. "I protect my investments."

Ivan snorted. "I think I speak for the group when I say none of us are buying that."

"There is a modicum of respect I demand from individuals when in the confines of my building, Ivan. I've earned it."

"I'm pretty sure I've earned the same, Mr. Chase, and I'm well compensated for it. I'm also good at reading people, and I can tell you're a man with an instinctual drive to protect. I admire it, but it's your Achilles' heel as well as your strength. And can you honestly say you're offended I want to cut through the crap?"

Far from it. In fact, he was actually starting to like the guy. The goddamn bastard was observant and he wasn't throwing any punches. He also wasn't a man who was easily intimidated. By anyone.

Jim cleared his throat. "I think what Ivan is trying to so eloquently say—" he cut his eyes at his military counterpart "—is that you need to level with us. We can't operate at top form without all the necessary information."

Hudson ran a hand back through his hair. Jim had a point. They couldn't be expected to deliver results without reading the fine print. "What do you need?"

"It would be helpful to know the nature of the blackmail as well as the extent of your relationship with Miss Sinclair."

Hudson joined them at the table. "Alessandra and I have been involved since shortly before Christmas. One of Julian's demands was that she end our relationship, which he and the press believe she did last night. He's made it clear he intends to use her status in the US to catapult himself to the equivalent of American royalty. He wants . . ." What's mine. "My shares of Ingram Media as well."

The three operatives listened as Hudson outlined the details of Julian's plan. No notes were taken, no paper trail created, but he knew they were absorbing and analyzing every detail. When he was finished, it was Jim who spoke first.

"What concessions are you willing to make?" he asked.

"Such as?"

Ivan piped up. "Keeping your distance from Miss Sinclair, restricting your . . . activities together. Perhaps even leaving the city."

"Our *activities* are none of your business. And while I'm equipped to work anywhere in the world, Julian's plan hinges on Miss Sinclair's ability to convince me to part with my shares of Ingram. Even if it didn't, there's no way I would leave town. I'll jump through the necessary hoops to convince Julian that Allie is following his directives, but the only way I'm staying one hundred percent away from her— " Hudson leveled his stare on Ivan "—is if I'm dead."

Jim's voice was solemn when he spoke. "Mr. Chase, if you don't do as we advise, that could be a distinct possibility."

"And if this Laurent character is as crazy he sounds, he already has your plots picked out," Ivan added.

Max cut Ivan a look.

"What?" Ivan said in return. "You know as well as I do what people are capable of. Hell, look at what this guy has already done."

"Nonetheless," Hudson said, "Julian is expecting me to pursue her. A certain amount of interaction will assure him things are progressing as planned."

"Which brings us back to the question of leverage," Jim said.

When Hudson hesitated, Ivan spoke up. "We're all in this line of work because we don't always play nice with authority," he said. "But discretion and confidentiality are nonnegotiable. We wouldn't last long otherwise. When you get our bill, you'll see our services come at a very high price. Might as well get your money's worth."

Hudson let out a resigned breath. "Julian is in possession of a surveillance video that could prove harmful to people Miss Sinclair cares about." That's all he said, and in his opinion that was all they needed to know. Aside from Allie and himself, Max was the only person who knew what was on that video, and Hudson intended to keep it that way.

"So you're looking for something to hold over his head," Jessica said. It was more statement than question. "A trade of sorts."

"Video can be forged and manipulated," Jim said. "Which is why copies can be easily discredited. The original footage is your primary concern."

"Max is handling that aspect of the investigation. Your objective is to locate evidence that connects Julian to the deaths of Richard and Victoria Sinclair. I need proof he was the executioner, and I need it before the police."

"Understood," the three of them said as one.

"Max." Hudson nodded to his right-hand man.

"These envelopes contain copies of the crime scene photos and police reports, along with the statements taken from Miss Sinclair, the housekeeper, and the neighbors." Max slid the manila envelopes across the glossy mahogany one at a time. Ivan slapped his palm down on top of the thick packet to bring it to a stop, then Jim and Jessica followed suit. "You will also find the full work-up of the subject, including the addresses of numerous properties, the various holdings in his family's trust, and a few of the more mundane facts as well: what he smokes, what he drinks, and his, ah . . ." Max cleared his throat. "Preferences."

Hudson knew Max was censoring himself for his benefit. The report inside those envelopes no doubt detailed Julian's "preference" for hookers or social climbing nymphets game for a threesome.

"Do we have eyes on the ground in France?" Jim asked.

Max nodded. "I've also placed someone here at Chase Industries and at Ingram for Miss Sinclair." Max twisted the gold band on his left hand. "If he has someone watching her—"

"He does," Hudson said. "Julian knew the second we landed at O'Hare and that we shared a limo to her house."

"Well, the guy now has a new shadow," Ivan said. "Round the clock. Julian's stooges don't only work the day shift, so neither do I. Although I'm not a morning person." He cracked some semblance of a smile. "And I'd like my coffee black."

Hudson fixed him with a hard stare. "I don't fetch coffee, GI Joe. And I'm not paying you to sit on your ass and drink it."

Ivan chuckled. "I'm liking your boy here, Max." His words were said without an ounce of condescension. "You've got balls of steel under that prissy Tom Ford, dontcha, Mr. Chase?"

"Ralph Lauren Black Label," Jim corrected. Hudson was impressed. The guy clearly knew his suits.

"Where do we go from here?" Hudson asked, refocusing the conversation.

"Jessica will be conducting back channel investigations," Max said.

"Most of its done on the dark web," she explained. "If there's a trail of cash, I'll find it there."

"We'll get started right away," Jim said, offering no details as to his role in the group.

"Good. I expect results." Hudson stood. "Funds will be wired to your specified accounts by the end of the day and Max has full authority to approve any additional expenses." He checked the Patek Philips strapped to his wrist. "Now if you'll excuse me, I have another meeting."

9

*T*he significance of the location Harper had picked was completely lost on Allie. She was so consumed with thoughts of Hudson and Julian and drug dealers and hit men and private military ops that she didn't make the connection. Not when she read Harper's text, not as she jogged through Lincoln Park, and not as she stood waiting on the corner of Division and Clark. It wasn't until they were standing in line that she realized they weren't meeting at just any Starbucks. They were meeting for coffee at the location where Nick Chase worked as the shop's newest barista.

Allie watched him, juggling orders at rapid speed while charming the female customers, and she couldn't help but smile. For as different as they were, there was still so much about Nick that reminded her of his brother. The same jawline and nose, the same dark, unruly hair, though Nick wore his much longer, and the same confident stride. Their eyes were the most notable exception; Hudson's being a clear blue while Nick's were a deep brown. But despite the difference in color, both men expressed themselves clearly with a single glance, and at the moment Nick's eyes were telling Allie all she needed to know about his feelings for her best friend.

He did a double take when he caught sight of Allie, but instead of flashing his trademark grin, his gaze immediately shifted, searching the crowd to her right and left until he found what he was looking for. Or rather *who* he was looking for. He locked eyes with Harper and a shy smile curved his lips. When Allie turned to her best friend, she discovered a similarly ridiculous grin had spread across her face. And had the cold air outside turned her cheeks a warm pink or was Harper actually blushing?

Oh, how the tables have turned.

"Is that Nick?" she asked.

Harper squinted and leaned to her left. "Is it?"

Enjoying their little game too much to end it just yet, Allie decided to play along. "I think so. Didn't he mention something on Christmas Eve about working here?"

"Did he?" Harper chewed on her lip. "You know, I think you're right."

Allie fought the urge to roll her eyes as they stepped up to the cashier. She placed her order first, then stood back to take in the scene unfolding in front of her, watching in fascination as Nick tried his best to play it cool, feigning total focus on the espresso maker as it hissed and squealed while stealing glances in Harper's direction.

"Hi, Nick," Allie finally said.

"Hey, Allie." There wasn't a hint of surprise in his voice or expression. Clearly he'd been expecting them. "Out for a run?"

"Just finished."

"Grande caramel macchiato," he called out to the waiting crowd before setting the beverage on the raised counter.

"Looks like you're quite the pro."

"I'm getting the hang of it." Nick reached for the cup marked with Allie's name and flipped it in the air. "But we'll see if I can stand up to the ultimate test," he said, catching the cup with one hand. He read the detailed drink specifications scribbled along the side of the cup and took a deep breath. "Here goes." He set the cup down, then proceeded to crack his knuckles as part of a dramatic preparation.

This time Allie did roll her eyes. "I'm not *that* bad."

Harper appeared by her side, tucking her wallet back into her purse. "Don't even bother. We both know you too well."

Nick looked up at the sound of Harper's voice. "Hey," he said. They stared at each other for a long beat until the milk Nick was steaming overflowed from the stainless steel pitcher he held in his hand. "Shit," he said, jumping back as froth splattered all over his green apron.

Allie covered her mouth to hide her laugh, and for about the hundredth time that day found herself wishing Hudson was by her side. Although for Nick's sake it was probably a good thing he wasn't. The teasing would have no doubt been swift and relentless. "I'll grab a table," she said, leaving the two of them alone at the counter. When Harper joined her a few minutes later, she acted as though nothing was amiss.

"Have you recovered from the jet lag?" she asked, as if everything were perfectly normal and she hadn't just outed the relationship she'd categorically denied. "I guess that's one good thing about a twenty-four-hour trip to Europe," she added, handing Allie her skinny vanilla latte. "My body never had time to adjust."

"Are we going to pretend like that didn't just happen?"

"What?"

"Oh please. To quote one of your favorite expressions, 'I saw the way you two were eye-fucking each other.'"

Harper sputtered into her chai latte, then stole a glance over her shoulder at Nick. He winked and held up a finger to indicate he'd be one more minute.

"So the guy you're *not* dating is joining us?"

"He has a break in a few minutes," she mumbled into her cup.

Allie gave her a self-satisfied smile. "And you just happen to know this how?"

"Fine," Harper said. "We may have been hanging out a bit over the holidays. But everyone else I know was out of town, and Nick's trying to keep his distance from—"

"Stop. I think it's great the two of you are . . . hanging out," Allie said, parroting Harper's words. "What I don't understand is why you keep denying there's more to it. Anyone can see the attraction between the two of you."

Harper's face split into a wide grin. "Really?"

"Yes." Allie smiled back at her friend. Despite the chaos in her life, at least one person she cared about was genuinely happy. Focusing on that was exactly what Allie needed. "Now tell me what's been going on with the two of you since Christmas Eve."

"I don't know, really. I certainly wasn't looking for anything when I showed up on your doorstep like a human icicle." Harper cupped her tea between her hands and rested her elbows on the table. "We just sort of clicked that night."

"I'd say so." The image of Harper and Nick sitting side by side in front of the fireplace on Christmas morning filled Allie's mind.

"Nothing happened. I swear all we did was talk."

"I believe you. Although it was pretty funny the way Nick jumped up so quickly when Hudson and I came into the room."

"Like a busted teen." Harper laughed. "Gotta admit, even I was a bit scared when Hudson walked in the room. That man intimidates the hell out of me."

"So is that why all the secrecy?"

Harper shrugged. "Nick's not supposed to be dating so soon into his recovery," she said, answering Allie's unspoken question. Obviously Harper knew about Nick's recent stint in rehab.

"And what, he's worried Hudson will be disappointed?"

"Yeah. I know they have that tough brother act down pat, but

Nick is really grateful to Hudson for everything he's done. Feels like he saved his life, ya know?"

Allie gave a somber nod. She knew all too well the lengths to which Hudson had gone to protect his brother.

"The last thing Nick wants to do is let him down."

Allie wasn't nearly done questioning Harper, but when she spotted Nick making his way toward their table, she knew the rest of her interrogation would have to wait.

Nick picked up a chair and spun it around. He straddled it, then crossed his arms over the wooden back and leaned forward. "How did I get so lucky as to have two of the prettiest girls in Chicago stop by my Starbucks?"

Allie met his gaze with wide, innocent eyes. "Oh, I don't know, maybe because one of them is your girlfriend?"

Nick's eyes darted to Harper, who sat gaping at Allie. "Guess we weren't too subtle." He chuckled. "I take it she knows everything, then?"

"Well, yeah, sort of—I mean no," Harper stammered. "I never said I was your girlfriend."

A lopsided grin spread across Nick's face as he watched Harper struggle. It was a grin Allie had seen before, when he was a young, carefree boy. Her heart swelled at the sight of that smile on his face again.

"It's all good," Nick finally said, putting Harper out of her misery. He reached for her hand, bringing their entwined fingers to his mouth and pressing a kiss to her knuckles. "That's what you are, right, babe?"

There was no mistaking Harper's reaction for windblown cheeks this time. Her face blushed as red as her hair. Allie smiled. Seemed the Chase brothers had more in common than just their looks. Her gaze shifted back and forth between the two lovebirds until she feared someone at another table might actually catcall "Get a room." She cleared her throat with an exaggerated cough.

ANN MARIE WALKER & AMY K. ROGERS

"Sorry," Nick said a bit sheepishly. "It's not that we didn't want you to know."

"It's okay. Harper explained."

Nick grew serious. "It's just . . . Hudson's been really good to me. I don't want him to think I'm not taking the program seriously."

"I get it."

He grinned. "I knew you would. So you won't say anything to my bro about . . ." His gaze shifted to Harper.

"I'm trying to keep my conversations with your brother strictly business." It wasn't the assurance Nick was looking for, but it was the best she could provide without outright lying to him. In reality she never again wanted to have secrets of any kind between her and Hudson. Not after everything they'd been through, and especially not in light of everything else they were dealing with.

"Yeah, about that," Nick began.

Allie shook her head. "Oh no, not you too?"

"It's my fault," Harper said. "I asked him to gang up on you."

"I'll remember this, Nick," she teased. "Don't even think about asking me for help when her birthday rolls around."

Harper frowned. "Can we talk about this seriously for a second?"

No, they couldn't. Allie couldn't seriously discuss a life without Hudson in it. She'd barely faked her way through the conversation they'd already had. Harper would surely see through her lies if she had to go into more detail about why she no longer wanted to be with the man she loved. "Harper, I—"

She was saved by the ping of an incoming text. It wouldn't be Hudson, since they had agreed on radio silence, and since Harper was sitting in front of her that meant it could only be the office. For once, whatever emergency awaited her was a welcome interruption.

But when she pulled her smartphone out of her pocket it

wasn't Colin or Ben whose name appeared on the screen. Instead the sender was listed as private.

Tic Toc, Alessandra.

Allie felt the blood drain from her face as she read Julian's less than subtle reminder.

"Everything okay?" Harper asked.

Allie looked up to see both Harper and Nick staring at her, concern written all over their faces. "Oh yeah, just a last-minute glitch on a contract I thought we'd already put to bed." She gathered her coat and coffee. "I need to head up to the office."

Nick stood when she did. "Want me to grab you a cab?"

"No, sit, enjoy the rest of your break. I'll call you later, Harper," she said as she dashed out the door. It took every ounce of strength to fight the impulse to run straight to the Palmolive building and into Hudson's arms. It had barely been twenty-four hours since they'd been together and already the separation felt like torture. She longed to see him, to feel his touch or just hear his voice. She stared down at the phone still clutched in her hand and sighed. Even a call was too risky. They still had no idea who was acting as Julian's eyes and ears, or to what lengths he'd gone to keep her under surveillance.

A taxi pulled alongside the curb and she ducked inside, stuffing her phone back into her pocket as she gave the driver the address of Ingram's headquarters. There might not have been any fires to put out, but losing herself in work sounded like a much better option than pacing the floor of her brownstone. She and Hudson had plans to rendezvous the next day, but for now at least, there wasn't anything she could do but wait.

10

*H*udson's shoes slammed against the pavement. His feet kicked up water from the slush, which splattered onto his sweatpants. His arms pumped, his fists clenched tight, and his breath shot out of his mouth in clouds of condensation.

Allie had to have been goddamn nuts to suggest this "random" run-in. For once the sun was shining and the sky was clear, but like hell if it was running weather. It was balls-freezing cold. And while there were enough obstacles to obscure the line of sight of someone spying on them from the street, Lincoln Park didn't render them invisible. God, he wished they were. Then they wouldn't have to keep creating these orchestrated accidents.

A gust of wind smacked into his face. The cold was rough and raw and would have penetrated his bones if he wasn't beating the shit out of his running shoes. As he pushed himself harder toward their designated meeting place, his irritation over the situation made every protective instinct roar. He wanted to tell, hell dare, that French fuck to untuck his nut sac and recite his demands directly to him, leaving Allie out of it.

When he reached the Lincoln Monument, Hudson paused.

He closed his eyes and stretched his arms above his head, lengthening his spine, and felt the pain in his chest that had been a near constant. It wasn't work stress—business was thriving, not to mention *Forbes* had started making inquiries—or Nick, who was owning the twelve step thing. No, the ache that tightened his chest had been there since the day he thought Allie had left him. Again. And now they'd embarked on a game of playing Julian for a fool, not to mention the society pages and their friends, family, and colleagues. The ruse felt too real at times, and it hurt, but not enough to make him regret doing it. If their charade was what it took to keep her safe and have her as his again, then so be it. He just had to keep reminding himself that when it was over, they would move on with their fucking lives. She was his future.

Hudson dropped his arms, then did a check of his watch. Right on time Allie rounded the turn, heading home via the farm and pond at the south end of the Lincoln Park Zoo. He watched for a second, the sight of her hypnotizing him to the point where the city around them receded into the background and the traffic bled into white noise. His body responded immediately in a way that translated straight down to his cock and it thickened, straining both the fabric of his track pants and his self-control. Christ, he was going to be pitching a fucking a tent in the middle of the park if his hard-on didn't bow out.

But God, he wanted her; wanted her naked and underneath him, her legs locked around his hips and her breath panting his name. And he couldn't stop thinking about the quickest way to strip her out of those tight running pants and plunge his cock into her fast, hard, and deep.

He cracked his neck to loosen it up as he timed her approach . . . three . . . two . . . then broke into a jog to close the distance between them until he was literally "running" into her.

Allie halted in front of him. Her cheeks were flushed and a sheen of sweat glistened across her skin. "This wasn't a good idea."

Hudson stood farther back than he would have liked, his

body coiled tight and the muscle in his jaw flexing. No one was close enough to hear what they were saying, but their body language still mattered. "I'm supposed to be trying to win you back. He's banking on the fact that I will pursue you like last time."

"Don't you mean stalking?" The corners of her mouth turned up. "If I recall, you were quite good at it."

"Don't smile—you're not supposed to like me, remember? Besides, when you're pissed off, it is unbelievably hot."

Allie looked off toward the lake and pressed her lips together, stifling what he knew without question was a mind-blowing smile. "You're not helping."

Hudson shifted closer, doing his best to suppress a grin of his own. "Then I'll step up my stalker asshole game and we can go back to my place and have angry sex."

Allie covered her mouth in a fake cough. "Still not helping." She bent over and braced her hands on her shins, giving her hamstrings a good stretch and Hudson a good view. His gaze fell instinctively to her ass, and he groaned.

"That's not helping, either." He scrubbed a hand down his face as if that would wipe away the utterly filthy image he had of her on her hands and knees, perfectly aligned to take him. He knew how slick, hot, and fucking amazing it felt to slip the head of his cock between her folds, teasing her before he fucked her.

Allie straightened. "Don't even think about it."

"Too late."

She shook her head. "What would you like to talk about?"

"Why, Alessandra, are you at a loss for words? Hell just froze over."

"Funny." Allie rolled her eyes. "Oh! I saw Nick yesterday."

"Going from angry sex to the subject of my brother is not the direction I had in mind," he said in a dry, deep tone.

"Believe me, I'm right there with you. But I'm trying to work with what we have."

"So where did you see him?" he asked in an effort to tow the line.

"Harper and I had coffee at the Starbucks on Division."

"Ah yes, my brother the barista. Did he take good care of my girl?"

"He did. And my best friend, the recent coffee connoisseur, as well."

"Does Harper take twenty minutes to order a coffee, too?" His mouth curved into a wry grin.

"She spent twenty minutes at the counter all right, but not debating her order."

He raised his brows and crossed his arms over his chest. "Is there something I should know about?"

"Seems your brother and my best friend have become something of an item."

"What? When did this happen?"

"While we were in Europe. One all-night conversation led to a movie and that led to—"

"I get the idea." Hudson cut her off. He didn't need that image sitting front-and-center scratching against his visual cortex. Shit, the notion was already singeing his retinas. "Fuck." He ran a hand through his hair. "I already told him not to pull his crap with your friend."

"I don't think he's pulling any shit. From what I saw, they really like each other."

Hudson looked up at the sky. The forecast was for more snow, which was going to give those pigs that must be flying one hell of a time. "This should be an interesting topic of conversation at dinner tonight."

"You can't say anything."

"Why not?"

"Because you can't tell him that you know. We're broken up, remember? And even if we weren't, they asked me not to tell you."

He cursed under his breath. "This is ridiculous."

"After everything he's put you through, Nick wants nothing more than to make you proud, Hudson. Surely you can see that. And he's worried that breaking the no-dating-during-recovery rule is going to disappoint you." Her voice softened. "Just let him tell you about this when he's ready."

"Fine. Is there anything else I'm not supposed to know?"

"I think that's it." She fought the grin he knew threatened to spread across her face, but the sentiment was definitely in her voice; the kind that told him she was enjoying his reaction to this news flash perhaps a little too much. God help him, he loved seeing her happy, even when it was at his expense.

"The rest of the time was pretty much their version of an intervention," she said.

"Intervention?"

"Mmmhmm. They don't understand why we're not together. Can't say I blame them, really. After seeing how happy we were at Christmas, I'm sure they think I'm a raving bitch for suddenly breaking things off."

"We can't tell them what's really going on. For now we have to play it out. It's for their own protection."

"I know." Allie looked down at the ground. When she lifted her head, he could see the despair in her eyes that came from being in a crappy situation that had no foreseeable end. But hell if he was going to let it settle there. This, them being apart, was temporary. He knew that without question, but it was still a head-fuck.

"I want to touch you." On impulse he stepped forward, and at the same time Allie shifted back. "Goddamn fucking hell." The words came out with sharp edges. "I know that was for the watchful eyes, but it's killing me, Allie." He ran a hand back through his hair and fisted the dark waves at the base of his neck.

"Me too," she whispered, blinking back tears.

He let out a resigned breath. "I'm going to work at Chase HQ as much as possible this week."

Allie nodded. "Of course. I'm sure you've got a lot to catch up on there with the holidays and then all this."

"Well yes, but mostly if we're seen together all week, Julian will wonder why you haven't laid out your terms." Also because it was torture to see her and not be with her. Even though her cold indifference was a farce, it was too close to the reality he never wanted to experience again in any form.

"Right." She dropped her stare once more and toed a small patch of ice with her running shoe.

Hudson cleared his throat. "We need to afford Max a bit of time for his team to work."

Allie's head snapped up. "Who does he have working on it? Does he think they can find something to connect Julian?" There was a flicker of hope in her eyes that went from spark to full-on blaze in no time flat.

"The less you know, the better." She was already in this mess far deeper than he had ever wanted. And if Max was blurring the lines of the law at his request, Allie didn't need blow-by-blow intel that could pin her to the wall as an accomplice.

"Don't give me that crap, Hudson. We're in this together." The words slingshot out of her mouth, and he couldn't stop the slight grin that tugged at his lips.

"Agreed."

"Then tell me what's going on. I've had enough people keeping me in the dark for whatever reasons they felt were justified." Her eyes clouded. "If Max has any leads, I want to know about them."

"He doesn't. Not yet. But I've asked them to use any means at their disposal." He fixed her with a hard stare. "I won't involve you with the details of their methods, but I assure you, if they yield any results I will notify you immediately. Now, as much as I hate to say it, you need to leave me standing here, hat in hand.

Fortunately your expression is already the perfect mix of frustrated exasperation."

Allie rubbed her gloved hand over her face, and he knew it was to hide the smile she'd failed to fight.

"One more thing," he said. "A courier will deliver a package tomorrow. It will contain an encrypted phone. Speaking might be too risky given we don't know who is on Julian's payroll, but we can text each other any necessary information." He smirked. "Or Shakespeare."

She shook her head. "You're lucky you're cute, Chase."

Hudson lifted a brow. "Cute? Not the adjective I would have chosen." He kicked his chin toward the Chicago History Museum. "Now go on before I drag you into that building and show you just how cute I can be."

Her cheeks were already red from the chill of the wind, but when the color deepened he knew without a doubt she was blushing. And when Allie turned and took off toward her brownstone as he broke into a run in the opposite direction, he knew she had taken a piece of him with her.

The run back to his penthouse had nearly put Hudson's balls into hibernation. Nearly. Toeing off his shoes, he stripped naked and let his longsleeve T-shirt and sweatpants drop to the floor in a wet heap. He walked to the shower, cranked on the dual heads, and stepped under the spray. Closing his eyes, he faced the onslaught and was immediately hit with a poignant sadness and a bone-splitting emptiness.

He tried to concentrate on the heat of the water beating against his chest and rushing over his tired, chilled muscles. Fuck him, it wasn't happening. Allie and this mess occupied every corner of his mind, and the fact that Max hadn't turned up shit on Julian was throwing his mood even further into the crapper.

As he started to run through the various scenarios that could nail the connection between Julian and the Sinclair murders, he felt a soft feminine hand on his shoulder, then felt the warmth of naked skin at his back.

Hudson turned, and as he did, Allie's hands drifted over the hard ridges of his stomach. "How did you get in here?"

"You gave me a key card, remember?" She leaned forward and pressed her lips to his chest.

"An excellent move on my part." His hands gripped her waist, then slid up her delicate rib cage. "Not that I'm complaining, but address the how."

"I took the tunnel under Lake Shore and cut through the Drake, then came up through the garage."

The pads of his thumbs circled her nipples and he felt them tighten under his touch.

Allie drew a breath before continuing. "Last time I saw the black SUV, it was stuck in gridlock. Now, do you want to discuss the traffic on Michigan Avenue, or do you want me to suck your cock?"

He cupped her cheek and brushed a thumb across her bottom lip. "I want your perfect lips wrapped around my cock. And when I come in your mouth, you'll remember who you belong to."

"As if I could ever forget." Her smile was absolute wickedness as she dropped to her knees and into every man's shower fantasy in flawless HD.

Water hit the back of his neck, sluiced over his shoulders, and dripped off the head of his cock as it jutted out from his hips, begging for attention. Anticipation shot down his spine, going straight between his legs and making him painfully hard. Goddamn, the bastard was pounding.

Allie kept her eyes locked on his as her fingers curled around his thick shaft. She licked her lips, then leaned forward and took the wide head into her mouth—so slick, warm, and wet. The sensations of her drove him half crazed. His stance widened as her hands slid up his thighs to his ass. Her fingers splayed, pulling him deeper until she'd taken all of him.

"Fuck," he hissed. The sight of her, on her knees before him while she deep throated his cock, almost had him losing it.

Hudson's palm slapped against the marble and his hips flexed, thrusting himself in and out of all that silky wetness. She pulled back, her tongue stroking his length and her teeth grazing his tip, then her cheeks hollowed as she sucked him back in again.

"Rougher." His breath punched in and out of his lungs, and when she cupped his heavy sac, a groan ricocheted off the walls.

Fuck him, he could spend eternity working her mouth. Her skill was downright deadly. His arms dropped, his hands seeking, finding, and fisting Allie's hair. Need surged in him, and he thrust himself even deeper, the drive to fuck overriding all else. An approving hum escaped Allie's lips as if she were savoring every inch of him, and the sound vibrated up his length. He knew how wet it made her to suck him off, and Jesus Christ, what a turn-on. He wanted to return the favor and go down on her, to taste her and feel her pulse around his tongue as she came. But her punishing rhythm and the graze of her teeth yanked him back into the present.

She fluttered her tongue along the underside of his cock, then her lips closed around the head and she sucked. His grip on her hair tightened and the muscles in his neck chorded. He was dangerously close to the edge, but she didn't ease up in the slightest. And like hell if he was going to slow things down.

He stole a glance at her as the water beat down around them. No makeup, her skin flushed, her lashes fanned against her face —she couldn't have been more beautiful. Add to that the visual of him moving in and out of her mouth, her cheeks hollowed, her hands gripping his thighs . . . his breath caught and his body locked as his orgasm shot down his spine. Allie moaned as his

ANN MARIE WALKER & AMY K. ROGERS

release filled her mouth in spasms. "Swallow it," he grunted. "Take everything."

Her throat worked his cock while her hands milked him, and damn it to fucking hell, even as his orgasm barreled out of him, he wanted her again. He wanted to press her tits against the cold glass and fuck her hard and fast, pulling her hips back and driving into her until she was shouting his name. And he would. He'd spend the rest of the day inside her. She was there, in his house, and every damn surface would be used without apology.

He had no idea what tomorrow held. But for now, she was his.

---

11

*A*llie looked up from her computer as Colin plopped a brown paper bag on her desk. Whatever was inside smelled delicious and her stomach growled in agreement.

"What's that?"

"It's called lunch," he deadpanned. "Traditionally served somewhere between breakfast and dinner."

"I know what lunch is." She rolled her eyes. "I meant why is there a bag of it on my desk?"

"Because when two o'clock rolled around and you hadn't so much as poked your head through that door, I figured you weren't going out for lunch. So," he said, snapping a paper napkin open with an exaggerated flourish and spreading it out in front of her, "lunch came to you."

"That's very sweet, but you really didn't need to do this," she said, although he was right about her skipping lunch. Again. In an effort to take her mind off Hudson, she'd spent the past week working round the clock. And while her frantic pace hadn't done anything to lessen the emptiness she felt inside, it had managed to make her forget a few meals.

"Oh, but I did. You're wasting away to nothing right before my eyes."

Allie snorted. "Hardly. And flattery won't get you a raise," she teased. "You haven't been here long enough." While it was true Colin had only been her assistant for a little over a month, he actually did deserve a raise. He'd already proven himself to be a trusted and invaluable member of her team. The scope of his duties seemed to expand almost daily to matters far more important than arranging lunch, although his thoughtfulness, not to mention the food, was certainly an added bonus. She made a mental note to speak to Ben about offering Colin a contract, something that would not only increase his salary but also secure his position. At the very least, she wanted to insure he was given adequate severance should push come to shove. Regardless of what lay ahead in terms of her future at Ingram, Allie wanted to make sure Colin's career wasn't affected by any fallout from corporate maneuverings.

He pulled a clear plastic container out of the bag. "Hope salad's okay."

"Perfect," she said. "And thank you. What do I owe you for all this?"

"Nothing. I charged it to your card." He dug into the bag for a second box. "And you bought one for me as well."

Allie lifted a brow but she couldn't hide the smile that tugged at her lips. "How generous of me."

"I thought so too." He returned her smile with an impish grin and held up the two containers. "Asian Veggie or Southwest Chicken?"

Allie reached for the Asian salad.

"We can make it a working lunch," he said as he took a seat across from her. "Go over your schedule for next week, maybe?"

"Great idea. But let's talk about the gala instead since it's only two weeks from tomorrow."

Colin passed her a can of lemon LaCroix and popped the top

on his Diet Coke. "Can take the girl out of the event planning business but can't take the event planner out of the girl?"

She laughed. "Something like that." But truth be told, a lot was riding on this event, and Allie wanted to make sure it went smoothly. The annual Ingram Foundation Gala was the single largest event the company held, both in terms of fund-raising as well as community relations. The event she'd organized in the fall for Better Start had been small in comparison, and whereas the proceeds from the dinner at the Field Museum had benefited only that one charity, the annual gala would fund all twelve of Ingram's charitable interests. With the board scrutinizing her every move, Allie needed to make sure the event was not only a success, but that it went off without a hitch. She was quite sure her father never took a hands-on approach to such matters, but given her background in fund-raising, she knew the board would hold her personally accountable if the evening was considered a failure, despite the fact that the planning had begun long before she ever joined the company. Which is why she'd handpicked her team, bringing both Harper and Colin in to oversee the final stages of preparation.

Colin wiped his hands on a his napkin and flipped open the cover to his tablet. For the next thirty minutes they munched on salads while he gave Allie a detailed rundown on everything from the crab claws the hotel was having flown in from Alaska to the color of the tablecloths.

"And each couple will receive gift bags with a pair of his and hers UGG slippers and a box of Godiva truffles as a thank-you gift when they leave," he added at the end.

A box of candy for the limo ride home and some comfy slippers to change into after hours spent networking and dancing was a very nice finishing touch. It seemed as though he and Harper had truly thought of everything. Allie was impressed. She was about to tell him so when he hit her with one last detail.

"Speaking of couples," he said, trying and failing to sound nonchalant. "Shall I put you down for a plus one?"

She decided to ignore the question behind the question and instead merely answered the one he'd asked. "No, I won't be bringing anyone. Between the board and the donors, I'll barely have a free minute. Plus, I want to be available if anything comes up last minute. If I brought a date he'd just end up feeling neglected."

"Harper and I can handle any issues that pop up."

"I'm sure you can." She gave him a genuine smile. "But I still won't be bringing a date." Without missing a beat she segued out of that minefield. "Thank you, by the way. I realize working with Harper on this event isn't technically part of your job description. I really appreciate you jumping in with both feet."

"Not a problem. And Harper's great. Planning this with her doesn't seem like work at all." Colin leaned back in his chair. He crossed one ankle over the opposite knee, giving Allie a prime view of his Gucci oxfords. No wonder he and Harper got along so well. They both had a penchant for shoes that cost them a week's pay.

"You still in for tonight?" he asked, referring to the plans they'd made with Harper. She'd been trying to set a date for the three of them to go out clubbing pretty much since the first time she and Colin spoke on the phone.

"Of course. Why wouldn't I be?"

He shrugged. "I don't know. Maybe you feel like having me there will keep you from switching out of work mode and cutting loose." His brows rose. "Or maybe you have a hot date?"

The plus one might have been Colin's idea of subtle, but this approach was an all-out freight train charging full steam ahead.

"Tell you what," she said. "I'll promise to forget about the office and resist the urge to dictate memos if you'll promise to stop fishing for details on my nonexistent social life and resist the urge to fix me up at the club."

He clapped his hands together as he stood. "No can do, Boss Lady. I'm on a mission to make sure your dance card is full tonight. You need to let your hair down and have some fun for a change."

Before she had a chance to object, he was halfway out the door. Allie sagged back in her chair. Colin was right about one thing: she could definitely use a night off from the worry and stress that had plagued her the last two weeks. But what she really needed was a night with Hudson.

It had been a nearly a week since she'd surprised him in the shower. Five days, to be exact. And as wonderful as it had been to spend a lazy Sunday afternoon at his penthouse, she'd taken a huge risk by sneaking into his building, one they both agreed she shouldn't repeat. So instead they'd spent the week apart, each working in their respective towers on opposite banks of the Chicago River.

Allie spun her chair around to face the windows. In the distance she could see the Chase Industries building. The mere sight of the postmodern structure, towering over the city in an architectural display of masculine power, sent a sharp pang of longing through her. Instinctively she opened her desk drawer and reached for the burner phone she kept tucked in a pocket of her purse. The text she sent was simple and to the point and told Hudson exactly how she felt.

I miss you.

She waited a few minutes, watching the screen for the tiny bubbles that would indicate Hudson was typing a reply, but none came. She knew she shouldn't have expected an immediate response. It wasn't as though he was sitting around his office waiting for a random message from her. He had a multibillion dollar conglomerate to run. Not to mention his responsibilities at Ingram and the investigation he was spearheading into Julian's involvement in her parents' murders. How the man found time to sleep, much less text, was a mystery.

Her thumb had just pressed the lock button when she heard a soft ping. His answer was equally direct.

`I want you.`

A feeling of warmth spread through her. Before she had a chance to reply, another message from Hudson popped up on the screen.

`Did you and Colin have a nice lunch?`

What? How the hell did he know about that? Was he at Ingram HQ while she was holed up in her office with Colin? She was about to ask when her phone lit up again.

`That color looks lovely on you, by the way.`

Her mouth popped open. `You can see me?`

`Yes.`

How? A thought occurred to her and she quickly typed a follow-up question. `Did you buy a telescope?`

`No.`

`Then how?`

`I may have procured some equipment from my recently assembled team.`

`Stalker.`

`Just utilizing available technology. Lift your skirt.`

`Pervert.`

`Do it.`

`Why?`

`Because I've been wondering all day if you're wearing garters.`

`Maybe.`

`Show me, Alessandra. Now.`

It was just a text, but as she read it she could almost hear the deep timbre of his voice commanding her to submit to his will, and a surge of heated pleasure shot straight to her core. Slowly, she slid the hem of her skirt up her thigh until the black garter was revealed, along with the lace edge of her stockings.

Her phone pinged. `Higher.`

She pulled the fabric higher, so her lace panties were visible.

`Fucking hell.`

`This isn't fair,` she typed.

`The fact that I'm now inconveniently hard and you're across the river? I agree.`

`That's your own fault.` She laughed.

`I meant that you can see me. All I can do is stare at granite and glass and try to picture you in your office.`

`And what are you picturing?`

A wicked smile curved her lips. Hudson might have started their little game, but two could play. `You at your desk. Me under it.`

`Now who's the pervert?`

She ignored his comment and continued to describe the image in her mind with a series of rapid- fire texts.

`Rather like that time in the chair.`

`But instead of riding your cock, I'd be on my knees . . . sucking you off while you rule over your kingdom.`

There was a long beat of silence, then her phone rang in her hand.

"I'm coming over," he said. His voice was tight with a barely leashed restraint.

"No, don't. It's too risky. We don't know who at Ingram is on Julian's payroll. And we've taken far too many chances as it is."

"I'm your business partner, for fuck's sake. Any number of issues can bring me to that building." His frustration was palpable, but they couldn't do anything to blow their cover or to encourage Julian to move up his timetable.

"If we're alone together too often, he'll expect progress, and we need more time."

"Then we'll stay in plain sight." His tone softened. "Christ, Allie, I need to see you. I'm losing my mind without you."

"I feel the same way, but . . ."

"But what?"

Her words tumbled out in a rush. "I can't bear to see you and not be able to touch you. And I don't want to have to pretend that I hate you. It kills me. Because even though you know it's an act, there's a tiny piece of you that still feels it. I can see it in your eyes and it breaks my heart."

He let out an resigned breath. "Tonight, then. Give me an hour or so to come up with a plan."

"I can't. I'm meeting Harper and Colin at a club."

"First lunch and now drinks? I'm starting to get jealous of your assistant."

Allie gave a small laugh. "Don't be. I'm not his type." She stood and walked over to the window. "I miss you," she said, echoing the words she'd typed at the start of their conversation.

"I miss you, too. More than you know."

She pressed her palm to the glass, and wondered if across the river, he was doing the same. "Tell me it will all work out, Hudson. Tell me the good guys will win this time. Tell me we'll end up with our happily ever after."

His voice was hoarse when he answered. "We will, Allie. I swear to you, somehow we will."

12

*A*llie eyed Harper over the rim of her glass. She was wearing a short sequined dress that caught each beat of the lights that pulsed over the crowd, and heels that, despite her petite frame, made her legs look like they went on for miles. Her cheeks were flushed, her eyes bright and glassy, and her toes tapped to the pounding bass. She was in total club mode. With one exception. Harper Hayes hadn't so much as looked at a guy. Not a glance, not a wink. Not even a smile. And she certainly hadn't passed her phone number to the bartender despite the fact that, as Colin was quick to point out, he looked like Ian Somerhalder. Even Allie had given him a second glance, but Harper seemed completely impervious to his devilishly handsome good looks, and for that there could be only one explanation.

Nick.

Harper hadn't said anything about her budding relationship with Hudson's brother, but Allie was confident he was the reason for her best friend's sudden lack of interest in the male population. At least when it came to finding a potential date for herself. She was having no problem using her well-honed skills to find Allie a man, and she'd been putting them to good use all night.

"There was nothing wrong with that one," Harper said as the guy in question moved on to another table. "And the first three were perfectly fine, too."

Allie wrinkled her nose. She didn't want perfectly fine, she wanted perfect. She wanted Hudson Chase.

"It's not like you're picking out china patterns," she said. "They just wanted to buy you a drink."

"I can buy my own drinks, thank you very much." Allie downed the last of her lemon drop martini, her third of the night. Usually she followed Harper's "martinis are like boobs" motto when it came to her drink of choice. In other words, one was not enough, and three was too many. But tonight she wanted to lose herself in that heady combination of drinking too much alcohol in a club where the music was much too loud. And for that, Asylum was the perfect destination.

The entire club pulsed with a hypnotic energy. Hundreds of bodies filled the circular dance floor in the center of the club, all writhing and swaying under the multihued lighting that kept time to the pounding music. Above them the ceiling soared three stories high, with the balconies on each level wrapping around all three hundred and sixty degrees, and in the distance a DJ held court on a raised platform.

"Well, the next one's on me." Colin caught the eye of their waitress and signaled for another round. "As for your many admirers, no offense, Boss Lady, but you really only have yourself to blame."

"First, we agreed I'm not your boss tonight. Second, how do you figure?"

"Well, if you didn't want to spend the night fending off guys left and right, then you shouldn't look so hot." He hid his smile behind his glass.

Allie gaped at him. She would have been offended if it weren't for the irresistible combination of amusement and affection that sparkled in his bright green eyes.

"What?" he asked, aiming for innocent and failing miserably. "You said you're not my boss tonight."

Allie laughed and shook her head. "Right, but the flattery-won't-get-you-a-raise policy is still in effect."

"Ah, but it's true. Look at you, hair in a perfectly disheveled updo, makeup completely on point with those smoky eyes and glossy nude lips. And that dress." His eyes raked over the slinky black halter dress that dipped low in the back. "I mean, damn, even I want to hit that." He smirked. "And you're lacking the proper anatomy."

"I think she's too busy pining away over the Muscled Mogul to give any of these guys a chance," Harper chimed in.

Aaaand we're back to the nicknames.

Colin choked on his vodka tonic. "Muscled Mogul? I take it she means . . ." He lifted his brows.

"Yes. Fair warning, Colin, Harper has a thing for nicknames." Allie shot her friend a look. "And apparently no one is off-limits."

Harper beamed back at her. "That's not even my best work. Personally, I thought the Tempting Tycoon was much better."

"Well, *I* think that all of this is just your way of diverting attention from the real issue."

Colin leaned forward conspiratorially, resting his elbows on their tall-boy table. "Oh, this sounds good. Do tell."

"Harper here has made it her night's mission to find a man for me so we won't notice the fact that she's now off the market."

"Am not," she protested. "I just haven't seen anyone I like."

"Bullshit. Damon Salvatore's doppelganger was mixing your Cosmo and you didn't so much as bat an eye." Allie laughed. "Admit it. You are one hundred percent head over heels for Nick Chase."

Colin slumped back in his chair. "Can't blame her there. Actually, I can't blame either of you. That gene pool definitely has an extra dose of tall, dark, and handsome."

"Here's an idea," Harper interrupted. "Let's talk about Colin instead."

He laughed. "Nice try."

"No, she's right." Other than what was on Colin's résumé and a few mundane details, Allie actually knew very little about the man who had become such an integral part of her daily life. "Tell us the Colin James story."

The waitress appeared at the table with a fresh round of drinks on her tray. Colin waited while she set the glasses on the table and cleared the empty ones. "Not much to tell, really." He lifted the lime wedge off the side of his glass and squeezed it into his drink. "Born and raised in the Midwest; three older sisters; loves Beyoncé, long walks on the beach, and Harry Styles's hair."

Harper cocked one perfectly arched brow. "Is that your match.com bio?"

"Saw it on there, did ya?" Colin shot back without missing a beat.

She lifted her new Cosmo in salute. "Touché."

Allie shook her head. "How did I end up with you two?"

"Luck." They said as one before clinking their glasses together.

"So, anyone special in your life?" Harper asked him.

"There was. But after we graduated, he took a job at a station on the West Coast. An Ingram affiliate, actually."

"Which one?" Allie asked.

"Seattle." Colin shoved a hand through the light brown hair that hung in an artful mess over his forehead. "We tried the long distance thing for a few months, but . . ." He gave a slight shrug and reached for his glass.

"Okay," Harper announced. "New plan. 'Operation: Find a Man for Colin' shall now commence."

"No need," he said, sliding off his stool and grinning. "I got this."

They watched as he strolled toward the bar.

"I like him," Harper said.

"But not as much as you like Nick." Allie didn't even bother to phrase it as a question.

"Back to that, are we?"

"Oh, that's rich. This from Miss Relentless?"

"Using my own tactics against me?"

Allie wasn't sure if Harper was referring to the persistent questioning or the annoying moniker. Perhaps both. "If that's what it takes." She licked a bit of sugar from the rim of her martini glass. The warm buzz of alcohol was making her feel loose and relaxed, but not so much that she was beyond pumping her friend for long overdue details. "You still haven't given me the full scoop."

"I like him," Harper said. "And yes, more than Colin." Allie expected a pithy quip, or at the very least an eye roll, but instead Harper grew uncharacteristically serious. "More than anyone I've ever known, actually."

The look on Harper's face told Allie all she needed to know. It was clear her friend had fallen hard for the younger Chase brother. But Nick had been through a lot, and there had to be a reason why his sponsor suggested avoiding new relationships during the first few months of sobriety. As much as Allie loved the idea of two people she cared about finding happiness together, it also made her worry. "How does he feel?"

"The same." She twirled the stem of her glass between her fingers. "Although he's not super talkative about his feelings."

Allie nodded at yet another characteristic the two brothers seemed to share.

A spark lit Harper's eyes. "But hey, he's willing to rent a tux for me, so if that doesn't say true love, I don't know what does."

"A tux?"

"Yeah, I was going to bring him as my date to the gala. If that's all right with you? I know I'm working and all, but he gets that. Our only concern was how you and Hudson would feel about it."

Nick in a tux? This she had to see. "If you two are happy, then I'm happy. I'm sure Hudson will see it that way, too." And if he didn't, Allie would just have to find a way to convince him.

"Have you talked to him at all since you've been back?"

"A few times, but only about work."

"Still not buying this," Harper said.

Allie decided it was best to change the subject before Harper dug too deep. "Looks like Colin found someone," she said, nodding toward the end of the bar where he stood talking to two unbelievably hot guys.

"Whoa, he has good taste."

As if feeling the weight of their stare, Colin glanced at them and smiled. After a few words to his two new friends, he sauntered back to the table. "C'mon, Boss Lady, time to dance. This one might be in a relationship, but you're not. And as luck would have it, my guy has a straight friend."

In the distance, one of the two men lifted his beer to her and smiled. She opened her mouth to protest, but the sight of Harper's suspicious gaze had her rethinking her answer. If she declined, it would only add fuel to the fire. If she wanted her best friend to buy the idea that she was over Hudson, then she had to at least appear to be moving on. And in this case it meant agreeing to a dance. She sighed in resignation. "Fine. One dance."

A wide grin spread across Colin's face. "To start," he said, taking Allie's hand and tugging her off the stool. The two men Colin had been talking to joined them, and together they weaved toward the dance floor. The crowd swallowed them, and in no time Allie found herself pressed between a mass of bodies, all writhing to the pulsing beat of the music. They danced more as a group than couples, moving as one in a current of hedonistic abandonment. But then one song morphed into another and a pair of arms wrapped around Allie from behind. At first she stiffened, but then a nod of encouragement from Colin forced her to relax. It was only dancing, after all, something she would enjoy if she were truly single.

The music pulsed through her body with every beat, and slowly she began to lose herself to the hypnotic rhythm. Closing her eyes, she surrendered to it, imagining Hudson's hands splayed across her hips, his body molded to hers. Every fiber of her being ached with a need for him that was so real, so tangible, she could almost feel his warm breath in her ear, his lips pressed to her neck.

"You're gorgeous," a deep voice vibrated against her skin.

Allie's eyes flew open at the unfamiliar sound and disappointment flooded her senses. The music slid into a slow, sultry beat, and the man behind her rolled his hips in a matching grind. "I'm going to sit the next one out," she told him, looking over her shoulder. He nodded as she wriggled free of his grasp. Within seconds he was absorbed back into the dense crowd.

She pushed her way through the crush of bodies. The moment she reached her table, the waitress approached with a fresh tray of drinks.

"Did you order another round?" she asked Harper.

"From the gentleman at the bar," the waitress answered. She set a Cosmo in front of Harper and a vodka tonic in front of Colin's empty chair. But instead of another martini, Allie was served a squat tumbler filled with amber liquid. She lifted the glass to her lips and took a small sip. Scotch. Johnny Walker Blue, if she wasn't mistaken. Not exactly her drink of choice, but it was . . .

Hudson.

Allie spun toward the bar. She saw a sea of faces, but not the one she hoped to find. Her heart sank. Of course it wasn't him. They had agreed to keep their distance. And while her head told her it was the wise decision, her heart still sank.

When she turned back to the table she noticed a single word written in pen on the cocktail napkin that had been beneath her drink. *Upstairs* was all it said, but the handwriting was as familiar to her as her own.

Upstairs? Not very specific. She slid her beaded clutch across the table and into her lap, discreetly checking the burner phone while pretending to rummage around for lip gloss. Sure enough, a text from Hudson filled the locked screen.

`Don't make me wait.`

Her gaze lifted to the spiral of balconies above the dance floor. There had to be dozens of booths and private lounges. She had no idea how she was going to find him, but she was damn sure going to try.

"I'll be right back," Allie said. "Gonna hit the ladies' room." She didn't bother waiting for a reply from Harper. Instead she melted into the crowd, her pulse increasing with every step as she made her way toward the stairs. The grates on the metal treads offered a dizzying view she would have found unnerving under any other circumstance, but at the moment they didn't even faze her. The only thing that mattered was finding Hudson.

The first balcony was essentially a wide catwalk with a row of circular booths. Each faced the center of the club, providing the perfect vantage point for watching the action on the dance floor below. It was doubtful Hudson would have chosen such a high-profile location, but she scanned them briefly before hurrying to the next level. The second balcony was deeper, offering private lounges with clusters of plush seating surrounding tables cluttered with bottles of premium liquor. A velvet rope hung across the staircase to the third balcony along with a sign that read PRIVATE EVENT. For a moment she considered the possibility that Hudson might have rented the entire floor, but then a ripple of awareness washed over her. Every nerve in her body sprang to life. He was close. She could feel his presence, his overwhelming desire, calling to her on the most base level.

Allie's eyes darted across the expanse of the club. Most of the VIP lounges had their privacy curtains tied back, but on the far side of the balcony one lounge remained closed. Her skin prickled with anticipation as she followed the narrow path. Max emerged from the shadows as she drew closer, greeting her with a slight nod before drawing the curtain back. Allie stepped inside. The sight that greeted her took her breath away.

She'd barely seen Hudson since they returned from France, and when she did it was mostly as the billionaire mogul, dressed in designer suits and ready to conquer the world. But the man before her was younger and more dangerous, his stance predatory and his eyes dark. Dressed in jeans and a black sweater, he was sex personified. Allie licked her lips in anticipation because, for the moment at least, the only thing he looked ready to conquer was her.

Lights pulsed and shot down in laserlike beams of various hues to the beat of the pounding bass, while sweaty bodies undulated to the rhythm. High above in the VIP section, Hudson stood with his arms crossed over his chest, a tumbler of scotch in his hand. He repositioned his grip and the muscles in his forearm flexed as his fingers compressed the crystal against his palm. The glass protested, yet bared the weight of his choke hold. It was all he could do to keep from going wrecking ball through the crowd to tear that smarmy fuck's hands off Allie.

Without ever taking his eyes off the scene below, Hudson brought the glass to his lips. He took a moment to savor the potent proof, letting it roll over his tongue before sliding in a comfortable burn down his throat. An ambient glow caressed Allie's skin, and when she slid her hand up the back of her neck to lift her hair, he could see a sheen of sweat glistening on her flesh. Her head listed back, and as her hips swayed to the music, he became even more aware of the heavy pulse vibrating down the length of his cock.

As if on cue, Allie returned to her table. The waitress weaved through the dense crowd and delivered another round of drinks per his instructions. Hudson watched until she found his message, then turned and casually strode into the VIP lounge he'd reserved for the night. The curtains, thick enough to provide total privacy, dropped in a rush behind him. He downed the rest of his scotch and set the empty glass on the coffee table. When he straightened, Allie was standing there, her eyes glassy from cocktails and her skin flushed from dancing. His gaze traced up her athletic legs—which he was dying to have wrapped around his hips, his face; he didn't give a fuck as long as he was buried inside her with either his tongue or his cock—to the hem of her dress that was way too fucking short for public consumption, yet perfect.

A heavy, inescapable lust permeated the air in the confined space, heightening their mutual desire. His hands fisted at his sides and the beast within the civilized shell awoke. A hunger for her slammed into him and reverberated through his body. Christ, he wanted her; craved her with a greed so acute he would take her any way he could get her.

Her lips parted and the delicate expanse of her shoulders began to tremble. Unable to wait any longer, he stalked toward her, void of thought or decision. She came at him in a rush and their bodies met in a head-on collision of hands and tongues and mouths. In spite of the stress they were under, in spite of the shit that was threatening their future, Allie was the love of his life.

And he wouldn't change a goddamn thing.

It felt like an eternity since they'd been together, and he was starved for a taste of her. Hudson sifted both of his hands through the sweat-damp roots of her hair and his tongue pushed past her lips. "I can't go this long without you," he rasped. As he deepened the kiss, he felt a primal need to erase the lingering palm prints of the guy who had touched her.

He pulled back, his chest heaving as he looked down at her

through hooded eyes. "I hated seeing him all over you." His hand smoothed up the back of her thigh and under her dress. "Touching what's mine." He palmed her ass and yanked her hard against the erection straining the fly of his jeans.

"I was thinking about you." Allie molded her soft curves against his hard edges. "I wanted it to be you touching me. I always want it to be you." The surrender in her voice charged his desire. He wanted to claim her as his, right there.

Hudson dipped is head and caught her bottom lip between his teeth. "Prove it," he challenged.

"A dare, Mr. Chase?" Mischievous intent, undoubtedly fueled by alcohol, glimmered in Allie's eyes. He loved her like this, willing to abandon her inhibitions and unapologetic about what she wanted from him. Only him.

He smirked. "If you can handle it."

Allie's hands came up and landed dead center on his chest. She pushed him backward and he obliged, taking a load off as soon as his calves hit the double-wide couch. He reclined and his knees fell to the sides. But instead of climbing into his lap, Allie stood in front of him, slowly inching her dress up her thighs. Christ, she was going to draw this out, tease him relentlessly. And all he wanted right now was her dropping down hard on his cock, her damp skin against his, and his mouth moving with hers if only to breathe the same air.

"Come here." His voice was a guttural growl.

She straddled him and ran her hands down his chest. He sucked in a sharp breath when she lifted the hem of his shirt and ran her fingers lazily across his abdomen. And she didn't stop there. Without trepidation she cupped him through his jeans and deliberately massaged his raging-hard cock.

"Take me, baby."

Allie smiled in the darkness as she slowly lowered the zipper of his fly. Painfully fucking slow. She freed him from the confines of his boxers and his cock punched out, laying thick and heavy against his stomach and glistening at the tip.

With his patience pushed to the limit, Hudson took control of their game. He slid his hands up the inside of her thighs and shifted her panties to the side. She was drenched. Her head listed back and her lips parted on a silent gasp as he glided his fingers back and forth between her slick folds.

"Pay attention, Alessandra, I'm only going to say this once." Her eyes opened, and when they met his, he knew he had her. Slowly, he slid one finger inside her, curling it forward. "This is mine."

"Forever." The word rushed out on a panting breath.

"You're so greedy." He eased out, then back in with a second finger, priming her as her hips circled and rocked into the heel of his hand. "I know you want to fuck me."

"Yes . . ." A strobe of light flashed through the curtains, highlighting Allie's face. He eased his fingers out, and with his eyes locked to hers he traced her lips, coating them with her arousal. He shifted a hand under the weight of her hair and curled his fingers around her neck. On a groan he pulled her to him and kissed her hard, his tongue licking the taste of her from her lips.

"Do it," he rasped against her mouth. He lifted his hips to push his pants farther down his legs. "Take me. I want to watch you."

The bastard in him wanted to tie her hands behind her back so all she had to take him with was her hot, soaking core. But he craved the soft, gentle touch of her hands, a dark paradox to her quest to be taken rough and hard. He watched intently as she wrapped her fingers around his achingly hard length and rubbed the head of his cock against her slick sex.

"Now, Allie," Hudson hissed through clenched teeth. He was way past the point of asking nicely.

She rose up on her knees and positioned herself, the thick head of his cock parting her lips. He swallowed hard as she lowered herself onto him. "Fuck," he bit out. "So tight." His fingers flexed restlessly against her thighs as she took more of him inside her, until with a final shift, he was balls deep.

In the dim, filtered light he watched Allie's back arch and her teeth sink into her lower lip. He moved his hands to her waist and squeezed. Her muscles flexed under his grip as she began to ride him in an easy, fluid movement, over and over. Outside the heavy curtains a sultry bass thumped throughout the jam-packed club. But inside that confined space, the world belonged to them, and before long, their slow teasing fuck turned into a raw, voracious need.

With a curse, Hudson's head kicked back, pressing into the cushion behind him. His breathing became rough and more ragged. Allie braced her hands on his shoulders and her body undulated in waves over him, rolling her hips into each downward stroke—harder, faster, deeper.

Fuck, she didn't stop. And he never wanted her to.

Panting, she leaned forward and her lips hovered over his. "Hudson . . ."

He took her mouth with a furious need, swallowing her cries. He could feel her impending orgasm pulsing around his shaft as his tongue thrust fast and hot over hers. His hips surged upward, pumping in and out of her with a perfect pounding glide that met her strokes with increasing force. Her fingers raked into his hair and clenched a handful of his dark waves, the sweet lick of pain a direct line to his groin.

His hand slipped between her thighs and his thumb circled the top of her sex, taking her higher and higher until her body exploded in an orgasm that had her fisting his cock like a vise. The sensation kicked off his own release in a razor-sharp flash of pleasure that shot straight down his spine. His hips locked against hers as he emptied himself inside her. And as he did, only one word came to mind. "Yours."

The panoramic view from Hudson's office displayed the urban sprawl of Chicago as a winter wonderland. Outside, snow swirled just beyond the thick glass in what must have been the coldest winter on record, at times nearly grinding the city to a halt. But inside it was business as usual. With his brow furrowed in concentration, Hudson's fingers hammered against his laptop at a vicious pace. Work had always been his savior, and with him and Allie at negotiated opposite ends, he was relying on it once again to encapsulate him into his world.

Hudson blew out a breath as he hit send on a lengthy e-mail, then moved to the next item burning up his inbox. With any luck it would preoccupy him for the rest of the day. Although in reality there wasn't a spreadsheet in the world that could keep his focus from shifting to the photo of Allie that sat framed on his desk.

Ever since Julian cornered her with his list of demands, they'd been sparring for public consumption while fucking each other senseless in private. Admittedly, the latter wasn't so bad, but the former had him on edge. The seconds, minutes, and hours they stole in hidden corners, dark offices, or late-night covert ops seemed to be the only thing holding them both together. But it wasn't enough. They needed a day—scratch that, a weekend—where Allie wasn't constantly looking over her shoulder.

Hudson's gaze fell to his calendar and an idea began to take hold. But as he reached for his cell phone, it vibrated against his desk. His little brother's name flashed up on the screen along with some selfie reminiscent of *Easy Rider* that he'd snapped on the Fat Boy Hudson had given him for Christmas.

"For Fuck's sake," Hudson muttered. When in the hell had he had enough time or ingenuity to do that? At least he wasn't flashing his ass . . . this time.

"Yeah, Nick." He shifted to a pile on the corner of his desk, lifting a contract off the top and slashing a red *X* through the black and white.

"How did you know it was me?"

"Modern technology."

"Whatcha up to?" Nick's over-the-top enthusiasm had Hudson wishing he'd dropped the call into voice mail.

"Working." Hudson flipped the page to annihilate another paragraph.

"You work too much. Get out, live a little."

"What do you want, Nick?" Giving up on the documents in front of him, Hudson leaned back in his leather chair.

"I wanted to, ya know, see if you wanted to get some grub. Feel like a little Al's Beef? Been craving that greasy goodness for days."

"I already ate."

"When?"

"I don't know, earlier. What's with the dietary interrogation?"

"What's with the 'tude? Allie would school your ass for being such a grumpy prick."

Hudson frowned into the phone. Nick had known Allie as long as he had and wasn't far off with that assessment. Her presence

—her smile, her laugh, all those soft feminine curves—would have straight-up given him an attitude adjustment. Not to mention her sharp tongue dropping the hammer on his shitty mood.

"Let's hang." Nick snorted into the phone. "You know, get outside the eighteen million rooms of your bachelor pad."

Hudson breathed deep through his nose. "I have work I need to get done."

"Come on, you're the big wig at that joint. Spare a couple hours and go shopping with me or something. You're always ragging on how I'm dressed. Thought you might get off on taking me to Banana Republic or some shit. Make me over into your mini-me."

"What's this about, Nick?"

"Nothing. Can't a guy just want to spend time with his brother?"

A chuckle reverberated in Hudson's chest. "Cut the bullshit, Nicky. What's your angle?"

Nick exhaled in a rush. "I'm worried about you, bro. You're isolating yourself back into your old habits. All work and no play make Hudson an asshole. Besides, you've always been lookin' out for me; now it's my turn."

Hudson could barely stand his own company these days. The air in his penthouse had become suffocating and stale, and work wasn't doing shit to smooth out his edges. Maybe an afternoon with Nick was what he needed. A grin curved his mouth. "I have an idea."

"What?" Nick shot back.

"You'll see." Hudson started the shut-down process on his laptop.

"Shopping? Food? Ice skating?"

"None of the above."

"What the fuck is better than you J.Crewing the hell out of me?"

"Pick you up in thirty." Hudson hung up, cutting off a string of curses mixed with pleas for a hint.

***

Hudson curbed the DB9 outside the apartment he'd rented for his brother. After his stint in rehab, the dive of a neighborhood he'd been living in was a no-go. Nick had balked at taking a handout, but Hudson had finally convinced him. In hindsight he should have just moved him into the penthouse, since that's where he was most nights anyway.

Nick was already waiting outside in some sweatpants and T-shirt ensemble that almost had Hudson rethinking the shopping idea.

Almost.

His clothes looked to have been salvaged from the hamper and his hair was a frickin' mess. As if someone had turned him upside down and mopped the floor.

Nick jerked the door open and plopped into the seat. "Oh yeah, the ass heaters are on," he said as he slammed the thing shut.

"Hey, easy on the door."

"Sorry, did I bruise your precious Assssston Martin?" Nick took a one-two at him. "You're all designer, mixy-matchy."

"I don't look like I rolled out of bed." Hudson's jaw tightened as he put the car in gear and hit the gas. The pistons churned and the engine roared to the perfect pitch of a finely tuned automobile. "Get your seat belt on."

Nick pulled the strap across his chest and the belt slid home with a soft click.

"So what's the plan? Saks? Neiman's?"

"No. Better."

"Better?"

Hudson glanced at his brother and his mouth twitched into a

slight grin. "Absolutely." The cityscape streaked by as he maneuvered the car through traffic with laserlike precision. Beneath them the tires crunched over salt-crusted roads, and outside tree branches twisted and curled like arthritic hands, begging for the renewal of spring. They reminded Hudson of the skeleton of a man he was without his heart; without Allie, he was a shell.

But what better way to burn off steam from sins of the past and frustrations of the present than . . .

"Holy shit," Nick said as the DB9 came to a stop in front of Chicago Fight Club. The sign on the North Elston gym read BRING YOUR OWN WEAPON with double fists as bullet points. "I know you've wanted to kick the shit out of me for a while now, but are you serious?"

"Does Pinocchio have a wooden dick?" Hudson cut the engine and yanked on the door handle. "Get your ass out of the car."

"Fuuuuuck," Nick cursed under his breath. "Never mind kicking the shit out of me; you're going to whoop me across the whole damn state." He got out of the car and slammed the door shut. Again.

Hudson glared over his shoulder as he strode toward the gym. "That's not working in your favor."

Nick dragged his feet, then jogged a couple steps to catch up. "Wouldn't you rather swaddle me in cashmere, then feast on Al's Beef—greasy, hand-dipped, succulent meat n' cheese? We'll be like ladies who lunch."

"No." Hudson held the door open. "Come on, go inside like a big boy."

"Ass."

"Inside princess."

"You're being a real jerk," Nick said, shuffling into the fight club.

"Take it out on me in the ring."

The second they walked in, Hudson heard the rhythmic

sound of jump ropes slapping against concrete; the goading, shit-talking trainers shouting out drills; and the even-tempered thump-a-thump of gloved fists working well-worn, bloodred punching bags that dropped from the sky. Chicago Fight Club was hard core, and belts hung on the wall to prove it. This was the joint he sought out to silence the torment between his ears. Because when you were stuck indoors after mother nature decided to send the city into a deep freeze, beating the hell out of something seemed like a better energy burn than hamster wheeling it on a treadmill.

They moved deeper into the place, toward a roped-off ring in the back. Hudson gave tight nods to various trainers, and regulars like himself kicked a chin at him or grinned with mouth guards puffing out their cheeks and brightening their pearly whites.

When he'd started there six months ago, Hudson wasn't into the formal training. He was a street fighter with defensive skills developed to survive one shitty neighborhood after another. But he quickly found sparring with an opponent channeled the simmering angst that always hummed in the background of his mind, endlessly shifting up and down like an equalizer. And working with a trainer honed his technique. His brother, however, was just as good, if not better, with the natural instinct. Despite the bitching and moaning, taking Nick into the ring had the potential to be one of his most challenging rounds yet.

"My brother the billionaire takes me to the nicest places. Couldn't we have gone to Equinox or some fancy gym where they offer massages and women wear spandex?"

"What's wrong with this place? You want to work up a sweat, you come here." Hudson unzipped his jacket, then with a shrug of his shoulders tossed it off and to the side.

"What's wrong? This is like some first-rule-of-Fight-Club place. And no, I don't want to 'work up a sweat.' I want to chow down with my big bro picking up the tab while I leave the tip." Nick looked up at the exposed support beams and the pipes that snaked around them, rattling and clanking from someone turning on the showers. The concrete was worn, the paint clean but peeling, and the walls bare. "At least they have hot water so I don't have to ride home with your stench."

"I shower at home." Hudson fisted a hand behind his neck, pulling his T-shirt over his head and throwing it on top of his jacket.

"Oh, fuck me. No way." Nick balled up his hoodie and dropped it onto a chair. "I'll cab it, take the bus, walk through the sn—"

"Shut up and get your gloves on." Hudson chucked his brother a set of gloves, derailing the next smart-ass comment that was without question about to fire out of Nick's mouth. With his own pair in hand, Hudson parted the ropes and ducked into the ring. He shoved his left hand into a glove, then his right. Going head-to-head with his fists, he knocked the padded gloves together. "I'm waiting."

Nick ducked into the ring with a glove on his left hand. "Violence isn't the answer, bro."

"Stop whining like a little girl." Hudson rolled his head from side to side, giving his neck a crack to loosen it up.

Nick stabbed his right hand into the glove, then shook the hair out of his face. "Fine. If taking a couple swings at me makes you feel better, let's do it," he said, squaring off. Hudson immediately recognized the reckless gleam in his eyes. It was a trait they both shared, one that pushed them to their own respective extremes.

"If I only wanted to swing my fists at you for a couple hours, I wouldn't need a boxing ring to do it."

"True that." Nick fanned his arms out to shoulder level. "So come on then, you thread-humping, designer-whoring pussy." He flashed a smug grin. "Give it your best shot."

Hudson chuckled as he watched his brother bounce on the balls of his feet. "Let's see if your jab is as quick as your smart-ass mouth." He stepped forward and raised his fists, keeping them tight to his chin. He knew his brother had game, but that didn't stop him from . . . "Trigger shy?" . . . taunting, antagonizing, firing him up to strike.

Nick snapped out a couple of punches that were met with a forearm block. Hudson was quick to retaliate and nailed a clear shot to his brother's ribs.

"Fuck, that hurt." A swift kick to the other side of Nick's torso had him ducking out of the way. "I thought we were going to just play around some, then go get you a fancy latte or some shit."

"Says the fancy-ass coffee slinger." Hudson was already balancing out his weight. He was like a bomb attached to an ignition switch and that bitch-ass bastard Julian was cranking the key. This was what he needed to level him out, to dull his mood into a tolerable state. Raw fucking would have worked, too, but one had to work with what he had. Besides, Allie had elevated the physical act into another dimension. There was no going back from that. She owned him—heart, body, and soul. Man, did he sound like a whipped son-of-a-bitch. As if he gave a flying fuck.

"All right, game on, bro. We're goin' to get scruffy now." Nick threw out a left jab and something hot ripped through Hudson's gut. He refocused, and with tremendous strength his muscles coalesced into the perfect uppercut that made his brother stagger as though he were drunk.

Hudson gave him a second to recover. "You good?"

"Yeah man, but who the hell pissed you off?"

"Clears my head." Hudson spun and kicked his leg in the air, and his brother dropped low, dodging what would have been a direct hit. "Come on, Nicky, you've been in barroom brawls that rival the Octagon."

"Hey, I'm a lover, not a fighter."

Hudson thought about what it would feel like to live a life

short on responsibility, and for a brief moment he envied his brother's freedom. "You must have some shit to work out."

"Evidently you do." Nick moved in fast with a hard punch forward, then threw out a combination that made Hudson step up his efforts with a left-right.

"I was dumped, Nick." As the words left his mouth a pain rolled through his chest and twisted down to his gut. And to top it off it was a lie, a total fucking lie that cinched up his stomach hard core. The devil knew his closet was full of skeletons, but secrets between brothers was something he'd never subscribed to. Nick knew his past; hell, they'd lived it together, and the cause and effect of it had bonded them tighter than most. But some lies were spun out of necessity.

"I know. It's a first for you. Shit, wait, third. Same girl, but still."

"Not funny." Hudson went at him in a meet-and-greet in the middle of the ring, force against force, with each of them trying to toss the other off like a set of magnets. Their biceps strained and the muscles in their forearms flexed.

Twisting himself free, Nick bounced back on his heels. His chest heaved and sweat ran down his temples. "Actually, I need your help with something."

"Christ," Hudson muttered under his breath as he threw out a roundhouse kick.

Nick caught him by the ankle. "What's that supposed to mean?" He laughed at Hudson jumping on one foot like a pogo stick before finally dropping his leg.

"Because conversations beginning with 'I need your help' usually mean you're in deep shit."

"Nah, nothing like that. I need a tux."

Hudson's guard dropped and his brow shot up to his hairline. "A what?" he asked just as Nick popped him a solid one in the jaw.

"Ha! Bull's-eye, motherfucker."

Hudson shook off the blow that had left him momentarily dazed. "Goddamn, good right hook."

"Thanks." Nick's mouth lifted into a broad grin. "And I need a tux."

"For what?"

"That frilly charity event of yours. I'm going too."

"For the love of God, Nicky. Allie and I broke up but I haven't sworn off women. I can get a date."

"Not with your sorry ass, dick. With Harper."

"Come again?" Sweet hell, Nick was going for the heavyweight title of shockers.

Nick cleared his throat. "I'm escorting the fair maiden, Harper Hayes," he said, trying to sound all regal.

"Quit talking like that. And 'maiden' and 'fair' aren't adjectives that describe the redhead." The woman was more of a wrecking crew with a bullhorn, but Hudson liked her. She didn't take shit even from hotheaded assholes like himself. "More importantly, when the hell did this happen?"

"Since Mother Nature played matchmaker on Christmas Eve. We've been hanging out."

"Hanging out?" Allie had given him a heads-up about his brother and Harper, but the news still . . . he ripped a glove off and ran a hand through his hair.

"Yeah, she's cool to talk to."

"How often are the two of you just 'hanging out'?" Hudson wanted his brother to be happy, but there were rules of the twelve-step variety that suggested getting into a relationship in the first months of sobriety wasn't a good idea.

Nick shrugged. "A few times a week, I guess." He glanced down at the gray mat sprinkled with droplets of their sweat. "I like her."

"When were you planning on telling me this?"

"I'm telling you *now*, aren't I?"

"Only because you've had the fear of the tux put into you. Christ, Nicky."

Nick flashed a cheesy grin. "So you'll help me get all spiffy like my big bro?"

"Ass kisser."

"Please."

"Of course."

"Thanks. Next week?"

"I'm out of town at the start of next week. But I'll make a few calls."

"Sweet." Nick laughed. "Now get your glove back on so I can knock your ass across this mat for being a prick."

14

*A*commotion in the hallway drew Allie's attention from the e-mail on the monitor in front of her. Hudson was in the building. She felt his presence before she even heard his voice. The hair on her neck raised and her skin tightened in anticipation.

Through the open door she saw him round the corner, his jaw tight and his brow furrowed. "No, absolutely not," he barked into the phone he held pressed to his ear. "I'm about to discuss it with her." He turned his attention to Colin, his tone tight and clipped. "Hold her calls," he instructed as he strode by his desk and into Allie's office, closing the door behind him.

"God, you're hot when you're pissy."

He lifted an amused brow. "That was for the benefit of the young Mr. James." With a push of his thumb he powered his phone off before dropping it inside his suit jacket. "Not to mention the other dozen or so I passed in the hall. Nothing more than a show so I might steal a moment alone with you."

"It was?"

"Hmm, but now I'm intrigued." A smile tugged at the corner of his lips. "Hot when I'm pissy, eh? Let's discuss."

"It turns me on when you go all alpha male," she said, shifting slightly in her chair.

Hudson's eyes flared as his shrewd stare picked up on her subtle movement. "Is that so?"

"You know it does." There was no denying it. Hudson had experienced her response to his more dominant side on numerous occasions. But the gleam in his eyes told her he was enjoying the turn in conversation far too much to let the subject drop just yet.

"I know you've had a taste of what it's like when I'm in control." He drew closer. "Let's hypothetical here. Suppose I told you to touch yourself?"

"Hypothetically . . . are you watching me do this?"

"Of course I'm watching."

"Then hypothetically . . . I would keep my eyes locked on yours and do what you asked." There was a time when Allie would have found the idea of touching herself in front of a man far too embarrassing to even consider. But Hudson once told her it was a fantasy of his to watch her pleasure herself, and his unyielding desire gave her confidence. It made her feel wanton and sexy and awakened a side of her she never knew existed.

"And what if I waited until you were about to come, then stopped you?" He rounded the desk. "And told you that if you didn't stop, you couldn't have my cock." In a swift move he spun her chair to face him. "How would that feel, being unable to release until I say?"

"I think I'd like that." Her voice had turned breathy and needy, betraying the growing ache between her legs.

"Then suppose I told you to finger yourself until you were about to come again." A rush of pleasure surged through her core and she pressed her thighs together in an effort to find some relief. But Hudson placed a hand on each of her knees and yanked them apart. "And then once again made you stop right before you slipped over the edge." His thumbs moved in small circles on her skin. "Teasing you little by little." His hands fell away and he straightened, his cock straining against the fabric of his suit. The conversation was affecting him as much as it was her, but he kept going, adding one more caveat to their little game. "And to be clear," he added, "you're not allowed to beg."

Allie bit her lip to stifle a moan. "Hypothetically this is making me wet."

He smirked. "Oh, I'm not even close to being done."

Evil bastard. "You're not?"

"No, because then I'd have you take your nipples, one at a time, and pull, hard, until I said stop." His words caused her nipples to harden against the rough lace of her bra. "All the while you're trying to forget how desperately you want to come."

"Even though I'd want to keep my hands much lower?"

He nodded slowly. "But you can't because I won't let you come if you don't obey. And make no mistake, Alessandra, you won't come until I decide you're ready to be fucked."

She swallowed hard.

"Still think you'd like being controlled?" He smirked. "Hypothetically."

All she could manage was a small nod.

His eyes narrowed briefly as he appraised the situation, then his expression turned into something darker. It was a look she'd come to know well, one that never failed to leave her breathless. "Take your panties off," he ordered softly.

Her mouth gaped open. "The door isn't even locked."

"It wasn't a request." His stance altered as he gazed down at her. "Do it."

He watched with hungry eyes as she reached under her skirt and slowly peeled the scrap of black lace down her thighs. "Spread your legs. Show me how much you want me."

A thrill shot through her at his rough command and she shivered. Being exposed to him, so open and vulnerable while he stood before her fully clothed was more of a turn-on than she would have ever thought possible. Parting her thighs, she revealed herself to him, and in return was rewarded with his sharp intake of breath.

"Beautiful," he murmured, dropping to his knees before her. "So swollen and wet." A single finger skirted her trembling opening. "You're aching to feel me inside you, aren't you?"

"God, yes . . ." She lifted her hips in a shameless plea for more, but he kept up the maddening pace, circling her in a lazy, leisurely rhythm. Every so often his fingertip would dip inside, only to withdraw and begin again. She was near mindless with the need to be filled when he finally pushed two fingers inside of her.

Allies' head fell back against the leather chair. She was wound so tight, she knew all it would take was one skilled flick of his wrist to send her spiraling over the edge. But instead his hand remained perfectly still.

"Don't come," he said. His voice was harsh with a barely leashed restraint. "Not until I say you can." With that his fingers began a slow and teasing pump in and out of her quivering flesh.

Somehow she managed to stop herself from grinding against his palm, resisting the urge to ride his fingers to the shattering orgasm she craved. But she couldn't hold back her plea. "Please, Hudson," she begged.

"When you come it will be with my cock inside you." His fingers moved in a circular motion. "And I don't think you're quite ready yet."

He added a third finger and a moan was ripped from somewhere deep inside her. She dug her heels into the carpet in an attempt to stem the wave of pleasure that threatened to consume her. He kept her on the edge, driving her mad but never giving her exactly what she needed to get her off. When the first tremors of orgasm grasped his fingers, he removed them, leaving her a quivering, panting mess. He held her gaze as he brought his fingers to his lips, tasting the evidence of her arousal. "Hmm, yes, I do believe you're ready now."

She nearly sobbed with relief.

"Bend yourself over the desk and lift your skirt."

All thoughts of office decorum left her and she hurried to obey. A second later she heard the faint click of his buckle followed by the metallic sound of a zipper.

"Hold on to the edge and don't let go," he ordered, his voice hoarse and urgent.

She did as he asked, her fingers curling around the mahogany top. His hands gripped her waist and she felt the blunt head of him slip against her as he guided himself to where she was wet and more than ready.

"Brace yourself." He spread her legs wider with a push of his foot against hers. "This is going to be hard and fast." With no further warning he surged forward with a powerful thrust of his hips.

Allie bit the inside of her cheek to keep from crying out. She loved it when he took her like this, rough and unapologetic in his use of her body to bring them both the pleasure they craved. His need to claim her, to make her his own, ratcheted her desire for him to an almost unfathomable level.

He growled her name as he eased slowly back, then with a shift of his hips slammed into her again. Over and over he took her, pushing her forward with each punishing thrust. "Hold on," he ground out between clenched teeth. She tightened her grasp on the desktop as he yanked her back to meet his hips, angling her body so she felt every hard inch of him. His drives were merciless and in no time she felt her insides begin to quicken.

Bending over her, his lips grazed her ear. "Now, baby. Come for me."

On command her body exploded with an orgasm so intense

her vision blurred. Hudson cursed and jerked against her, driving to the hilt one last time, then stilling as he followed her over the edge. She was vaguely aware of movement as he fell back in the chair, pulling her with him and cradling her in his arms. They sat like that for several minutes while their breathing calmed. When Allie finally lifted her head to meet his gaze, she found his eyes filled with nothing but warmth and tenderness.

"How was that?" he asked, pressing a soft kiss to her lips.

"Amazing." She leaned her head against his shoulder and a quiet giggle escaped her lips. "Adventurous. Arousing . . . Awesome."

He chuckled quietly. "Allie's orgasm brought to you by the letter 'A'?

She looked up at him and smiled. "More like the letter H. As in holy hell, Hudson." She laughed. "That was intense."

He met her grin with one of his own.

"You supposedly came in here to argue with me," she reminded him. "Hope you have a decent poker face, Chase, because right now you look like a man who's thoroughly pleased with himself."

"Perhaps they'll believe I got what I came for."

Allie rolled her eyes. "That was bad."

"Terrible puns aside, I actually did have something to discuss with you."

"Oh?"

"I'm taking you to the lake on Friday," he said. It wasn't a question, and from the way he said it, there wouldn't be much discussion either. Still, Allie protested.

"You know I love your lake house, Hudson, but—"

"But nothing," he said, cutting her off before she had a chance to list the numerous reasons why they couldn't go away together. "I'm tired of stealing time. I want a whole weekend with you, a three- day weekend, no less. I want to go to bed with you and wake up with you and fuck you senseless during every hour in between."

Her breath caught. "When . . . who . . . I mean how . . ." she stammered, her mouth trying to catch up with her brain.

Hudson laughed. He planted a swift kiss on the top of her head before hauling her to her feet. "Trust me, I have a plan."

15

*A*llie's schedule was tighter than ever. With the holiday weekend approaching, Colin had extended her calendar well into the evening hours. From breakfast meetings to late-night e-mails, work consumed her every waking moment. It should have made time fly. But the end of the week held the promise of uninterrupted quality time with Hudson Chase. No sneaking around, no stolen moments behind closed doors, no covert texts or furtive glances. Just three days alone with the man she loved. The thought was never far from her mind, and so despite its hectic pace, the week crawled by. And by late Friday morning it seemed as though time had actually ground to a halt.

Hudson had been vague about their plans, saying only that they would be going to his lake house and that he would take care of the rest. She'd assumed he'd give her some sort of instructions during the week, but so far she hadn't heard a word from him, much less the details on how or when they were escaping the city for the peace and tranquility of his Lake Geneva cabin.

Allie's thoughts drifted to the time they'd spent there in October, and all at once memories bombarded her senses. The sight of Hudson straddling his motorcycle, looking every bit the bad boy she once knew; the scent of pine trees mixed with the rich smell of leather as she rode on the back of his bike; the feel of the sun on her face and his muscles flexing beneath her palms; the sound of his laughter mixed with her squeals. The day had been perfect in every way, but it paled in comparison to the night. Because there, on the floor in front of a roaring fire, Hudson had let his guard down. He'd opened up to her and shared glimpses of his past; his thoughts, his fears, his emotions. It was the night she'd always longed for. The night she knew they'd have.

"Big plans for the weekend?" Colin asked, interrupting her daydream.

Allie looked up to find him standing at the door to her office holding a large box in his hands. "What? Um, no. I mean, why do you ask?"

"Just figured with three days blocked off, you must have something exciting planned."

"Not really." She shrugged. "I just need a few days to unplug and recharge."

"So you're not going anywhere?"

"The only trip I plan on taking is from the bed to the couch and back again. Eat, sleep, repeat." It wasn't a total lie. She merely omitted the part about it being Hudson's bed. The one she'd been tied to while he teased and tormented her with his fingers, lips, and tongue.

Jeez, snap out of it Sinclair.

"What's in the box?" she asked, attempting to refocus her attention on the here and now.

Colin strode toward her. "No clue. It was just delivered via messenger, marked 'personal and confidential.' Again." He set the box on her desk and lifted a brow. "If I didn't know better I'd say you have a secret admirer." An audible gasp escaped his lips, and a look of conspiratorial mischief lit his bright green eyes. "Is it the guy from Asylum?" he asked in a dramatic whisper.

"Who?"

"That hunk of handsome you were pressed against Friday night."

"He didn't even know my name."

"I could enlighten him if you'd like?"

"Don't you have a memo to type or something?"

Colin laughed. "Okay, okay. Consider it dropped."

Allie waited until he'd closed the door behind him before tearing into the package. Inside the box was a camel-colored top coat along with a pair of Chanel sunglasses and a red knit hat and scarf. One by one she placed the items on her desk. She even removed the tissue paper but found nothing underneath. No note, no instructions. While she was fairly sure who was responsible for the mysterious delivery, she had no idea the purpose of its contents.

The burner phone. The thought had no sooner occurred to her when she heard a soft ping. She opened her bottom drawer of her desk and dug the phone out of her purse. A text from Hudson lit the screen.

`Did the package arrive?`

She smiled as she typed. `The eagle has landed.`

`Amusing yourself, Miss Sinclair?`

`Have to distract myself somehow, Mr. Chase.`

`From?`

`Thoughts of you.`

`Anything specific?`

`Specifically naked,` she replied.

`I like where this is going.`

`All weekend.`

`I'll pack light, then.`

`In fact, I may tie you to the bed.`

`That's my line.`

`Fine,` she typed, `you can tie me to the bed.`

`Fuck.`

`What?`

I'm hard.

She giggled. Let's leave now then.

We can't.

Why not?

Because the plans I have for smuggling you out of the city won't be in place until this afternoon. So as much as I'd love to have my face between your thighs . . .

Fuck.

His reply was immediate. What's wrong?

I'm wet.

There was a pause while she waited for his reply, during which she imagined him cursing as he adjusted his trousers. Behave.

Not sure I can.

Did you growl before you typed that? Because you know what that does to me.

Work, Alessandra. Get back to it.

Yes . . . sir.

That's not helping.

She smiled. It wasn't meant to.

Payback will be swift and decisive.

A wave of heated anticipation rolled through her and she found herself pressing her thighs together in an effort to find some relief. It was her own fault, really, since she'd been the one to start their little game. So instead of protesting the fact that she had to wait several hours for said payback to begin, she simply answered with the truth. I can hardly wait.

4:00. Wear the items from the box. A taxi will be waiting. Further instructions then.

She almost made a joke about how very 007 this all sounded when she realized that the team Hudson had working for him might very well have been former MI6. With that sobering thought in mind, she got back to work, trying her best to remain focused on the e-mails and contracts and conference calls that filled the rest of her afternoon. When four o'clock rolled around, she did exactly as she'd been instructed, donning the coat, hat, and sunglasses in Ingram's lobby before pushing through the revolving doors.

The sun was still shining as Allie stepped out onto Michigan Avenue, making the sunglasses seem less out of place in January, but the bite of cold wind stung her face. She pulled the scarf up over her mouth as she scanned the row of cabs idling at the curb.

A driver climbed out of the one directly in front of the door. "Miss Sinclair?" At Allie's nod he hurried round the front of the car and opened the back door for her. Allie slid inside, then pulled the burner phone out of her purse. She'd dialed Hudson's number before the driver was even back in the car.

"Anxious to see me?" he asked. She could hear the smile in his voice.

"Says the man who answered his phone on the first ring."

"I've never claimed to be anything but when it came to you." A warmth spread through her at the gentle caress of his voice, dampened only by the realization he was speaking over a Bluetooth system.

"You're driving?"

"The Range Rover, yes. Why do you ask?

"No reason."

"Alessandra?" She could tell by his tone he was expecting an answer.

"I just had a different picture in mind, that's all."

"Did you now?"

"Mmmhmm. You, me, the back of the limo." She cut her eyes to the front seat of the taxi. The driver seemed far too busy maneuvering into traffic to pay her much attention, but she still turned her head and lowered her voice. "Something about your face and my thighs."

"Believe me, I'd like nothing more than to start the trip by spreading you out on that bench and fucking you with my tongue until we reach the state line."

A jolt of pleasure arrowed straight to her core, and she let out a frustrated groan. "You're an evil bastard, do you know that?"

He chuckled softly. "Yes, but I'm your evil bastard. And I'll make it up to you when you get here." His voice dropped to a sexy rasp. "Thoroughly and repeatedly."

"That's not helping," she said, echoing his words from earlier.

This time he didn't even bother to temper his laugh. "It wasn't meant to."

"Wait," she said, his words registering, "When I get there? Where are you?"

"At the moment I'm at a red light in front of that little candy shop you were so fond of last time."

Allie remembered it well. She could picture the charming pink and white building clearly, right down to the woman spreading velvety chocolate across a cool marble slab. And while her mouth watered at the thought of the creamy fudge, her heart sank at the thought that Hudson was already in Lake Geneva.

"I would have preferred we drive up together," he said as if reading her mind. "But the risk was too great."

And there it was, the harsh reality that shadowed them. No matter how hard they tried, it was always there, threatening to end their happiness once and for all. Allie stared out the window at the pedestrians clogging the intersection, people rushing home to start their weekends without threats of blackmail or bodily harm. "I know," she whispered. It was impossible to mask her disappointment, though she knew he was right.

"And I need the time to prepare," he added in what was obviously an effort to steer them away from the dark turn the conversation had taken. It was also clear that he was taunting her, but she couldn't stop herself from asking. "What are you up to?"

"Anticipation, Alessandra."

She knew from experience there would be no further explanation. Resigned to her two-hour torture, she sighed. "So what's the plan?"

"You're about to turn onto lower Wacker," Hudson began. She almost asked how he knew that, but then she remembered the spy gadget that allowed him to see across the river and into her office. Tracking her location was child's play.

The taxi grew dark as the driver veered onto a ramp that took them beneath the city. The winding tunnels were a much quicker option than the congested streets of the Loop as the fast-paced traffic and unmarked alleyways were far too daunting to the inexperienced driver. Only those well acquainted with the bowels of the city took the shortcut known as the Chicago Autobahn.

"From there you will be taken to a parking garage, where you will transfer to another car." The cab took a sharp right. After circling one level they pulled alongside a black limousine. A blonde stepped out of the back wearing the exact same coat, hat, scarf, and sunglasses as Allie.

"Both the limo driver and the woman are members of Max's team," Hudson said. "Jessica will be taking the taxi you're in to your brownstown, where she will remain for the duration of the weekend. Take whatever you need out of your purse, then give it to her along with your keys and cell phone. Keep the burner with you."

Three days off the grid with Hudson was exactly what Allie wanted, but still, the thought of being completely out of touch with the rest of the world gave her pause. "What if there's an emergency. Or a break in the case?"

"She will be monitoring the incoming call log and voice mails and, if necessary, has instructions on how to reach us. We don't know if Julian is using your cell phone to track your movements, but in the event that he is, having it in her possession not only protects you, it aids our ruse."

"You've thought of everything, haven't you?

His voice dropped to a seductive purr. "You have no idea."

The promise held in those four words not only made her toes curl, it made the two hour drive to Lake Geneva seem more like eight.

Allie peered through the tinted window when the limo finally rolled to a stop in the center of the quaint town. With the exception of the dusting of powdery snow, it was exactly as she remembered. Rows of pastel-colored shops lined both sides of the street —everything from high-end art galleries to extreme sports rentals —all catering to the affluent crowd who used the lakeside community as their chance to get away from the stress of the city. The streets were crowded with those taking advantage of the three-day weekend. But unlike the couples who strolled hand in hand down the cobblestone sidewalks, pausing to window shop or duck into a café for a latte or a scoop of hand-churned ice cream, she and Hudson had no desire to venture into town. The only destination on their agenda was his cabin, and knowing he was already there, waiting for her, sent waves of adrenaline coursing through her veins.

She could hardly sit still as the limo crawled along the narrow road that hugged the shoreline. And she was already unbuckling her seat belt as the driver turned through the stone walls flanking both sides of the winding driveway. At the top of the hill the peaks of Hudson's wood and stone house soared high above the pine trees, the windows aglow like a beacon, calling her home.

When they pulled into the clearing she saw him, watching from the balcony that wrapped the length of the house, the wood plank door standing open behind him. He was down the stairs in no time, and had the limo door open before the car had even rolled to a complete stop.

"I thought you'd never fucking get here," he growled, reaching for Allie's hand. With a sharp tug he pulled her body flush against his, crushing his lips against hers in a ravenous kiss. His raw hunger ignited a flame that rushed like wildfire across her skin. Spending the week apart was a torture that had clearly taken its toll on both of them.

Allie melted into the kiss, carried away by the combination of lust and love she felt for the man who owned her, body and soul. Her hands clutched his dark, unruly hair, holding him to her as if he might slip through her fingers; a dream that might vanish into the night. He groaned in response and his hand cupped her ass, obliterating whatever distance remained between them with a seductive roll of the hips. But it wasn't enough. It would never be enough. Not until his skin was pressed against hers and he was buried deep inside her.

When he finally broke their kiss, she was a panting, quivering mess.

"I want you naked all weekend," he said, rubbing the tip of his nose against hers.

She grinned. "Is that so?"

"Hmm, I plan on taking you in every way imaginable in each and every room."

"Deal." Pulling back, she reached for his belt, grasping the buckle and tugging him toward the open car door. "We can start with the limo."

"While I welcome your initiative," he said as his fingers curled around hers, "I have plans for you. Inside." He dropped a swift kiss on her pouting lips. "Come."

Allie let out a small whimper as he stepped away. "That was the plan."

Hudson chuckled, then in a sudden move bent down, wrapped his arm around her thighs, and scooped her over his shoulder.

Allie let out a surprised squeal. "What are you doing?"

"Expediting matters," he said, matter-of-factly.

She slapped his behind. "Put me down."

"I didn't realize you were into spanking, Alessandra." Hudson laughed as he turned toward the stairs. "Although I do believe you've got the roles reversed."

"You're acting like a caveman," she said, holding onto his hips to keep from bouncing off his shoulder as he strode up the stairs. When he reached the top he set her on her feet, letting her slide slowly down his body so that she felt every hard, muscular inch.

"God, I've missed you," he breathed.

She smacked him playfully on the chest. "You could have been with me the past two hours."

"There were preparations to be made."

Allie narrowed her eyes, assessing him. "What have you been up to?" The scent of tomatoes and basil wafted through the air. She inhaled deeply and her mouth watered. "And more importantly, what smells so delicious?"

"Dinner. Are you hungry?" When her stomach growled, he smirked. "I will take that as a yes."

She blushed. "I may have worked through lunch."

A frown marred his handsome face. "Alessandra, we really need to have a discussion about your eating habits." His hands skimmed over her hips. "I like your curves just the way they are," he said, accenting his opinion with a gentle squeeze of her ass.

"It wasn't intentional." She reached up and smoothed the crease between his brows with her fingertip. "But yes, I will make more of an effort to eat regular meals, starting now. What did you order for us?"

"No delivery. I cooked."

When her mouth popped open, Hudson threw his head back and laughed. It was a deep, sexy sound that had literally become music to her ears. "Don't look so shocked," he said.

"I've seen you make coffee. And popcorn. Neither experience bodes well for this dinner."

Hudson placed his hand over his heart. "So little faith. I'm wounded. I think you may be pleasantly surprised." He nodded toward the kitchen. "Although I had hoped to have the mess cleaned up before you arrived."

Allie followed his gaze to the state-of-the-art kitchen. Although she was the only guest Hudson had ever invited to his lake house, the architect had clearly designed the space with large gatherings in mind. The beamed ceiling and planked floor of the living room flowed into the open space, and the same multicolor stones on the two-story fireplace created a similar hearth around a twelve-burner cooktop. A large island sat in the middle of the room with copper lights strung above it and a slab of marble on top that was bigger than most dining room tables. But it wasn't the sight of the six distressed wood barstools that prompted Allie's question—it was the dozen or so pots and pans strewn about the countertops that had her asking, "How many people are you expecting?

"It may have taken a few attempts," he mumbled. "But the final batch is nearly as I remember."

"As you remember?" Allie's heart swelled. Hudson mentioned his past so infrequently, any detail was precious to her simply because he was willing to share it. "Is this a family recipe?"

"Yes. My mother wasn't much of a cook, at least not that I can remember. But every now and again she would make my grandmother's Bolognese."

A wide grin spread across her face.

"Don't get too excited," he warned. "You haven't tasted it yet."

"I'm sure I'll love it. Do I have time to change before we eat?"

Hudson nodded. "I thought we could have some wine and relax a bit before dinner." He pressed a quick kiss to her lips. "Go ahead and freshen up while I try to restore a bit of order to the kitchen."

Allie hurried upstairs and showered quickly before changing into a pair of well-worn jeans and a soft cream sweater. She loved how relaxed and casual they both were at the lake. Far from the boardrooms and ballrooms, Hudson's cabin was a place where they could be themselves, eating Chinese takeout on the floor or dancing barefoot across the living room. Her lips curved into a giddy grin just thinking about the time they'd spent there in the fall, and she was still smiling as she made her way back down the stairs.

Soothing strains of classical music filled the room, and a cluster of candles flickered on a tray that rested atop a tufted ottoman. The tapestry pillows that normally dotted the leather sectional had been piled in front of the fireplace along with a soft throw. The kitchen was cleared of everything but one All- Clad pot, and a bottle of red wine had been opened and left to breathe on the island alongside two stemless glasses. Everything was perfect with one exception. Hudson was nowhere in sight.

Allie wandered into the kitchen. The sauce Hudson made had been turned to a low simmer. She lifted the lid and was tempted to sneak a taste, but decided to wait for him before sampling his efforts. As she recovered the pot, something caught her eye through the window. Hudson was standing just outside the French doors leading from the kitchen to the expansive deck. The torches on the railing posts were dark, but she could see him in the moonlight that shone down from the clear night sky. He had his back to her, but she could tell that something was bothering him. It was evident in his stance and the tension in his shoulders. Allie frowned. This was Hudson's favorite spot, the one place in the world he felt truly at home. The fact that something from her world could spoil even a moment for him here made her heart ache with sadness.

"What are you doing out here?" she asked, tugging on a parka she'd grabbed off one of the hooks by the door.

"Enjoying the view." Hudson turned, and at the sight of her all the tension left his frame. "Although I admit it's improved significantly now." He pulled her in front of him and wrapped his arms around her from behind. "I'm so glad you're here."

"You seemed upset before I came out here. Were you worrying about Julian?"

"Your safety is never far from my mind, Alessandra. But no, that wasn't what I was thinking about."

"What, then?"

He nuzzled her hair. "Are you happy?" His voice was hoarse against her ear.

Allie turned her head, pressing a kiss to his jaw. "Very. Despite everything that has happened over the past two months, I've never been happier than I am when I'm with you." She placed her hand on his cheek, urging him to look at her. "I love you, Hudson."

His gaze was soft on her face. "I love you too, Allie."

She let out a contented sigh as she leaned back against his chest. The sun had long since set but the moon glittered across the half-frozen lake. "And I love being here with you. It makes me feel like no matter what waits for us back home, it will all work out because we have this, we have us."

"There's something I need to . . ." His voice trailed off and his arms released their hold on her. Allie felt the warmth of his body leave her as he stepped back.

"Hudson?" When his eyes met hers his gaze was distant, almost lost, and the blood had drained from his handsome face. Panic gripped her, tightening her throat as she choked out the words. "What is it, what's wrong?"

"I was going to wait until later, but . . ." Hudson swallowed hard before dropping to one knee. "Alessandra Sinclair, I love you. And I want to love, honor, and cherish you for the rest of our lives." From the pocket of his jeans he pulled out a small, red leather box. He flipped it open to reveal a stunning diamond solitaire. This time when his eyes met hers, they were filled with a mix of adoration and nervous anticipation. "Marry me?"

16

---

*H*udson gazed up at Allie, who had a look of complete shock on her face. As he knelt in front of her, the reality of the situation sunk in and anxiety hit him hard. She wasn't saying a word. Silence . . . more silence.

"I'm on my knees here. Say something. Tell me no, or to go to hell, but I'd rather a yes."

"I don't know what to say."

"Not the reaction I was hoping for." Hudson stood up.

"It's not that . . . yes, I love you . . . but it's just . . . I mean, you hardly know me . . . and we've barely been together six weeks . . . and technically we're not even together right now and . . ."

"To the outside world we're not, but we're together in the only place that matters—in our hearts. That's one thing after all these years that's never changed. I lost you twice before and I'm a man who learns from his mistakes. Hell if I'm going to lose you again. And despite the litany of reasons you just provided for why we shouldn't marry, I'm fairly sure I heard a 'yes' somewhere in the middle. So let me do this again."

Allie laughed despite the tears that filled her eyes. "You want a do-over, Mr. Chase?"

"I believe our entire relationship is a do-over, Miss Sinclair." Hudson took a step back and dropped to one knee. He cleared his throat as he held out the red leather box again. "Alessandra Sinclair—my love, my life—will you marry me?"

"Yes, yes, I will marry you." When he stood up, Allie launched herself at him, hitting his chest so hard they took a couple steps back. His hands shot up to cup the sides of her face. He brushed his mouth against hers before pressing a tender kiss to her lips.

"Say it again," he whispered.

Tears spilled down Allie's cheeks and a huge smile spread across her face. "Yes, I will marry you. Big wedding, small wedding, whatever you want." She laughed. "But please don't say the Drake."

Hudson chuckled. "Hell no." He ran a hand back through his hair. "I was actually thinking we could get married here."

"At the lake?"

He nodded. "The weekend we spent here in October, the time we shared . . . something changed between us that last night. I suspect that's the night you realized you loved me. Without a doubt it's when I knew I loved you, and that I always had." He took a deep breath. "I take risks on a daily basis, Allie, but I will never again take one that jeopardizes what we have. Nothing in the world is worth more than that. I'm just sorry I wasn't man enough to admit it then."

"Shh," Allie pressed her fingers to his lips. "I think this would be the perfect place to get married."

Hudson dropped a quick kiss to her mouth and grinned like a son of a bitch. "It's settled then. We'll marry at sunset tomorrow."

"Tomorrow?" Allie's voice reached a pitch he was certain only mammals of the four-legged variety could hear.

"Yes," he said emphatically.

"We're in the middle of this huge mess with Julian."

"All the more reason. Despite the uncertainty in our lives right now, there's one thing I'm sure of, and it's that I intend to spend the rest of my life with you. I see no reason to postpone that simply because Julian wants to maintain some fucked-up love triangle. Besides," Hudson flashed a broad grin. "I'm a man of opportunity, and when I see one I take it. Tomorrow will be our wedding day. I want to say vows to each other; I want you to take my name, become Mrs. Hudson Chase." Allie opened her mouth, but he kept talking. "I won't argue with you if you choose to hyphenate, but—to our family, friends, colleagues—you'll bear my name as my wife. I am madly in love with you, Allie, and I need to start the rest of our lives together immediately. I can't wait."

"I don't want to wait either, but have you forgotten we're not even dating at the moment?"

"How could I forget?" The muscles in Hudson's jaw flexed.

"I know we don't have much family between us, but I'd like to at least have Nick and Harper here."

"So would I, but we can't tell them."

"Harper is going to be pissed. We sort of have this whole maid of honor pact going."

"Nick will no doubt hang this over my head until I'm six feet under. Once this whole mess is resolved we can marry again in front of our friends and family, as many times as you want, anywhere you want. Whatever your heart desires, I'll give it to you. We can announce our engagement in the newspapers, take publicity photos; hell, I'll even argue with you over seating charts if that's what you want. And you can invite all of Chicago, I don't care. But tomorrow will be about us, for us. I want you to be my wife, and the only person I need in attendance is a minister. Everything else has been taken care of—flowers, dresses, hair, and makeup—whatever you need has been arranged."

"That confident I'd say yes?"

He grinned. "That hopeful."

"Wait, did you say dresses?"

"In the guest bedroom. I had a local shop send over several for you to choose from. Don't worry," he added quickly. "Even I know that the groom can't see the dress. Though I look forward to seeing you out of it." A sinful grin curved his lips. "Take a look at them after dinner. If none suit your taste, I'll have more brought in tomorrow."

A slight blush colored Allie's cheeks. "I thought you knew my taste," she teased.

"Oh, I do." Hudson's lips brushed her jaw. "Exquisite perfection. Sweet, and all mine." Allie sank into him as he ran his open mouth down her throat. "But when the woman started to mention fabric choices and bodice cuts, I threw my hands up in surrender."

She laughed as he found that sensitive spot beneath her ear. "Well, you men have it easy. The black tux or the black tux?"

He smiled against her skin. "You never know. I could have opted for the powder blue."

Allie reared back and a frown creased her brow. Hudson reached up to smooth the velvety skin with the pad of his thumb. "I'm playing, Allie."

"No, not that. What if . . . Well, it's just that you and I, we're always in formal attire for one event or another. But the weekend we spent here in yoga pants and jeans, it was one of the happiest times I've ever known. I want to start our lives off the exact same way."

He cocked a brow. "Are you suggesting we marry in jeans?"

Allie nodded. "As much as I love you in a tuxedo, I love you like this even more."

"Are you sure you wouldn't rather wear a fancy white dress? Don't little girls dream about that sort of thing?"

"This girl has spent ten years dreaming about being with you again. And now I'm going to be your wife. The clothes we wear are irrelevant. I can wear a proper wedding dress when we do this again for our family and friends. But tomorrow, like you said, is just about us. And this is who we are."

Hudson dipped his head and his tongue did a slow sweep along the curve of her lip before he sealed his mouth over hers in a kiss. His shoulders rolled as he wrapped his arms around her and pulled her tighter against him. As he poured everything he felt for her into this kiss, he thought about the woman Allie had become—forgiving, compassionate, beautiful, intelligent—and he was one lucky SOB that she loved a shell of a man like himself. Life was way too fucking short, and one lifetime with her wasn't ever going to be enough. He would marry her every damn year to prove that he was done searching. She was it. Such a fucking sap he'd become. Like he gave a shit. Hudson broke the kiss and traced her now- reddened, swollen lips. "The rehearsal dinner is at seven with rehearsal for the honeymoon to follow."

"Oh, no."

"What?"

"Not until the wedding night."

"You're shitting me, right?"

A glint of amusement lit Allie's hazel eyes, the gold flecks brightening over the asinine idea. "We may not be the most traditional couple, but I'm not having sex with you the night before our wedding."

"That's fine, you can just fuck me."

"Hudson," Allie admonished.

"Make love?"

"Seriously."

"You expect me to sleep in the same bed with you and not touch you? Fuck, Allie, it's been a week."

"No. I'll sleep in one of the guest rooms."

"The guest rooms are wedding central at the moment."

"Then I'll sleep on the couch."

"Like hell you will." Hudson exhaled a harsh breath. "You

can have the master bedroom and I'll take the couch. But for the record, this no-sex rule is horseshit."

Allie fought a smile and failed miserably. She was mocking him, for Christ's sake. "Sorry."

"No, you're not." Hudson grinned. "But I'll let you make it up to me."

"Is that so?"

"Hmm. But for now, dinner with your fiancé."

She giggled. "Short engagement."

"Indeed." They turned back toward the house and he gave her a quick smack on the ass. "Enjoy your last night as Miss Sinclair, baby."

17

*A*llie's eyes flew open and she froze. Her heart raced as she listened through the darkness, praying the sound that woke her had been merely in her head. But then she heard it again, a guttural moan of tormented pain.

"No . . . leave him alone . . . don't take him."

Hudson's cries had her bolting out of bed. When she reached the top of the stairs she saw him on the couch, his fists clenching the sheet beneath him, his body twisting as if being pulled. At first she assumed the nightmare was about losing Nick, that he was reliving that horrible moment when his brother had been literally torn from his arms. But then he said something else. Something that stopped her in her tracks.

"His eyes are open . . . make him breathe . . . Dad!" The last word came on a primal scream that hit her like a physical blow.

"Hudson! Wake up." But his eyes remained closed, his head thrashing and his legs kicking. She ran to him, dropping to her knees beside the couch and shaking him. Beneath her hand she could feel his heart pounding against his sweat-soaked T-shirt. "Hudson, wake up. Please."

He bolted upright, his lungs heaving for air. The look in his eyes was wild and scared as his gaze darted frantically around the moonlit room before finally coming to rest on Allie. "What is it," he gasped. "What's wrong?"

"You were having another nightmare."

Hudson let out a heavy exhale and rubbed a hand over his face. "I'm sorry I woke you."

Allie sat down on the sofa beside him. "Do you want to talk about it?" she asked, already knowing full well the answer.

"No."

"It might help."

"I said I don't want to discuss it."

"You can't keep boxing these things up, Hudson."

"I'm fine," he said. "Let's just go back to sleep."

"But you're not sleeping." Her voice grew quiet. "And I'm worried about you. How long has this been going on?"

"Most of my life."

"How often?"

"It depends. They had stopped for a while."

"When did they return?"

Hudson pinched the bridge of his nose. "Recently."

"Since we flew back from Europe?

"Yes." He ran a hand back through his sweat-slicked hair. "It's my anxiety over your safety. Once this mess is resolved I'll be fine."

"Stop staying that." She could see the nightmare clinging to him. He wasn't fine, and he wouldn't be, not until he dealt with his demons once and for all. "The situation with Julian may be what brought them back, but you said yourself, you've had these all your life."

"And I've managed." He made a move to stand, but Allie stopped him.

"I've only witnessed a handful of these," she said. "But from what I've seen, they're tearing you up inside. Please, talk to me. Tell me about your nightmares."

"Trust me, you don't want a front row seat for the fucked up show inside my head."

"Then tell me about your past." Allie knew whatever haunted Hudson stemmed from his youth. Perhaps if she could convince him to talk about those early days, she could get to the root of what plagued him. "I'm marrying you tomorrow, Hudson." She reached for his hand. Turning it palm up she traced the spot where there would soon be a wedding band. "We're going to exchange rings and vow to be partners . . . in everything. For better or worse. Please, let me in."

His eyes shifted from where her fingers traced his hand to her pleading gaze. "What do you want to know?" he asked, his voice hoarse.

"Tell me about your family. What was it like when you were young? From what little I know, it doesn't sound like things were always bad."

The tension in his shoulders eased ever so slightly. "Everything was perfect, actually. I mean, we didn't have money to burn, but we were happy. And my parents were truly in love with each other. Hell, for my mother, the whole world revolved around my dad. I came earlier than planned and Nick, well, he was a surprise. But both of us always felt wanted."

Allie knew very little about their father other than he'd been out of their lives since Hudson and Nick were very young. "What was your dad like?"

A small, wistful grin formed on Hudson's lips. "He was the ultimate. Complete hands-on. He looked a lot like I do, but had a better sense of humor. And he could play just about any song on the guitar after hearing it one time."

"He sounds great."

Hudson nodded. "He worked hard to provide for us—nothing fancy, but life was good."

"So what happened?"

His brow creased and his smile faded. "I fucked everything up, that's what happened." He was quiet, and for a moment she thought that was as much as he would say, but then he surprised her by continuing. "We were driving back from a camping trip. Extravagant vacations weren't an option. We did road trips with the whole roughing it thing. It was late and we stopped so my dad could fill the tank up with enough gas to get us home, but I was starved and wanted some junk food from the store. My mother told me no, that she'd fix me and Nick PB&J's on white when we got home." He grimaced. "White fucking bread. Can't stomach the stuff now. But the selfish bastard I am, that wasn't good enough for me. I pitched a goddamn fit until my dad caved. He told me to pick something out for Nicky, too, but while I was debating the choices, a guy burst in waving a gun."

Allie couldn't stop the gasp that escaped her lips.

"He kept shouting for us to get down on the floor and not to make a fucking move or he'd cap a bullet in our skulls." Hudson swallowed hard. "I was pants-pissing scared, but my dad was so fucking calm."

"Were you the only two in the store?"

He shook his head. "There was a lady trying to buy a pack of smokes, from what I could see, and some old man jonesing for his Colt 45. The guy with the gun kept yelling at the cashier to pop open the register, but the poor kid was shaking like a leaf, dropping the money, change clattering all over the floor. I thought maybe he'd hit some sort of panic button or reach for a gun of his own, but he was just scared shitless like the rest of us. There was only about fifty bucks in the drawer, so the guy started barking at him to open the safe. The kid tried to reason with him —kept saying he didn't know the combo, only the manager did —but the guy was out of his fucking mind."

Allie held her breath. In that moment she would have done anything to rewrite history and change what she now realized would be the end of the story. But all she could do was listen as Hudson recounted the horrible details of that night.

"My dad was all calm and cool. Goddamn fucking hero tried to talk some sense into that piece of shit, even offered to give him the last of our cash just to get him the hell out of the store. But when my dad reached for his wallet, the guy swung his gun around and fired without even thinking." Hudson's entire body tensed. "The round nailed him in the chest and he hit the floor. I didn't know what to do. He was struggling to breathe and there was blood everywhere, so I pressed my hands on the wound." His voice cracked. "I couldn't stop it. The blood kept oozing between my fingers."

Allie's throat tightened as the scene Hudson was describing played out in perfect clarity in her mind.

"The guy took one look at my dad and ran like hell. My mom and Nick had watched the whole scene from the parking lot. Someone must have kept Nicky back but my mom was right there in seconds, screaming and crying. The whole thing was total chaos but slow-mo at the same time. People shouting, sirens in the distance, and blood . . . so much fucking blood." His grip tightened on her hand. "My father died before the paramedics arrived. I'll never forget the moment his eyes lost focus and his hand let go of mine."

Hot tears slid down Allie's cheeks. "I'm so sorry, Hudson."

"If I would have been content with a fucking peanut butter and jelly sandwich, my dad would still be alive. My mother would still be alive. Nick would have never spun out of control. Everything about our lives would have turned out differently. We could have been happy, but I fucked everything up."

"You think everything that's happened since then is somehow all your fault?"

He gazed at her incredulously. "The chain of events started that night."

And there it was, the sobering guilt that Hudson carried on

his shoulders. It was what drove his every action, what haunted him even in his sleep.

"You were just a kid. That's what kids do, they harass their parents."

"They're dead because of me. Nick was taken away because of my actions. There isn't an apology adequate for what I caused, nor any forgiveness for it."

"That's where you're wrong, Hudson." Her voice was soft, but the unwavering conviction was clear. "Your mother obviously had problems that ran far deeper than this, but Nick certainly doesn't blame you. In case you haven't noticed, he thinks you hung the moon." She gave him a small, reassuring smile. "And from what you've told me about your dad, I imagine the last thing he would want is for you to be putting yourself through this hell." Allie rested her free hand on the back of Hudson's neck, her fingers stroking through the damp hair at his nape. "You have to forgive yourself."

He frowned. "Easier said than done."

They were quiet for a few moments before Allie broke the silence. "Thank you."

He met her gaze with questioning eyes. "For what?"

"For trusting me enough to let me in. I want to share everything with you, Hudson, the good and the bad. And I want to help you work through this, but I'm not a professional. Will you at least consider talking to someone about this?"

He let out a resigned sigh. "I'll consider it. For you."

Allie knew he needed to seek help for himself, not just because she wanted him to. But she also knew it had been a huge step for him to open up to her, and that considering therapy was an even bigger leap. For that she was profoundly grateful. "I can't tell you how much it means to me."

The look that flashed in his eyes told her he was back from the darkness. "Enough to drop this whole sex embargo?" he asked, cocking a lopsided grin.

"Not a chance." She laughed, then her expression softened. "But I'd like to stay here with you for a bit if you don't mind."

Hudson smiled as he pulled her to lie next to him on the couch, her back to his front. "I thought I made myself clear last night," he said, nuzzling her neck. "I want you to stay with me forever."

18

*A*llie squinted at the clock above the fireplace mantel. The bright light filling the room told her it was at least late morning, but still, she hadn't expected both hands to be pointing to the twelve. Normally she didn't sleep half the day away, but the past few weeks had obviously taken their toll. And talking with Hudson in the middle of the night had brought her a sense of peace she hadn't felt in a very long time. There was still so much that was unresolved, but the last barrier had fallen. They were a team, and they would face their obstacles together, head-on.

Beside her, Hudson stirred in his sleep and his arm tightened around her waist. Allie closed her eyes and relished the feel of his body pressed along the length of hers. Lying next to him in that sleepy fog that hovered just at the brink of consciousness was one of her favorite ways to start the day. And this wasn't just any day. It was her wedding day.

Her wedding day.

The last remnants of sleep vanished instantly and Allie bolted upright. Her hands flew to cover Hudson's face. "Don't open your eyes."

Hudson groaned and a sleepy smile curved his lips. "I do

have blindfolds for this kind of thing, Alessandra," he said, his voice thick with sleep. "Although I'd prefer if you were the one wearing it."

Allie rolled her eyes even though she knew he couldn't see her. "That's not what I meant. I don't want you to see me."

He chuckled. "I promise to still marry you despite your bedhead."

"Funny, Chase. But unless you want to postpone the wedding to another day, keep your eyes closed. It's bad luck for the groom to see the bride before the ceremony."

"You're not seriously subscribing to that superstition, are you?"

"Given our track record, I'm not taking any chances. We need all the good mojo we can get. So do we have a deal?"

"Far be it for me to mess with mojo." He smiled beneath her hands. "I will keep my eyes closed. You have my word."

Allie slipped from the couch and scurried to one of the guest bedrooms. Once she was locked safely inside, she called out to him. "All clear."

A moment later there was a tap at the door. "How long do you plan on staying in there?" Hudson asked from the other side.

"Well, that depends. How long until the ceremony?"

"Four hours."

"Then I plan on staying in here for four hours."

A deep laugh vibrated from the other side of the door. "No need. I have a few last-minute arrangements to see to. Give me a few minutes and then the place is all yours."

"Arrangements? What are you up to?" But from the other side of the door came only silence. After what seemed like an eternity, she heard the sound of footsteps on the stairs and a clatter of dishes in the kitchen.

What the hell is he doing?

Her answer came in the form of a note slipped under the door. Lunch is in the kitchen and a bath is waiting upstairs.

Meet you at the altar.

—H

Meet me at the altar? What altar?

"Hudson?" She waited a few minutes, and when no reply came, cracked the door open to find . . .

Nothing. No sign of Hudson, but also no further explanation. There was, however, a lovely lunch of fruit and cheese and crusty bread arranged on the kitchen island, along with a can of her favorite sparkling water. Seemed her fiancé had thought of everything. As for the rest of the arrangements, she just had to trust that all would be revealed when the time came.

Allie made herself a small plate of food and took it with her to the master suite. As promised, a bath had been drawn, and judging by the delicious scent that filled the air, jasmine and vanilla scented oils had been added to the water. The two-sided fireplace that separated the bathroom from the bedroom had been lit, and a cluster of candles flickered atop the slate tiles that ran along the tub's edge.

In almost no time Allie's clothes were in a pile on the floor and she was soaking in the oversize copper tub. The warm water felt like heaven on her sore muscles, and before long the aches she'd incurred from a night spent sleeping on a couch began to fade. She rested her head against the edge of the tub and closed her eyes. Thoughts of the evening to come filled her mind, and she smiled. Before the night was through, Hudson would be her husband. They would exchange rings and vows as they pledged their lives to each other.

Her eyes popped open. While she was confident Hudson would have provided his and hers wedding bands, the subject of vows hadn't been discussed. Would they be repeating traditional vows after the minister or would they be reciting their own? Deciding to be better safe than sorry, she sat up in a rush, sending water sloshing over the side of the tub, and reached for a towel.

Telling Hudson how she felt about him was going to be the easy part; keeping it to a reasonable length would be the challenge. As she wrapped herself in a white, fluffy robe, she began to laugh. *This* was her stress—writing vows that didn't drag on until dawn. The contrast to her previous foray into wedding planning was so extreme it was comical. And for the hundredth time that day she knew she'd made exactly the right decision.

Despite her initial reaction to the contrary, she loved the idea of eloping. From the moment they'd met, there had been forces at play keeping them apart. After all they'd been through, all they'd overcome and still had yet to face, it made perfect sense to start their lives together on their own terms.

And the location Hudson had chosen was perfect. He was right—this was where she knew with all certainty that she loved him. They would no doubt marry again for the sake of family and friends, but she loved the idea that their first vows would be spoken at a place that meant so much to both of them.

With those thoughts in mind, she grabbed a paper and pen from the kitchen and began to put her feelings down on paper. In the end she decided on two versions: one that was a set of vows she could recite in a timely manner; the other an outpouring of her thoughts and emotions in the form of a letter she would give to her new husband as a wedding gift later that night. *Her husband.* Would she ever get used to calling him that? A warmth spread through her at the realization that she would have a lifetime to find out.

When she was finally finished writing, it was nearly two o'clock. Hudson had said the ceremony was at four, which left her plenty of time to get ready. He'd offered to have the Grand Geneva Hotel send over a few members of the spa team to pamper and prepare her, but Allie had declined his sweet offer. Preserving the intimacy and privacy of the day was important to her, which meant keeping outside involvement to the bare minimum.

So instead of lying back while a bevy of white coats fluttered around her, Allie got ready for her wedding alone, with a thousand butterflies fluttering in her stomach and Frank Sinatra crooning from her iPod. She kept her makeup light and natural, the way she knew Hudson liked it, and arranged her hair in a pile of loose curls held in place with tiny, pearl-tipped pins. A few tendrils hung down to frame her face, and a pair of simple diamond studs adorned her ears. She sat back and admired her reflection. Even she had to admit she was glowing, although it had nothing to do with the bronzer she'd brushed over her cheeks and everything to do with the man she was about to meet at the altar.

Speaking of her mysterious man . . .

What the hell has he been up to all day?

There was only one way to find out, and with hair and makeup done, it was finally time to get dressed.

The walk-in closet was full of clothes, with everything from ski pants to lingerie lining both sides. At the very back hung a row of long, white garment bags. Allie unzipped them one at a time. There was no denying that the wedding dresses the store had delivered were absolutely stunning. Elegant gowns in fabrics ranging from silk to tulle, some with elaborate beading and others more simple in their stylish sophistication. Any one of them would have been a wonderful choice. But instead Allie selected a white angora sweater that hung with the more casual outfits and paired it with her favorite dark jeans. And instead of crystal Jimmy Choos she donned a pair of fur-lined boots that laced to her knee. The outfit was a far cry from the gown she was to have worn when she married Julian, and it couldn't have been more perfect. Because today, Alessandra Sinclair wasn't becoming the Marquise Laurent in an elaborate ceremony that was nothing more than a glorified merger. Today, Allie Sinclair was becoming Mrs. Hudson Chase in a simple exchange of vows with the man who was not only her first love, but her last.

But when she emerged from the bedroom she found the house was still empty. Hudson was nowhere to be seen, and there certainly wasn't an altar. Perhaps he was outside again? When she reached the kitchen she opened the French doors that led to the deck. It was empty and the lanterns on the posts remained unlit. She was about to go back inside when she heard the unmistakable neigh of a horse. She followed the deck as it wrapped around to the front of the house. There, at the foot of the stairs, sat a horse-drawn sleigh. The majestic Clydesdale greeted her with a whinny and a shake of his head, causing a giggle to escape her lips.

"Right this way, Miss Sinclair," the driver said, gesturing to the small set of stairs waiting alongside the gleaming white sleigh.

"Let me just grab a coat."

"No need." He reached for a white parka and held it open for her. She might have been getting married in jeans and a sweater, but her thoughtful fiancé had made sure to provide outerwear that was bridal white. "There's a blanket on the seat," the man added as he helped her into the coat.

Allie took his hand as she climbed into the sled. Sure enough, a luxurious, white faux-fur throw sat folded on the crushed velvet seat. Hudson's attention to detail astonished her, right down to the bouquet of white roses hand-tied with a wide satin ribbon.

With a snap of the reigns, they were on their way, the sleigh gliding through the woods behind the house. The sun had nearly set and the fresh snow glittered a silvery blue beneath the runners. After a few moments a small, rustic barn appeared in the distance. Through the frost-covered windowpanes, Allie could see the flicker of candles. She smiled to herself, knowing inside that barn stood the man she loved, waiting for her to walk down the aisle and into his arms. But when the door swung open, her breath caught and her steps faltered. Though she'd been thinking about this moment all day, nothing she'd imagined came close to the sight that greeted her as she walked into the barn.

Candles covered nearly every flat surface, casting the barn

with a soft, warm glow. Above them tiny lights twinkled like stars stretched across the night sky, and white blooms cascaded from the hay lofts, creating the feel of an indoor winter wonderland. A white runner dotted with rose petals formed an aisle that ran from the door to the far side of the barn, where more flowers formed an arch over the minister. But it was the sight of Hudson that had her frozen, barely able to breathe, let alone walk. His eyes met hers and the smile that stretched across his face told her he felt it, too, the longing that had pulsed between them since the day they'd first met. It was a tangible force, a magnetic pull bringing them together no matter the obstacles or odds. Only now it was even more than attraction and lust and desire and need. Now it was love.

19

*F*ucking breathe, Hudson had to remind himself. His heart pounded in his chest like a jackhammer. Ten years and inconsequential months, hours, days, minutes, and seconds blurred into I-don't-give-a-shit.

This was it. Showtime, Chase.

He stood at a makeshift altar under a canopy of flowers and strands of lights, surrounded by dozens of candles that cast the vintage barn in a warm glow. Beside him, the minister stood ready to perform the ceremony, while outside snow flurries had begun to fall. Hudson looked at his watch, then stole a glance through the frosted window. The woman he loved was out there somewhere in a horse-drawn sleigh. Any minute now the doors would swing open and she would walk down the white runner that stretched the length of the floor.

The thought of her standing in the doorway did nothing to ease the tightening in his chest. Hudson lifted his arm to run his hand through his hair, but caught himself. When Allie showed up, he didn't want to look like he'd just rolled out of bed. Goddamn, he was nervous. If he'd been wearing a tie he would have straightened it, repeatedly. But in true form, Allie had surprised him yet again. So instead of a monkey suit, he stood waiting for his future wife in jeans and a cashmere sweater. His wife. The words hit him hard. He rocked backed on his heels and blew out a deep breath. He was throwing off anything but cool, calm, and collected, and he needed to get a grip ASAP.

The minister chuckled. "Relax, son. It's just you and your bride up here."

No shit. It was just him and his bride in the whole place. Hudson rubbed his brow and a slight frown pulled at the corners of his mouth. Under different circumstances, Nick would have been standing at his side, busting his chops or cracking jokes about losing the rings. Truth was he felt like a bastard for not telling his brother what he was doing, but it was mission critical that their nuptials remained a secret. It was necessary; didn't mean he liked it. In fact, he hated that a minister and a cellist would be the only two people to witness the moment when Alessandra Ingram Sinclair became his wife.

Right at the moment the double doors parted, the cellist began to play, and Hudson's nerves vanished.

She was beautiful. No, that didn't cut it. Exquisite. Fucking hell, perfect.

He watched her make her way toward him to the cellist's rendition of "Thinking Out Loud" and couldn't help but recall the first time he saw her. She was walking on the beach—tan legs, sundress, light freckles across her nose, and blond hair high-lighted by the sun. He never dreamed he'd be worthy of her, let alone that one day she'd be his. He was a punk back then and hadn't improved much over time, but he'd spend the rest of his life trying to be the man she deserved.

God, he loved her. What was taking her so long to get down such a short aisle? He had to ground himself to keep from meeting her halfway, but there was nothing he could do to stop the ridiculous grin that spread across his face. And damn if it didn't grow wider with every step she took. "Hurry," he finally mouthed.

The smile she gave him in return started out shy, just a twitch at one side, then spread until she was full on beaming at him. "I love you," she mouthed back. She looked so beautiful, yet nervous, and that wasn't how he wanted her to feel at that moment.

"Breathe, baby," he whispered.

The music slowed to a stop and then . . .

"Today you celebrate one of life's greatest moments," the minister began, "and give recognition to the value and beauty of love as you are joined together in vows of marriage. Words can be beautiful, but actions are meaningful. It is one thing to talk, and one thing to promise; one thing to experience, and one thing to savor. This day is one thing; your lives another. The past is important, but it is in the future where your lives lay."

Hudson's hand tightened around Allie's. Standing at the altar with her felt like they'd climbed Mount Everest and had finally reached the top.

"You are entering into the holy estate, which is the deepest mystery of experience, and which is the very sacrament of divine love. No other human ties are more tender, no other vows are more sacred, than these you are about to say. Do you have the rings?"

Hudson pulled a leather box out of his pocket and opened it to reveal two platinum bands resting inside. Allie lifted his out of the satin, which was holding the ring securely in place, and Hudson did the same with hers before tucking the box back into his jeans. He turned back to Allie with the ring suspended between his fingers and held her gaze as if he were holding her in his arms.

"I, Hudson, take you Allie, to be my wife. It is by this ring and this ceremony that I make you that which you should have been so long ago. I promise to be your lover and your companion, your greatest fan and your most challenging adversary." His lips twitched into an amused grin. "And to communicate truthfully and fearlessly." His eyes roamed over Allie's face as he slipped the band on her finger. "As I join my life with yours, take this ring as a sign of my love and commitment."

Allie reached for Hudson's left hand and looked into his eyes as she began to recite her vows. "I, Allie, take you, Hudson, to be my husband, secure in the knowledge that you are my one true love."

A smile tugged at Hudson's lips. Without even discussing it, they had both written their own vows, opting out of the traditional.

"I give you my solemn vow to be your faithful partner in good times and in bad, to stand by your side in sickness and in health, and in joy as well as sorrow. I promise to love you without reservation, comfort you in times of need, and encourage your dreams and goals. I will laugh with you and cry with you, grow with you in mind and spirit, and above all else, cherish you for as long as we both shall live." She slid the ring on his finger, and despite the multitude of problems they still faced, everything felt right in the world. "Take this ring as a sign of my never-ending love."

Hudson held her hand as they stood staring at one another. The emotion that shone in his new bride's eyes reflected the way he felt. She was his love, his life, his home. They stayed like that, lost in the moment, until the minister cleared his throat.

"Having heard the pledges of your affection, and the vows of your fidelity, I do therefore by virtue of the authority vested in me by the state of Wisconsin, pronounce you husband and wife." He glanced back and forth between the two of them and smiled. "You may now kiss your bride."

Hudson wrapped his arms around Allie and drew her close.

"Finally, you're mine," he whispered just before he slanted his mouth over hers in a slow, languid kiss. When he pulled away, he noticed a warm flush had spread across her cheeks. He trailed a finger along her jaw. "You look beautiful."

"So what now?" she asked almost shyly.

Hudson smiled. "The rest of our lives, Mrs. Chase."

20

_T_he ride back to the lake house was a blur of falling snow, gentle touches, and whispered words. Allie and Hudson couldn't seem to take their eyes off each other, much less their hands, which was why she barely noticed the lanterns that lined the driveway until the sleigh pulled to a stop in front of the house.

She turned on the crushed velvet bench. More candles encased in beveled glass dotted the stairs. "It looks beautiful," she said.

Hudson climbed down from the sleigh, and when he held his hand out, the moonlight glinted off his platinum wedding band. The sight of her ring on his finger made Allie's stomach flutter. It was official. He was hers. Forever. When she met his gaze she knew he'd read the thoughts as they'd flickered across her face. And the glow that lit his blue eyes as he waited for his new bride to climb down out of their wedding carriage told her he was feeling the exact same thing. She was his and nothing in the world mattered more to him. In that moment she didn't think it was possible for him to look any sexier. But then he spoke and her insides melted.

"Come, Mrs. Chase," he said, the corner of his mouth turning up into a mischievous grin. "Your wedding reception awaits."

Allie lifted a brow in question as she placed her hand in his. "What have you been up to?" She'd no sooner set one foot on the side rail when he bent forward and swept her into his arms. "Hudson," she squealed. "What are you doing?"

He chuckled. "Carrying my bride across the threshold." He held her tight against his chest as he carried her effortlessly up the stairs. When they reached the top he pushed the front door open without ever tearing his gaze away from hers. "I love you," he whispered just before their lips touched. The kiss started softly, almost reverently, but then Allie's hands found their way into his hair, holding him to her as his tongue slid greedily over hers. His arms tightened around her as he deepened the kiss. She felt his every thought, every emotion, in the way his mouth moved with hers. Tasting her, consuming her, loving her.

When he finally pulled away, she could hardly catch her breath.

"That's quite a smile," he said. "And you haven't even seen my best work yet."

Allie knew she was grinning like a fool, but she didn't care. She was married to the only man she'd ever truly loved. And she was about to spend the rest of the night showing him just how much. "So I was thinking . . ."

"I'm usually wary when you begin a sentence like that, Alessandra," he teased.

She gave his shoulder a playful shove. "I was thinking that one good thing about a private ceremony is now there's nothing to keep me from getting you naked. Pronto."

A laugh vibrated deep within his chest. "As much as I appreciate your enthusiasm," he said before his gaze darkened and his voice grew gruff, "and as much as I can't wait to claim you as my wife, there are a few traditions that need to be upheld."

He set her on her feet, and for the first time Allie took in the sight of the living room. A small round table had been set up in front of the fireplace, where flames danced over two birch logs. White linen was draped over the tabletop and a bowl of white roses sat between two elegant china place settings. As she drew closer she could see that dinner had already been served, and an open bottle of champagne waited in a silver ice bucket. Whatever team of "elves" Hudson had assembled to pull off this very private reception hadn't been gone long.

"It's perfect," she murmured.

Hudson pulled out Allie's chair and waited while she sat. But instead of rounding the table to take his own seat, he reached for her butter knife and began clinking it softly against her glass.

"What are . . ." She giggled as the answer to her unfinished question popped into her head. Hudson matched her grin with one of his own as he leaned down to place a soft kiss on her lips. "Wow, you weren't kidding about the traditions, were you?"

"Only the beginning, baby." He gave no further details, but rather went about the business of pouring them each a glass of champagne and offering a toast that made her heart swell and her toes curl. They dined by candlelight, making small talk about the ceremony and laughing over what the minister's reaction must have been to seeing her walking down the aisle dressed in jeans. Or how the sleigh driver must have considered them worse than a pair of horny teens. But mostly they just gazed at each other with an unspoken appreciation of the moment.

Allie had just finished her last bite when Hudson reached across the table and took her hand. "I love the way my ring looks on you," he said, his thumb brushing back and forth across the platinum band.

"Staking your claim?"

He chuckled. "Something like that. Since I'm assuming a tattoo that says 'Mine' is more than likely out of the question."

Allie frowned.

"Hey." He gave her hand a gentle squeeze. "I was just teasing."

She cracked a small smile. "I know."

"Then what's wrong?"

Her gaze fell to their entwined fingers. "I always thought once I put a wedding band on I would never take it off." She gave an apologetic shrug.

Hudson lifted her hand and pressed his lips to the band. "The day will come when this ring is never off your finger." His gaze darkened momentarily before a lighthearted mirth lit his eyes. "But for now, time to cut the cake."

"Cake?"

He pushed back from the table and stood. "Oh, yes. I might not be a professional event planner, but even a mere mortal such as myself knows a bride and groom need to cut a cake."

Allie turned and watched her husband stroll into the kitchen, completely smitten by him. The fact that he'd made the effort to incorporate so many traditions into their makeshift reception was all kinds of cute. Still, she couldn't help but think of the traditions they were missing out on, ones they couldn't have had either way. Even if they'd invited half of Chicago to their wedding, Allie's father still wouldn't have been there to walk her down the aisle. Hudson still wouldn't have been able to dance with his mom.

She straightened in her chair and shook the unsettling thoughts from her head. While it was true that she and Hudson had lost a great deal, they had each other, which was far more than either of them had thought possible a short time ago. And they had Nick and Harper. A slight frown tugged at the corner of Allie's mouth at the thought of not sharing the occasion with the two people who meant the most to them.

Hudson was suddenly behind her, his lips at her ear. "We'll do this again with the people we care about," he said in yet another example of the uncanny knack he had for reading her mind.

The cake he set on the table in front of her looked almost too beautiful to eat. With three layers and a cascade of flowers shaped out of what smelled like her favorite buttercream icing, the miniature creation was exactly what she would have chosen, just appropriately sized for a reception for two.

"I believe the honors go to the bride," he said, passing her a cake knife with a white satin bow tied around a crystal handle. Allie took it from him, noticing the interlocking A & H engraved on the wide blade along with the date.

"I *believe* we're supposed to do it together."

Hudson placed his hand over hers as they cut a single wedge of cake. He broke off a small piece with his fingers and lifted it to her lips. "Open for me, baby." The tenor of his voice matched the mischievous gleam in his eyes.

Allie pulled back and fixed him with a hard stare. "Don't even think about it, Chase." Smashing cake in each other's faces was one tradition Allie was more than happy to skip.

"Or what, *Chase*?" His serious expression dissolved into an amused chuckle. "Relax. While I did enjoy the end results, a repeat of our cookie decorating is not what I have in mind for tonight."

"And what do you have in mind for tonight?"

"Cake, Alessandra," he said, ignoring her question.

Allie resisted the urge to roll her eyes and instead simply held his gaze as he eased the bite into her mouth. "Delicious."

"Let me have a taste." Hudson buried his fingers in Allie's hair and pulled her to him. His lips moved softly over hers as his tongue dipped inside her mouth in a leisurely kiss. When it ended she was more than ready to leave the reception and head straight to the honeymoon suite, but Hudson seemed to be in no rush. He reached for a remote that had been resting on the table and pressed a button. "Time for the first dance." Over the speakers Ed Sheeran began to sing the same song the cellist had played as Allie had walked down the aisle.

A smile spread across her face as she took Hudson's hand. "You really have thought of everything, haven't you?"

He lifted Allie's arm above her head and spun her into the middle of the living room. "I wanted tonight to be special for you." He slid his hand to the small of her back and eased her against him. "For us."

She gazed up at him. "Every night I spend with you is special."

"Ah, but this is your first night as my wife." He spun her away and then yanked her back against him. "Had to up my game." An almost boyish grin lit his face. It was the same one from long ago, somehow both devastatingly handsome and curiously shy. Ten years had done nothing to lessen the effect it had on her, and she knew in her heart no amount of time ever would.

They swayed in time to the music, sweeping across the living room as Sheeran crooned about never-ending love. Hudson's arm tightened around Allie's waist and he dipped her low, slanting his mouth over hers in a passionate kiss. "Hmm." He hummed against her lips, then in a quiet murmur quoted the song as it drew to a close. "Till we're seventy."

"I want much more than that, Mr. Chase. Ninety is the bare minimum."

Hudson laughed, but when he pulled her back up, his gaze was soft on her face. "Forever wouldn't be enough," he said. He traced her bottom lip with his finger, then dipped his head to brush his lips softly against hers. It was the briefest of contact, but enough to make every nerve in her body come alive. He teased her with gentle licks, then covered her mouth with his, kissing her long and slow and deep. She moaned softly as his tongue moved against hers in lush strokes, and when his hand slid down her backside, she pressed against him, longing to feel his bare skin against hers.

The soft click of a camera came from beside her. Allie turned her head to discover Hudson had snapped a picture of the two of them with his phone. "Smile pretty for the camera," he said. They were the same words he'd spoken when the photographer interrupted their dance at the Field Museum. As the camera flashed, Allie couldn't help but think about how far they'd come since that chance encounter three months prior. Deep down she knew they still had so far to go, but she pushed those unwelcome thoughts out of her mind. This was her wedding night, and the only thing that mattered was the man with his arm banded around her waist and his temple pressed to hers.

"I'm sure that the next time we do this, we'll have enough professional photos to fill your entire tablet," he said. "But I wanted this one just for me."

"Taking that picture reminded me of the one the paper ran back in September," she said.

Hudson powered off his phone and tucked it back in the ass pocket of his jeans. "Made you think about how much you wanted me that night, too?"

This time she did roll her eyes. "Actually, I thought you were a pompous ass that night."

He grinned. "But you still wanted me."

She bit her lip. "Perhaps."

"Well, I thought you were a spoiled, uptight bitch that night." Allie's mouth popped open in feigned exasperation but Hudson merely smiled and finished his thought. "And even more beautiful than you were when I first met you. Which, for the record, I wouldn't have thought possible."

"And now?" she asked

"And now I can't believe I'm the lucky bastard who gets to see that look in your eyes."

"What look?"

"The one that says you want nothing more than to have me buried deep inside you."

A small gasp escaped her lips. "Well, if I'm that obvious, what the hell are you waiting for? Let's consummate this already."

Hudson's head fell back and he laughed. "Ever the romantic, Mrs. Chase." In a swift move he grasped her behind the knees and lifted her into his arms.

"What are you doing now?"

"We've been over this," he said, striding toward the stairs. "I need to carry you over the threshold."

"Of the bedroom?" A small giggle bubbled up from inside her. "I thought that tradition only applied to the front door."

"Laugh all you want, but I believe you were the one who pointed out the need for superstition." He grinned. "Or mojo, as you called it."

Allie wrapped her arms around Hudson's neck as he carried her upstairs to his bedroom. The team of wedding planning elves had apparently been busy on the second floor as well. Rose petals were spread across the white duvet, and a hurricane glass with a cluster of flickering candles rested atop the nightstand.

He lay her on the king-size bed, then joined her, and together they began to remove each other's clothing. Frantic hands and fumbling fingers blended with anxious groans and soft laughter to create a scene more in keeping with the two teens in the backseat of a car than a couple on their wedding night.

When they were both naked, he moved over her body with a measured control that was a complete contradiction to the frenzied pace in which they'd undressed, not to mention the erection pressed against her thigh. All laughter faded and the only sound that remained was their deep, stuttering breaths.

Hudson brushed her hair away from her face, his thumb lingering to caress her cheek. "If ever any beauty I did see / Which I desired, and got / 'Twas but a dream of thee."

Tears welled in Allie's eyes as John Donne's words washed over her heated skin like a caress. Hudson wasn't the type of man to quote poetry, which made the gesture all the more moving.

And the words he'd chosen to whisper to his new bride were not only beautiful, but appropriate. To the outside world Hudson Chase had everything he could possibly desire, and yet he'd made it clear time and time again that Allie was the only dream that ever mattered. The poetic reminder that the man she loved cherished her above all else took her desire for him to an almost debilitating level. She couldn't wait any longer. She needed his hands and lips and tongue on her. She needed to be one with him through the most primal connection. She needed her husband. "Love me, Hudson."

"I do," he murmured. His voice was thick with emotion. "Those words will never be enough, but God help me, I do."

With that, Hudson lowered his mouth to hers. She moaned, and when her lips parted he deepened the kiss, his tongue claiming her with an undeniable possession. "I've been waiting for this all day," he rasped. His body arched over hers as he sucked and licked his way down her throat. "The moment when I make you mine."

He dipped his head and his tongue flicked across one nipple before catching it between his teeth. Her body shuddered as he tugged hard, the sensation echoing through her core. Then he kissed his way to the other side, laving the hardened peak with lazy circles before sucking it deep into his mouth.

Allie's fingers trembled against his skin as they skated over his shoulders and across his chest. His stomach muscles tensed as she smoothed over the ripples of his abs, and when she took his hard length in her hand, he drew a sharp breath.

"I love touching you," she whispered. Her fingers curled around him, gently squeezing and stroking from root to tip. The feel of him throbbing and pulsing in her hand drove her wild, and before long her hips began to move in a silent plea.

Hudson gazed up at her with dark, hungry eyes. "Not yet," he murmured. "First I need to taste my wife." The delicious promise held in his words made her entire body clench with need. Or maybe it was just the sound of Hudson calling her his wife that caused a soft whimper to escape her lips. Either way, anticipation thrummed through her veins as he shifted fast and smooth between her thighs. He lifted one leg over his shoulder, spreading her wide, and dragged his tongue up her center. Allie's breath hitched and the air rushed out of her lungs as his tongue lashed across her most sensitive flesh. There was nothing gentle about the way he devoured her—licking, nipping, and sucking her as if consumed by a desperate need to bring her pleasure.

"Oh God," she moaned. Her fingers dug into his hair, holding him against her as she began to quiver.

"That's it, come on my tongue. Let me taste you." His words vibrated against her and she cried out, splintering apart in a mind-blowing orgasm.

He kneed her legs apart. "Spread for me. I need to be inside you." The weight of his body settled over hers and his erection lay hot and heavy just where she needed him most. He gazed down at her as he brought their bodies together. Once he was buried deep, he stilled. "Mine."

"Yours," Allie whispered in return, relishing the feel of him and knowing their connection was complete. He brushed his lips against hers as he began to slowly move, pulling back and then flexing into her with a deliberate, unhurried rhythm.

She groaned, needing more, needing him. "Please, Hudson . . ."

With a growl he slid deeper. Allie gasped, her swollen flesh tightening around him as he drew back. Their kiss deepened as he began to really move, his tongue fucking her mouth in time with each possessive thrust of his hips. Allie felt her insides begin to quicken as his body rolled against hers with measured determination. Her hand clutched the white sheet, her grip tightening with each relentless drive. She felt herself climbing higher and higher, then Hudson changed his angle, hitting a spot deep inside her, and a keening cry escaped her lips. Her head tipped back and her eyes drifted shut.

"Open," he grunted.

Her gaze met his as a fiery orgasm rolled through her body, obliterating everything but the man moving hot and slick above her. "Fuck, Allie. That's it. Look into my eyes as I come inside you."

He came long and hard, his hips jerking in a powerful, unforgiving thrust as he poured himself into her. "I love you," he whispered as he collapsed against her. The weight of him, pressing her into the mattress, soothed the aftershocks that racked her trembling frame.

"I love you, too," she said. Her voice quivered as her body shuddered.

Hudson rolled onto his back, pulling her with him without ever breaking their connection. Allie nuzzled against his chest as he cradled her in his arms, and felt the pounding beat of his heart beneath her cheek. They lay in silence, neither one speaking as their collective breathing slowed, and all thoughts left her but one. Hudson was right: a lifetime would never be enough.

She wanted forever.

21

Sunlight streamed through the window, waking Allie from the most amazing dream. Snow and candles and vows and tears and whispered words of love. Except it wasn't a dream at all. It was her life, and she would spend the rest of it with the wonderful man asleep beside her on the bed.

He was draped across her with his head on her chest, one arm wrapped possessively around her waist and his legs entwined with hers. Allie stroked her fingers down his back and a ray of sunlight caught the facets of the diamond on her engagement ring. She lifted her hand. The ring Hudson had given her was absolutely perfect. An understated yet flawless oval solitaire set on a thin platinum band covered with smaller stones. It was simple and elegant and exactly what she would have selected.

"Do you like it?" Hudson asked, blinking up at her.

Allie met his gaze. The love reflected in his clear blue eyes took her breath away, leaving her momentarily speechless.

"If you'd rather something else," he said, propping up on one elbow, "we can go back to the store together and—"

Allie pressed her fingertips to his lips. "I love it." She leaned forward, replacing her fingers with a soft kiss. "But I love the man who gave it to me even more."

"Mmm." A low sound of approval vibrated in the back of his throat and his arm tightened around her waist. "And I you, Mrs. Chase."

Warmth bubbled up inside her and a soft giggle escaped her lips.

Hudson reared back to look at her, lifting one brow. "Are you going to have that reaction every time I say your name?" The amusement in his voice made her smile widen even more.

"I just might."

"Then I will have to make a point to keep saying it." He tucked a strand of hair behind her ear. "Every day for the rest of my life."

"I like the sound of that," she said, leaning into his touch. "So tell me, what's the plan for day one of the rest of our lives?"

Hudson settled back on the pillow and pulled Allie across his chest. "I'm fine staying here all day."

"Well, we have to eat at some point."

He exhaled a heavy sigh. "Married not even twenty-four hours and already I'm second to food."

"Hardly." She laughed.

Hudson's brow knit together. "To be honest, I hadn't really given today much thought. I was so focused on the proposal and wedding, I didn't plan anything for the rest of the weekend." He smirked. "Aside from the obvious."

"Sounds like the perfect honeymoon," she said, her finger trailing over the defined slope of his pecs.

"Indeed. But you're correct. We will need to eat something besides leftover wedding cake, which means we'll need to go out." He sucked in a sharp breath when she brushed over a particularly ticklish spot she'd recently discovered just below his ribs. He caught her hand and entwined his fingers with hers. "I'd take you into town, but—"

"But we can't risk being seen."

"Precisely."

"Motorcycle helmets would make for a nice disguise, but it's not exactly the weather for taking your bike out."

"Enjoyed that, did you?"

"I did."

An almost childlike enthusiasm lit Hudson's face. "Get up," he said, flinging the covers back. "Dress warm."

With that, he climbed out of bed. The sight of his very fine, very naked backside as he strolled into the closet had Allie wishing she'd never mentioned food in the first place. And dress warm? What was that all about? Allie was positive Hudson wouldn't risk a ride on his bike in the dead of winter. He'd been emphatic about safety when talking to Nick. So where the hell was he taking her?

A moment later Hudson emerged from the bathroom wearing a pair of dark jeans and a blue sweater that did crazy things to his eyes. "Meet you out back," he said as he strode out of the room.

Allie scrambled out of bed and sifted through the closet for the warmest clothes she could find. Once she was dressed, she made her way downstairs and out onto the deck that circled the house.

The backyard, as Hudson called it, was acres of Wisconsin wilderness. Gently rolling hills stretched out as far as she could see, dotted with pine trees and covered with several inches of fresh white snow. Allie found her new husband at the foot of the rear staircase, just outside the garages that made up the first level of the three-story home. He was wearing a fitted black parka and a black motorcycle helmet with the tinted visor flipped down. If it weren't for the fact that he was straddling a snowmobile instead of a motorcycle, she would have sworn she was living her very own *Grease 2* fantasy.

"Where did this come from?" she asked.

Hudson flipped up his visor. His blue eyes sparkled in the late morning sun. "I purchased it when I bought the Harley. Wasn't sure I'd have much use for it, though, until today."

Allie smiled. "Guess it's true what they say about boys and their toys."

"That word evokes something entirely different in my mind," he said, holding her gaze until the heat of his stare had her shifting on her feet. "Why Alessandra, is that the wind turning your cheeks pink, or have I made my wife blush?"

"You're a naughty boy, Hudson Chase."

"Hmm, you don't know the half of it. Yet." The rough timbre of his voice sent a shiver of desire through her. But instead of elaborating, Hudson merely reached for the extra helmet on the back of the Ski-Doo. "Here," he said, as though he hadn't just reduced her to a puddle. "These ought to keep anyone from recognizing either of us."

She took a deep breath. "Where are we headed?"

"There's a little ski town not too far north. We can follow the trails through the backwoods." Hudson turned a key, and a second later the snowmobile roared to life. "Hop on," he yelled over the engine. He held his hand out to help her climb on, then waited while she secured her helmet. "All set?"

Allie nodded, then squealed as the snowmobile took off like a shot, kicking up a plume of snow in its wake. With her arms wrapped tight around his waist, she snuggled against his back, partly to protect herself from the wind and partly just to be closer to him. She molded herself against his body, absorbing the hum of the engine as it vibrated through his frame. Everything Hudson Chase did was an aphrodisiac to her, but there was something particularly sexy about riding behind him on his bike. Turned out the same applied to a snowmobile.

After cutting through the field behind Hudson's cabin, they veered into a more wooded area, zigzagging between trees and snow drifts until they reached the trails. The ski resort Hudson mentioned was bustling with tourists, none of whom paid any attention to one more couple on a snowmobile eating lunch in the lodge and purchasing supplies at the general store.

The sun was setting over the lake when they finally arrived back at the house. Hudson pulled alongside the front staircase and held her hand as she climbed off the back of the snowmobile. "Go on in and get warm. I'll put this away."

Allie pulled her helmet off, her loose blond curls cascading over her shoulders. A smile curved her lips as she scurried up the stairs, already knowing exactly how she planned to warm them both up.

The cold cut through Hudson's clothes as he moved across the driveway. His heavy boots crunched into the layers of snow, and when he hit the stairs leading to the front door he stomped them against the wood to avoid tracking the nasty mess all over the floor.

A blast of heat hit him as he opened the front door. The house hadn't seemed that warm before they left, but now it felt downright tropical. Hudson stepped inside and a lone female snow boot nearly tripped him. He caught his balance, and as he did his eyes locked on the shoe's partner and the twin socks strewn just beyond it. Next were jeans, a black sweater, lace panties and a matching bra. All blazing a trail that stopped at the threshold of glass doors that led to the deck, and a hot tub where his naked wife sat waiting.

Fuck. He was instantly hard.

Hudson made his way to the open doors. Steam billowed and curled upward around Allie's face. She was slick, flushed from the heat, and so goddamn beautiful. He stood there with a case of the struck- stupids while his hard-on kicked behind his fly, more than ready to go for a swim.

"You told me to get warm," she said. Her voice was low and seductive.

"That I did." Hudson's lips curved into a lazy, sinful grin. "And I like where you went with it. Very thinking outside the box."

She pushed her hand through the swirling water, and as she did, her breast rose out of the bubbling foam, revealing a taut pink nipple just begging for his mouth. "Are you going to join me?"

She didn't have to ask twice. Hudson stripped out of his wet coat and gloves, dropping one on top of the other and not giving a shit about the puddle they were leaving on the floor. His shoulders rolled and his biceps thickened as he pulled his sweater over his head, taking the T-shirt underneath with it and adding them both to the pile.

Allie's gaze raked over him as he popped the buttons on his fly, the avid hunger in her stare making the need between them a living, breathing thing. He yanked his jeans and boxer briefs down in one swift move, and his cock sprang free, jutting out from his hips. Her jaw went slack and her tongue swept the curve of her bottom lip. Sweet hell, he could practically feel the glide of it along his achingly hard length.

With his eyes locked on hers, Hudson stepped into the hot tub and lowered himself into the water. "Come here, Mrs. Chase." He pulled Allie across his lap and her thighs parted over his. Her forearms came to a rest on his shoulders and her fingers played with the hair curling at his nape.

"I like hearing that."

He brushed his lips against her mouth. "I like saying it."

"Say it again," she whispered. Her wet hand slid down his chest, forging a heated trail to his cock, and when her fingers grasped him, he hissed.

"Two hands, Mrs. Chase." He smirked as he said the name that now linked them together. She took him in both hands and squeezed, her thumb brushing across the wide crest. Fuck, she knew exactly what he liked.

Allie arched her back, and with his tongue leading the way, Hudson latched onto her breast. He palmed the heavy weight in his hand as he teased the taut peak, his lips soft and gentle and his suction greedy. When he caught her nipple between his teeth, her breath rushed out and her hands tightened on a downward stroke of his shaft.

"Christ, Allie." He was too goddamn hard to think straight, but he had just enough blood running to his brain to know he was dangerously close to the edge. And there wasn't a hand job in the world that could replace the feel of her coming all around him. "Put me inside you, baby. Take what's always been yours."

She hovered over him, her body glistening in the warm glow emanating from the house; then, in a lithe move, she eased down on his cock. Hudson's head fell back on a groan. She was tight, even hotter than the water that licked their bodies, and so fucking silky. He gripped her hips to halt her for a split second while he regained his control. When the urge to come too fucking soon passed, he began moving her up and down with smooth, measured strokes.

"I love you," she gasped as he filled her again and again, planting her palms on the thick muscles of his chest as he drove them both higher. The rhythm was inexorable, and as she began to move on her own volition, his hands drifted up her waist and over her ribs, her sleek muscles flexing and releasing under his hands.

"I love you, Mrs. Chase."

Allie smiled, then her head lolled back and her eyes fluttered closed. He pumped his hips faster and deeper, wanting her to feel every damn inch of his cock. With every thrust his pecs tightened and his abs flexed.

The motion of their bodies sloshed the water over the sides of the hot tub, splashing all over the deck and dripping through the cracks to melt the snow below. Steam rose all around them and sweat gleamed on Allie's face. He was drunk on the sight of her and the feel of being deep inside her was the chaser.

"Hudson." Allie's fingers dug into his shoulders. "Oh . . . God." Her eyes met his and her breath hitched in her throat as her body began to quiver.

"That's it, give it to me," he commanded. The muscles in his neck chorded with the last vestige of restraint. "Now."

Her orgasm shot through her so violently that she shouted his name. Her release ricocheted and pulsed around his cock; all the while her eyes remained locked to his. Every sensation and every emotion manifested into this one perfect moment. Their life was a complicated mess, but the truth of their love was simple.

Raw and unchained, Hudson's own release shot down his spine. "Fuck," he cursed on an explosive breath. His hips locked to hers and his erection kicked deep inside her as he came long and hard.

Incredible. Absofuckinglutely incredible.

They rode out their orgasms together, and when they finally stilled, Allie's head collapsed on Hudson's shoulder and her body melted against his chest. His arms tightened around her, and for a moment he felt as though he could keep them connected like that forever.

But the next morning, reality crashed in and twisted up hard in his gut. They ate breakfast in near silence, then waited for the driver to arrive to take Allie back to Chicago. Alone. The weekend might have been perfect, but their lives were far from it. And going their separate ways after a one-day honeymoon wasn't the natural fucking order of things. They should have been jetting off to a tropical island, or at the very least hibernating in his cabin for the next two weeks.

Instead Hudson found himself kissing his new bride good-bye. Allie's lips lingered on his for a moment, and a single tear slid down her cheek.

"Hey." His voice was soft. "I'll see you tomorrow."

"I know." She lifted his hand and kissed his wedding band. "I love you."

"I love you too, Mrs. Chase." He mustered a reassuring smile. "Call me when you've arrived home."

"Of course." Allie slid into the backseat, and Hudson leaned down to press one last kiss to her lips before shutting the door. He knocked his knuckles against the roof, then watched as the car pulled away, taking his heart with it.

22

----

*A*llie kept her head down as she made her way to the back of the conference room. Since they'd returned from Paris there had been plenty of occasions where she'd had to pretend Hudson meant nothing more to her than any of the other board members. But this time it was her husband who had just strolled into the room. The sight of him dressed in a navy pinstripe suit and wearing her favorite crystal blue tie hit her like a brick wall. Every instinct told her to go to him, to touch him, to kiss him, or hell, to even just talk to him. But she couldn't, not without raising suspicion. So instead she turned on her heel, seeking refuge at the small breakfast buffet Colin had ordered for the morning's meeting.

She felt Hudson's presence as he drew closer, and by the time he was standing next to her, every nerve in her body had sprung to life. In a subtle move his fingers brushed the back of her hand as he reached for a coffee cup. "I missed my wife this morning," he murmured, his voice caressing her heated skin.

Allie's lips parted on a sharp intake of air. Hearing Hudson call her his wife was bittersweet, a double-edged sword that both warmed her heart and pierced it. Her gaze met his for the first time, but Ben Weiss walked up behind them before she could reply. Not that it mattered. The look in Hudson's eyes told her he knew exactly what she was thinking.

"I believe we're ready to begin," Ben said.

Hudson and Allie took their seats at the opposite ends of the conference table. At times it felt as though they were in a scene from an old Western, locked in some sort of standoff at high noon; but Allie loved every minute she spent sparring with Hudson across the glossy mahogany. He would grumble about how she was the proverbial thorn in his side, but she knew he loved it, too. They challenged each other, brought out their best, and then took it to an even higher level.

If only the other board members saw it that way.

While Allie had enjoyed a sweet victory when it came to preserving the print edition of their flagship paper, most other votes hadn't gone her way. For that she had two people to thank. One was Duncan Wentworth, a man with money older than most anyone else in the Chicago. Wentworth wielded an undeniable influence despite never having worked a day in his life, and he never missed a chance to patronize Allie's efforts.

The other member blocking her at every turn was Melanie McCormick, a woman who'd earned her seat on the board through a string of successful divorces. To Melanie, the climb up the corporate ladder had come in the form of wedding vows spoken to men with ten times her net worth. Previous targets had been twice her age, but if her unabashed appreciation for Hudson was any indication, this time she'd set her sights on a much younger man.

Melanie slithered up to Hudson the moment the meeting ended. Having seen the same less-than- subtle maneuver played out at nearly every gathering, Allie had expected nothing less. But there was something different this time. Allie could see it in her eyes. Melanie was upping her game, and Hudson Chase was the coveted prize.

Allie took her time gathering her belongings until she and Hudson were the only two who remained. "What was all that about?" she asked as he strode across the now empty conference room.

"It seems our fellow board member has found herself without an escort for the Ingram Gala this weekend. She asked me to do the honors."

"She asked you out on a date?" Allie squeaked.

"Don't look so horrified, Alessandra." Hudson smirked. "I've been told I'm quite a catch."

"You're a married man."

He chuckled. "She doesn't know that. But I doubt in her case it would make much difference."

"That's not making me feel any better."

"I'm sorry." His eyes were lit with amusement. "Although jealousy is quite becoming on you."

Allie glanced down at her bare left hand. When she spoke her voice was barely a whisper. "I hated taking my ring off this morning."

His gaze softened. "As did I."

For a brief moment the world around them fell away and they were back in the candlelit barn. The intimacy that passed between them made her chest tighten to an almost unbearable ache. Hudson lowered his head, his lips inching closer to hers.

Behind them someone cleared his throat. "Sorry to interrupt," Colin said.

Allie stepped back. "It's fine. Just going over a few additional items," she turned, giving him her full attention. "What's up?"

Colin's eyes darted to Hudson then back to Allie. Her assistant was far too perceptive to have missed what was going on. But he was also proving to be fiercely loyal. She felt confident he would never breathe a word of what he now surely suspected. "Detective Green is here to see you."

"Show her to my office and offer her something to drink. I'll be there in a minute."

"Will do."

"What's that about?" Hudson asked once they were alone. The frown that creased his handsome brow revealed his unease.

"No idea. This meeting wasn't scheduled."

He gave a tight nod. "She has news then. She wouldn't stop by to tell you things were status quo."

"Do you think they've connected Julian to all this?"

"Don't get too far ahead of yourself. See what the woman has to say first," he cautioned. "And call me as soon as she leaves."

"Absolutely."

They stared at each other for a moment more until Hudson blew out an exasperated breath and ran a hand back through his hair. "These platonic good-byes are growing tiresome."

Despite her agreement, his frustration actually made her smile. "And if people knew we were married you'd what, push me up against the wall? "

"For a start."

"I think I'm going to like working with my husband. With any luck this charade will be over soon."

"One can only hope." Hudson's words echoed in Allie's head as she made her way back to her office. *Hope.* It was what got her through the past few weeks. Hope they would finally be free of Julian's threats; hope her parents' murderer would be brought to justice; and most of all, hope that she and Hudson would finally have the future they never thought possible.

But when she stepped into her office, all hope faded. Detective Green sat in one of the chairs in front of Allie's desk, her back straight and her expression grim. As had been the case every other time they'd met, the middle-aged woman was dressed in a conservative suit, and her sandy brown hair was pulled back in a tight bun. Her green eyes still cataloged every detail of her surroundings, but when she met Allie's questioning stare, her gaze no longer possessed the confident reassurance that had carried Allie through the darker moments of the investigation. This time her gaze was filled with nothing but apologetic disappointment.

She stood the moment Allie entered the room. "Thank you for seeing me on such short notice."

"Not a problem." Allie shook the detective's outstretched hand, then rounded her desk. "I was hoping your visit meant there'd been a break in the investigation. But judging by your expression I'm assuming that's not why you're here." She gestured toward the empty chair. "Please sit."

"I wish that were the case." The detective's suit jacket split open as she sat in one of the leather chairs, offering Allie a glimpse of the badge she wore clipped to her waist and the gun she kept holstered at her side. She drew a deep breath through her nose. "There's no easy way to say this, Miss Sinclair, but we've hit a dead end."

Allie's heart pounded in her chest. This couldn't be happening. Julian wasn't going to get away with murder. "I thought you identified the shooter?"

Green nodded. "Yes. But we can't find anything to link him to a third party. No bank deposits, no calls or recent trips out of town."

Then you're not looking in the right place, she wanted to scream. But she couldn't tell the police what she knew, not without incriminating Hudson.

"At this point all indications are he was working alone."

"With what motive?"

"It could have been a robbery as we first suspected. But without any further information, we may never know if he was working on his own or not."

Allie's eyes drifted shut as she took a moment to compose herself. When she opened them, the detective was standing in front of her desk.

"There are no victories in my line of duty, Miss Sinclair;

195

nothing I can do to bring back lost loved ones. But I work hard to try and bring them justice, and a sense of closure for their families. I'm truly sorry I haven't been able to do that for you."

"Thank you, Detective Green. I know you've dedicated a lot of time and effort to this investigation."

"If there are any new developments, you'll be the first to know. But for the time being, at least, the department considers this case closed."

Allie waited until the door clicked closed, then rested her elbows on the desk and dropped her face into her hands. That fucking bastard. Without a doubt there would be no further developments. Julian had covered his tracks too well. The team Hudson had assembled was the only remaining hope. If they could find something, anything, she could use as leverage against Julian . . .

The shrill ring of a phone cut through the quiet office and Allie jumped. At first she ignored it, hoping Colin would pick up, but then she realized it was her father's direct line. Who even had that number? Allie had certainly never given it to anyone. She reached for the handset and answered with a tentative "Hello?"

"Bonjour, Alessandra."

Speak of the devil. Literally. Allie grit her teeth. "Julian."

"So tense, ma cherie." A short, harsh laugh came across the line. "What's the matter, still chafing over your loss?"

"My what?"

"Today's vote." A lighter clicked near the mouthpiece of his phone. "Couldn't quite convince them."

How the hell did he know that so quickly?

"No matter. Once I'm in control, I would have reversed it. Terrible idea."

"Are you spying on me?"

"Keeping an eye on my company." He blew out a harsh breath that was undoubtedly a plume of smoke.

"It's not yours yet," she muttered.

"You're losing too often to that mongrel."

"You called to tell me I'm not winning enough battles in the boardroom?"

He snorted his derision. "I have better things to do with my time than spend it hurling insults, Alessandra. Not much sport either. As you Americans say, shooting fish in a barrel."

"Then why did you call?

"Because your litany of failures is altering my timetable. I fear the board will oust you before they convene in March. If they appoint your former lover as the permanent CEO, he'll never sign over his shares, no matter how wide you spread your legs." The lascivious tone of his voice sent a cold chill down her spine. "I'm returning to Chicago on the first of the month. I want this mess resolved by the time I'm back."

"But that's only—"

"Eleven days. Use them wisely."

23

*E*nough of this bullshit, Hudson thought. Nick was late. Again. The sun had set and the last of the hazy orange rays reflected off the surrounding skyscrapers, making the Magnificent Mile look like a fiery planet. Which was deceptive since the chill that descended barged in like an unwelcome houseguest.

Hudson's living room became as dark as his frame of mind when the last of the light faded. The cavernous room felt more like a cell made of glass than a luxury penthouse overlooking the urban sprawl of Chicago. A cell, a cage, a prison—all adequate terms to represent the grip Julian had on his balls; the one that had him in a constant state of revisit and revise.

He stood in front of the Art Deco bar in a black, custom-tailored Brioni tux and a motherfucking bow tie, dressed for yet another goddamn event. The silver lining of the night was that he would be in the same room as Allie. The bad news? He wasn't going to be able to touch his own wife. But the thing that dumped his mood even further into the shitter was not being introduced as her husband. He knew the situation was only temporary, but that didn't mean he had to like it. And to make matters worse, he was escorting a woman he could barely tolerate in a professional setting.

Hudson glanced down at the crystal decanters gleaming like jewels in the low ambient light. A stiff three fingers would go a long way toward taking the edge off of an evening with Melanie McCormick. That or ear plugs.

"Yo, Hudson." Nick called out from the foyer. "Where ya at?"

So much for that drink. Hudson slipped the wedding band off his finger and tucked it into the breast pocket of his jacket. "In here. You're late."

"I couldn't work this fucking piece of shit into anything resembling a bow. It's like navigating a pussy; do you start from the bottom or the top? It's different every time."

"Nice, Nick. But the similarity lies in that it takes practice. And it's not a piece of shit, it's a Tom Ford." Hudson turned and his eyes shot to . . . "What the hell is that under your arm?"

"This?" His brother had a shit-eating grin on his face as he hitched the furry creature up. "This is a Yorkie. Her name is Harley." Nick waved the tiny dog's paw. "Say hi to your Uncle Hudson."

"Are you shitting me? And what kind of name is that?"

"It was Harper's idea."

"The name or this . . . thing?"

"Nah, the name was my idea. She needed a big name to rep her personality. The dog was Harper's idea. She thought it would be good for me to have something to take care of."

"A plant would have been an excellent start. Animal control doesn't get involved if you forget to water it."

"Yeah, but plants don't talk to you, they just sit there."

Hudson lifted a dark brow. "And the dog?"

"Talks in her own way." Nick dipped his head toward the pooch. "Don't you, pretty girl?" Harley wriggled in his arms and her little tongue flicked out, frantically licking his face.

"By pissing and crapping on the floor."

"Don't be such a grump, bro. She's cute." Nick nuzzled the puppy. "Aren't you a cutie? Yes, you are." The more his brother progressed with the godforsaken baby talk, the faster the little thing's tail swished back and forth.

"For fuck's sake, put the dog down and get over here so I can choke you with that tie for bringing that creature over to ruin my hardwoods."

"Puppy pads, dude. Kind of like diapers for the floor." Nick put Harley down and pulled the ball that was his tie out of his pocket.

"This way." Hudson turned on his heel and strode down the corridor to the master suite. Nick followed, and right behind him was Harley, clumsily working her tiny legs as fast as she could to keep up.

Hudson came to a halt in front of the full-length mirror, and at the same time the *tap-tap* of puppy nails stopped. "Stand here."

"Damn, you're in a pissy mood tonight." Nick moved to the spot Hudson had pointed to and forked over the strip of fabric.

Hudson eyed the wrinkled mess. "What did you do to it?"

"Can you just tie the frickin' thing on me, please?"

Hudson popped his brother's collar and slung the tie around his neck, positioning the ends so the left side hung about two inches longer than the right.

Nick watched in the mirror. "This is where the train went off the tracks for me."

Harley began to paw at Hudson's leg. He shot the dog a look. "Down."

She sat immediately and cocked her head to the side.

"Damn, you're like the dog whisper. I've been trying to get her to do that for days."

Hudson's lips curved into a smug grin. "It's all about the delivery."

"Nah, you're just a bossy motherfucker."

"That too." Hudson crossed the ends over one another, then threaded the longer piece through and pulled.

"Dude, not so tight." Nick made a choking sound for effect. "Hey, can I ride with you, limo and all?"

"Are we picking Harper up on the way?"

"I'm meeting her there since she's working the event." Nick lifted his chin higher. "You going stag?"

"I have a date."

"No shit?" Nick dropped his chin. "With who?"

"Melanie McCormick."

"Details?"

Hudson pushed Nick's chin back up. "Not much to tell. She's on the Ingram board. Attractive, older." He had to force the words out of his mouth. She wasn't unattractive, and in practical terms they were a match made on paper. But he hated this. Loathed it. There was nothing redeeming about what he was going to subject himself to that night. "She asked me to escort her to the event."

"Code word for sleep with her."

"That wasn't agreed upon," Hudson said tightly.

"Yeah," Nick snorted. "Whatever you say. Sure you want me to tag along in the limo? Ya know, in case you want to hit it on the way? 'Cause you seem wound a little tight, bro."

Wound was an understatement. His skin was tight and his blood was heated to a near boil. And now he was attending a geriatric festival where prestige was granted in exchange for cash. All for a good cause, of course, and with a woman on his arm who wasn't his wife. Though logic and her track record would indicate she considered the evening a dry run. Yeah, he was an asshole. Stag would have been honorable, but the charade had to be maintained.

Hudson swung the dangling end of the tie counterclockwise and threaded it through the loop he'd created at his brother's neck. He pulled the tie tight, then straightened it. "There, done. Looking sharp, Nicky."

"Damn, bro." Nick admired his reflection. "You're good at this knot tying biz."

Hudson smirked. "Another thing that takes practice. Let's go," he said when his cell vibrated. "Max has the car ready."

Nick crouched down and picked back up with the baby talk routine. "You're going to be a good girl while I'm out kickin' it with Uncle Hudson, aren't you ?" The dog's butt moved to the fast beat of her tail.

"Tell me you're not planning on leaving that *thing* here?"

"She'll be fine. She's got the whole pee pad thing down."

"Christ," Hudson muttered as he strode back into living room.

Nick caught up to him at the elevator. "If she pisses all over the place, I'll clean it up," he said as they stepped inside.

"I'll hold you to that." Hudson punched the button for the garage and put on his best game face. Tonight he needed to be Chicago's most eligible bachelor; the womanizing playboy he used to be instead of the devoted husband he now was.

*A*llie's first public appearance with her new husband was far from how she'd imagined. Not that she'd really ever given the idea much thought. Or even considered any future where she was Mrs. Hudson Chase, for that matter. Just as it had ten years ago, a life with Hudson had seemed like an unattainable fairy tale. At least it had until she'd turned around to find him on bended knee. In that moment she believed anything was possible. And when he slipped the diamond and platinum band on her finger and vowed to love her for the rest of his life, she knew she never wanted to spend another day without him. Which was why she'd found herself saddened by the fact that he wasn't there to zip up her dress, why her heart sank as she rode without him in the limo, and why her fingernails dug into her palm as she'd watched him stroll into the Palmer House with Melanie McCormick on his arm.

Allie sipped a glass of champagne as she took in the sight of the ballroom, aglow with the flickering light from dozens of floral-wrapped candelabras. She smiled to herself. Harper and Colin had done a wonderful job with the event. Her eyes darted to where the two of them huddled with the auctioneer. Nick stood a few yards away, tugging on his bow tie and looking like he would rather be just about anywhere but a black tie event.

Not unlike his brother.

Almost involuntarily she sought out the man she loved. He was standing by the bar, a squat tumbler of scotch in his hand and Melanie at his side. The conniving witch was all over him, although not in the obvious way Sophia would have been. While her agenda was the same, Melanie's approach was more subtle. And if her string of marriages to powerful men was any indication, it was quite successful as well.

Hudson took a sip of the amber liquid, and as he did, his eyes met Allie's. They narrowed almost imperceptibly and she could have sworn she saw a smug grin curve his lips just before he lowered the glass. She watched as he bent closer to Melanie's ear, whispering something to her before making his way across the ballroom, weaving through linen-covered tables while cleverly avoiding unwanted conversations with a curt nod of his head.

Allie sipped her champagne, and for a moment her gaze shifted back to Melanie. Her frustration and disappointment were evident even from the other side of the room, and Allie had to fight the smile that tugged the corner of her mouth. But the satisfaction she took from the scowl on Melanie's face cost her. By the time she turned her attention back to Hudson, he was gone.

"Excuse me," she said, stepping out of the circle that had formed around her. She handed her empty champagne flute to a passing waiter and lifted the hem of her silver gown as she hurried in the direction Hudson had been heading. But when she pushed through the ballroom doors, he was nowhere in sight.

"Looking for someone?" Hudson was suddenly behind her. His voice was a seductive purr that under any other circumstance would have turned her into a puddle. But Allie held her ground.

"My husband. Have you seen him? Tall, dark, gorgeous, reveling in the attention of Chicago's most notorious gold digger." She turned and smirked at him. "Enjoying your evening with Melanie?"

Hudson frowned. "No, not particularly." He grabbed her by the elbow and guided her toward the coat room.

"You could have fooled me," she said as he pulled her past the velvet curtains. "Looked like—"

In one swift move he had her pressed against the wall, and then his mouth was on hers, silencing her with his untamed lust. Allie's mouth fell open on a gasp and Hudson took full advantage, his tongue stroking hers with expert skill. On instinct her body went lax, surrendering to the moment, and when he finally broke the kiss she could hardly catch her breath.

He pulled back just enough to see her face. "As much as I enjoy you in this shade of green," he said, his finger stroking her cheek, "you have no reason to be jealous."

Her fingers curled in the hair at the nape of his neck. "I hate watching her fawn all over you."

With a roll of his hips he ground the thick ridge of his erection against her. "You are the only one who does this to me." He took her mouth again, his taut body pinning her, and she moaned with a desperate need. She loved it when he was like this, so raw and untamed in his desire for her. It made her entire body come alive.

But they were only steps away from hundreds of guests. "We can't be seen together," she reminded him, though her voice lacked conviction.

Hudson loomed over her, his mouth just inches from hers. "Julian is expecting me to try to convince you to take me back." His lips curved into a grin that was somehow both sinful and playful all at once. "Consider yourself being convinced."

Allie returned his smile with one of her own. "In the coat room at a company party? Rather cliché, wouldn't you say, Mr. Chase? One step up from nailing me on a copy machine at the office Christmas party."

Hudson chuckled. "Not my style, but multiple copies of my wife's ass are tempting. I simply thought you might need a reminder of—"

Now it was Allie's turn to interrupt. "Then remind me already," she said, her voice taking on a more serious, seductive tone. She knew she should stop, straighten his tie and smooth her dress and get back to the three hundred patrons mingling in the ballroom. But hearing Hudson call her his wife was like an incendiary device to her already overheated skin. All she could think about was how desperately she wanted him.

His eyes grew dark as he pressed a key card into her hand. "Meet me upstairs in five minutes. Room 2305." With that he turned, parted the curtain, and was gone.

Allie waited several beats before stepping out into the corridor. In the distance the hum of quiet conversation mixed with the strains of a string quartet. They had twenty, maybe thirty minutes until dinner was served. Once that happened, their two empty chairs would no doubt raise suspicions. Anticipation thrummed in her veins as she quickly made her way to the elevator bank, glancing over her shoulder every so often to ensure no one saw her leaving the event.

Within minutes she was standing in front of the door to Hudson's suite. She slid the card in the lock and stepped into the room. A sliver of moonlight streamed in through the partially drawn curtains, casting a cool glow across her skin, but other than that the room was engulfed in near total darkness.

"Strip for me," Hudson ordered from somewhere in the shadows. His voice held that hard authoritative edge that never failed to send a jolt of pleasure straight to her core. "I want to see what's mine."

Her mouth went dry as she reached for the zipper that ran the side of her gown. The fitted bodice was tightly ruched from breast to hip, but when she lowered the zipper it fell away easily, the silver fabric gently billowing to a puddle at her feet. Beneath the gown she wore nothing but a white lace thong.

In the distance she heard Hudson's sharp intake of air. "Everything but the shoes," he said.

Slowly she peeled the scrap of material down her thighs. Her breathing grew shallow as she stood waiting for his next command. Knowing he was watching her, his eyes raking over every inch of her bare skin, made her feel beautiful and sexy and wanton. In moments like these his hold on her went far beyond the physical. She was his, body and soul.

The stillness in the room seemed to stretch on for an eternity until the sound of a chair skidding across the marble floor finally broke the silence. Hudson was on her in a heartbeat, shoving his hands into her hair and tilting her head to the angle he wanted. His mouth covered hers, his skilled tongue invading, exploring, dominating. But instead of stating his claim on her, he offered the reverse.

"You own me," he said. The roughly spoken words caused everything below her waist to tense with need. "Just because I'm not wearing my ring tonight doesn't make it any less true."

He stepped back and she heard the faint sound of a zipper. "I'm going to fuck you now for as long as it takes to remind you of that, and I don't give a shit who notices we're gone."

Grasping the back of her thighs, Hudson lifted her legs, wrapping them around his waist.

He took her mouth again, his tongue thrusting between her lips. Allie kissed him back, one hand fisted his shirt while the other tangled in his thick, wavy hair. The fact that she was naked while he was still fully dressed ratcheted her desire to an almost debilitating level, the rough fabric of his tuxedo brushing against her bare skin in testament to their unquenchable desire.

With a flex of his hips he pressed her against the wall, the head of his cock laying hard and hot at her entrance. Allie whimpered, her body moving of its own volition as she tried to get more of him inside her.

"Are you ready for me?" he said. His voice was low and hoarse. "Because I can't wait any longer."

"Yes," she panted, needing the connection as much as he did. "Now, Hudson. Please."

He surged forward, and in one lithe movement thrust inside her with the full force of his body. Allie's head fell back against the wall on a loud moan. He pulled back, and with a shift of his hips pushed even deeper. "So good," he growled.

Then he was fucking her, pounding into her with slick, relentless drives until all thoughts of the party below them left her. All that mattered was this man, this moment, and how perfectly they fit together.

"Oh, God." Her breath caught on a particularly skillful stroke and her eyes closed, relishing the feel of him as a white-hot rush began to consume her.

"Look at me," he ground out.

Her hazel eyes met his fiery blues. The intensity that burned in his gaze as he moved inside her was too much. Her fingers clutched the shoulders of his jacket as she spiraled into an orgasm that had her entire body quaking in his arms. Hudson drove to the hilt once more and stilled, emptying himself deep inside her.

"Forever, Allie." He let his forehead rest against hers as he struggled to catch his breath. "Forever."

Allie stepped off the elevator and right into the Irish Inquisition.

"For a minute there I thought you were going to skip dinner," Harper said. "Can't say I would blame you, really. If I saw the man I loved with that viper, I'd drag him off for a quickie, too."

Allie tried her best to keep her face impassive. Harper was

fishing. Maintaining an air of indifference was her only hope. "Don't you have work to do?" she asked.

"There you are." Colin rounded the corner as if on cue, and immediately began giving Harper the run down. "The entrees are being served, the manager found the extra case of Bollinger, and the band is ready to roll as soon as they begin serving dessert," he said, ticking the items off on his fingers. "Do you want to go over the thank-you speech now?"

"Sure." Harper's gaze shifted to Allie. "Unless you or Hudson would rather say a few words?"

Allie smiled at her friend. For as much as the woman could talk, Harper was still so uncomfortable with public speaking. "You got this," she told her as they made their way back to the entrance of the ballroom.

She waited until Colin and Harper had disappeared into the crowd before scanning the room for Hudson. He was seated at one of the round tables near the bandstand. Melanie had resumed her post at his side, chatting away about God knew what, but Hudson only had eyes for Allie. He kept his gaze locked on hers as the waiter poured a sample of cabernet into his glass. Allie stood transfixed, watching as he swirled the liquid in the glass before bringing it to his nose. Satisfied, he took a small sip, then his tongue darted out to lick his lips. The gesture was small, but the look in his eyes told her it was her taste he was imagining on his tongue.

A warm blush spread across Allie's face and a small gasp escaped her lips. Needing a moment to gather her composure, Allie looked away. When she turned back, Julian was standing directly in front of her.

"Good evening, Alessandra." A sneer curled his lips.

"Julian, what are you doing here?"

"Dining on a meal that should have been served to inmates."

"I mean . . . I thought," she stammered. "Didn't you say you were flying to Chicago on the first?"

"And yet here I am, a week early." He smirked. "Have you forgotten who is in control? I set the timetable, Alessandra. It's mine to adjust as I see fit. Now give me an update, and do try to keep it brief."

"Haven't your lackeys been keeping you apprised of my every move?"

His lips pressed into a thin line. "It seems we have some training to do after the ceremony." He stepped closer, and the cloying scent of his cologne invaded her senses. She could practically taste it. "You will speak to me with respect. Always."

Bile rose in her throat and her heart rate accelerated. "I need to get back to the guests. If you'll excuse me . . ." She stepped to the side but he caught her arm.

"Not so fast."

"Don't make a scene, Julian."

He dropped his hand. "Then answer my directive. Have you presented the ultimatum?"

"Not yet.

He stiffened. "What the hell are you waiting for? He's been following you around like you're a bitch in heat, just as I knew he would. It's time for you to . . . what is that expression you Americans love? Ah yes, lay your cards on the table. Do it, Alessandra." Julian nodded toward Hudson and Melanie. "And I'd hurry if I were you, before he loses interest." His eyes narrowed as he watched them. "I wonder how Melanie feels about conjugal visits?"

"I'll invite him to dinner and lay everything out then."

"Soon. I'm growing impatient, and you know the impulsive decisions I tend to make when I get this way." His veiled threat was less than subtle. She was out of time.

"I'll set it up for tomorrow night."

He gave a tight nod. "See that you do." His expression changed as his eyes roamed over her in a long, leering glance. "You're flushed, Alessandra. If I didn't know better I'd think you found my proximity arousing." Julian raised his hand and she flinched. His eyes flared at her defensive move. The sick bastard was getting turned on. She hated herself for reacting almost as much as she hated the satisfied smirk that curved his lips. Of course he wouldn't strike her, not with so many witnesses, especially not ones he deemed America's "faux nobility." No, Marquis Julian Laurent was far too concerned with his image to hit a woman in public. He was more the type to beat a woman in the privacy of her own home.

But when Julian touched her face, it might as well have been a slap. The sensation echoed the night he sent her flying across the living room of her brownstone. She could almost feel the blood dripping down her cheek as the back of his knuckles brushed over her skin, and when he leaned closer she could definitely smell the same stench of alcohol and cigarettes on his breath.

"Perhaps there will be some benefits to this merger after all." He dropped his hand, replacing his fingers with his lips. Allie's stomach turned as he kissed her cheek. "I'll be in touch," he said before strolling off in the direction of the bar.

Allie turned to find Hudson with his stare locked on hers, and all she could think about was how badly she wanted to feel his arms around her. At least now she had a reason to speak with him. In fact, Julian was probably watching her from somewhere in the room, waiting for her to do just that.

She made a beeline for his table. An hour ago the sight of Melanie, throwing her head back in a soft laugh as her hand came to rest on Hudson's wrist, would have made Allie see red. But at the moment she had far greater concerns.

Hudson stood as she approached, surprising Melanie, who from the sound of it was mid-sentence.

"Will you excuse us," Allie said, not giving a shit that she was interrupting the woman who quite literally had her claws in her man. "I need to speak with Mr. Chase." The words were hardly out of her mouth before he had her in motion. His hand barely touched the small of her back as he ushered them to a corner of the ballroom, but the contact was enough to soothe her.

"Two more minutes and I would have ripped his arms off," he spit out under his breath.

"We're out of time."

"What did he say?"

"Ladies and Gentleman," the bandleader interrupted before Allie could answer. "Before we begin, our hosts would like to say a few words."

Colin and Harper both stepped onto the dais, but it was Harper who took the microphone. Allie felt a sense of pride as she watched her friend conquer her fear.

"On behalf of the Ingram Foundation, I'd like to thank everyone for coming this evening. Your generous support funds over twelve charities, ranging from charter schools to cutting-edge cancer research to shelters for battered women and children." The latter had been a new addition to the Foundation's mission, one Allie had personally suggested. To her immense satisfaction, she had already secured the necessary donations to launch the program later that spring.

"Before I leave you to enjoy a bit of chocolate and a spin on the dance floor—" she dropped her voice "—and to drink enough wine that you bid ridiculous amounts for the items up for auction." She smiled at the round of quiet laughter her teasing nudge received. "I would be remiss if I didn't offer a special thanks to the Ingram board, particularly the CEOs, for their unwavering commitment."

The double meaning in her words was impossible to miss, but to further prove her point, Harper raised a brow in Allie's direction as she introduced Allie and Hudson to the room. The spotlight blinded them, the crowd clapped, and then the band began to play.

"I believe it would be customary for us to dance," Hudson said.

Allie nodded. Thanks to Harper's little stunt, there was no doubt Julian was watching them. Hell, the entire room was. If anything, a dance would reassure him she was making the progress he'd demanded.

Hudson offered his arm and Allie curled her hand around his bicep. She could feel the tension in his muscles through the fabric of his tuxedo jacket. When they reached the center of the parquet floor, he pulled her into his arms. She wanted to mold her body against his, to feel their connection from head to toe, but she kept a respectable distance fit for public consumption.

After a few bars of the song, other couples joined them on the dance floor, and the low murmur of conversation once again filled the room. Hudson pulled her closer and pressed his cheek to her temple. She knew it was to muffle their conversation, but the skin to skin contact made her shudder nonetheless.

"What did that asshole want?" he murmured into her hair.

"Results. I'm supposed to invite you to dinner tomorrow night and give you the ultimatum."

"I'll make a reservation."

"It needs to be somewhere visible, so he can see. Otherwise . . ." She pulled back to look at him. Hot tears pricked her eyes as she met his concerned gaze. "He's getting impatient, Hudson. He started making threats."

Hudson pulled her closer, and the hand holding hers tightened. "I'll take care of it," he said. After a beat, he added, "I'll take care of everything."

*A*llie eyed the small gadget Hudson held suspended between two fingers. "What is that?"

"The latest acquisition from Max's team." He dropped the tiny object back into the inside pocket of his suit jacket and smoothed his tie. "Some sort of noise distortion device. It will allow us to speak freely."

The tiny bistro was already buzzing with sounds of every kind, from the clanking of dishes to the animated conversations at the crowded bar. It was difficult to even hear the person across from you, much less at another table. Unless . . .

"Do you think Julian bugged this place?"

"I never underestimate the competition, Alessandra. And at this point there's no telling the lengths to which he will go." Hudson poured more Chianti into her glass. "Whoever is watching us tonight will only be able to decipher our conversation through facial expressions and body language."

She nodded, and her gaze instinctively shifted to the large window beside their table. Outside people hurried down the sidewalk and cars clogged all four lanes of traffic. In the distance, tourists milled about in front of the historic Water Tower, posing for pictures or embarking on carriage rides. Hudson had not only chosen the restaurant for its proximity to the busy plaza, but he also made sure they were seated right in front of the glass. The hostess seemed surprised that he preferred the fishbowl location over the intimate booth she'd been leading them to, but the fifty slipped discreetly into her palm settled the matter rather quickly.

"Relax, Allie." Hudson's tone was meant to reassure her, but it did nothing to quell the anxiety buzzing through her veins. Someone was out there watching their every move. Making small talk was proving more difficult than she'd anticipated.

She poked at her wood-fired pizza. The combination of burrata, arugula, and white truffle oil was usually one of her favorites, but tonight it sat largely untouched.

"Tell me about last night's projections," he said in what was obviously an effort to distract her. "Did they hit their target?"

Allie reached for her wine. Despite taking a hefty gulp, she barely tasted it.

"Exceeded, actually. And by quite a bit. Of course that was largely due to the generous check you wrote."

"Worth every cent to see my brother in a tuxedo."

A thought occurred to her, and for the first time since they sat down, a genuine smile curved Allie's lips. "I heard he got a puppy."

A crease formed between Hudson's brows. "Yes, seems the redhead thought it would be good for him."

"Hudson, you know her name is Harper."

"Fine. *Harper*," he said, stressing her name, "can clean up after the thing next time. The little mutt relieved herself everywhere but on the damn pad."

Allie covered her mouth with her napkin.

"I know the napkin trick, Alessandra. You're enjoying a laugh at my expense." His gaze softened. "But I'm glad you have a reason to smile."

"You've given me so many reasons to smile, Hudson."

"And I plan to keep it that way."

The waiter appeared at the table with the check. After handing over his credit card, Hudson turned his attention back to Allie. "But for now, I believe it's time for you to lower the boom."

"Well, seeing as how you need to look somewhat upset over what I have to say, shall we discuss last night's Bulls' game?"

Hudson frowned. "The refs decided that game, not the players."

Bingo. Within no time Hudson was leaning back in his chair, his arms crossed over his chest and his brow knit together. To prying eyes he looked like a man who'd just been given an ultimatum.

He stood in a rush when Allie rose from her chair. "My limo is outside," he said, tossing his napkin down on the table.

Her eyes darted to the window. "Do you think that's wise?"

"You supposedly just gave me the opportunity to win you back. I don't believe a ride home would be out of the question." He placed his hand on the small of her back and guided her out of the restaurant. Max was already standing on the sidewalk with the rear door held open. Allie slid inside, waiting while Hudson exchanged a few hushed words with his right-hand man before joining her on the leather bench. The door had no sooner closed when she crawled into his lap, taking full advantage of the privacy afforded by the dark tinted glass.

"Hold me?"

His arms were already encircling her. "You don't ever have to ask."

Allie rested her head on his shoulder. Normally his mere proximity had her melting against his chest, but even that wasn't enough to ease the tension racking her frame. "Did Max have any news?"

Hudson exhaled. "Unfortunately, no. Although he did spot a supposed tourist taking photos of our table."

"One of Julian's men?"

He gave a tight nod. "Appears so."

"He's going to want an update. The board meeting next month is making him anxious."

"Tell him I've agreed."

Allie lifted her head. "To give me your shares of Ingram?" Her voice sounded several octaves too high. It was a ridiculous concession, one she would never take him up on. But still, to hear him agree, even in theory, took her aback.

"Yes, Julian knows how I feel about you. His entire plan hinges on his belief that I will do whatever it takes to win you back. He will be expecting nothing less. There's no predicting his actions if it even appears as though I might not agree." Allie opened her mouth but Hudson answered her unspoken question with his next breath. "It won't accelerate his timetable. He knows how long it takes to have paperwork of that nature drawn up and processed. If anything, the false sense of progress might get him to ease up on you a bit." His fingers stroked rhythmically down her back. "In the meantime, I've put every resource at Max's disposal. If there's proof to leverage against Julian, he will eventually find it."

"That's just it, Hudson—I'm starting to think there's nothing to find. The shooter is dead and no one in Julian's inner circle is going to risk ending up with the same fate. Your team has been working on this for weeks and we're no further along than we were when this whole mess started." She let out a stuttering breath. "He's going to get away with it."

Hudson reached for her hand. "He won't. We'll figure something out."

Hot tears pricked her eyes as she pictured the smug expression on Julian's face that afternoon at his chateau. "If you could have seen the way he gloated." Her words shook with emotion. "He talked about planning their murder like it was one of those crime dramas he loves so much." An idea hit her like a physical jolt and she sat up straight. "That's it," she said, her voice strong and clear for the first time all night. "I need to get him on tape bragging about it."

"Absolutely not."

"It's the only chance I have to end this once and for all."

"No fucking way."

"Why not?"

Hudson stared at her as though she'd lost her mind. "Aside from the obvious?"

When she didn't budge, he let out an aggravated breath and continued. "Even if this wasn't out of the question, and even if you were successful, there's no guarantee the courts would allow it. That type of evidence is evaluated on a case by case basis."

She shook her head. "It doesn't matter. I wasn't planning to march into the police station with it or he might retaliate against you and Nick. I just need to hold it over his head. A trade of information."

Beneath her, Hudson's entire body tensed. "Goddammit, Allie," he practically shouted as he shifted her off his lap. "You can't be fucking serious." His words came in an angry rush. "That asshole is a loaded gun waiting to go off. There's no telling what he'll do if he feels backed into a corner. If you think I'm letting you put yourself in that kind of danger, even for one minute . . ." A muscle in his jaw ticked, and she knew the image of Julian forcing her over the back of the sofa filled his mind the same as it did hers.

"Julian needs me. He can't do anything to me or his whole plan goes up in smoke." She cupped his face between her hands, forcing him to look at her. When his eyes met hers they burned with rage, but more than that, what she saw in them was fear. He was afraid for her, and that was an emotion she understood all too well. "He won't hurt me," she whispered.

His voice was hoarse when he spoke. "Last time he almost . . ."

"I know," she said. "But he's on best behavior right now. He can't risk blowing everything by being arrested for battery."

"Fuck, Allie. Battery would only be the tip of the iceberg."

She swallowed hard. "Hudson, I have to do this. It's the only hope we have left."

A few tense moments passed. Allie held perfectly still, letting him reach what was the only logical conclusion on his own. When he finally spoke, it was on a heavy exhale. "I don't like this, Alessandra. Let me make that perfectly clear."

"I'm not happy about it either, but it's the only way."

Hudson shoved a hand through his hair. "We do this on my terms. I don't want anything left to chance."

"Yes, of course," she agreed without hesitation.

For the remainder of the ride Hudson laid out his conditions. The meeting would take place in public, Allie would wear a wire as well as a tracker, and Max would coordinate the entire operation. His team of trained professionals would not only coach her, they would have her under close surveillance at all times.

"I'll begin making the necessary arrangements first thing tomorrow," Hudson said as they rolled to a stop in front of her brownstone. He walked her to the door and said good-bye with a simple kiss to her cheek. "I fucking hate this," he growled in her ear before turning and jogging down the steps. She didn't know if he was referring to the plan or the chaste good night, but in all likelihood it was probably both.

She'd barely unlocked the front door when her phone began to ring.

"A kiss at the door? How sweet." Julian's words dripped with sarcasm. "I thought I made myself clear in regards to rutting with that mongrel."

"It was a kiss on the cheek, Julian. He's supposed to think I'm taking him back, remember? And it's working. He's agreed to have the papers drawn up."

"Excellent. When will they be ready?"

"I don't know. He said he would start the process tomorrow. I should know more soon."

"See that you do," he barked before hanging up.

"Well, good-bye to you, too. Asshole," she muttered under her breath. She shed her coat and scarf before making her way to her bedroom. On the way she grabbed her laptop off the coffee table. There were likely a dozen or so e-mails requiring her attention before the work week began in the morning. With any luck they would distract her from the thoughts that robbed her from sleep most every night. It seemed the only restful nights she'd had since Europe were when she'd shared a bed, or couch, with Hudson at the lake.

But instead of the comfort of her husband's arms, she would have to settle for a hot shower and a mug of her favorite green tea. She bent to pull a T-shirt and a pair of flannel sleep pants out of the dresser drawer, and when she turned toward the bathroom, she had to stifle a scream.

Hudson stood just inside her bedroom door. "I'm sorry. I didn't mean to frighten you." He'd changed out of his jacket and tie and now wore a quarter zip fleece along with a baseball cap pulled down low over his brow.

"You just . . . you changed . . . and I wasn't expecting you . . ." Her heart and mind still raced from the shock. "How did you get in here?"

He tossed the cap on her nightstand and ran a hand through his unruly hair. "I came up the back. Julian's guys aren't hard to spot. Their car is right out front."

"I think obvious is the point. He wants me to know he's watching me, which is why you can't stay."

"The hell I can't. I haven't slept with my wife since our honey-moon, if you can even call it that." He yanked both the fleece and his shirt over his head in one move, revealing the hard contours of his pecs and the ripple of his washboard abs. "Once this mess is over, I'm taking you on a proper honeymoon, somewhere warm and tropical. No clothing required."

The sight of Hudson's bare chest combined with the thought of lounging naked with him on a sandy beach distracted her, and before she even realized what was happening, he was completely naked. She drank him in from head to toe, her gaze lingering on the erection straining toward her in a mouthwatering display of virility and desire.

"See something you like, baby?"

She looked up to find his brow arched and his mouth curved into a wry grin. "You know I do, but . . ."

"I'll leave in the morning after your tail has followed you to work. But for now, I want to make love to my wife and fall asleep in her arms."

There was no point in fighting him. Not when what he was offering was exactly what she needed. "You're a persuasive orator, Mr. Chase. A master of linguistics, one might say."

He licked his lips as he sauntered across the bedroom. "Oh, Mrs. Chase, you have no idea."

26

*A*llie had never liked Monday mornings. Not as a little girl being chauffeured to school, and not as grown woman commuting to work. But Monday mornings were especially brutal when you had to leave Hudson Chase asleep in your bed. Naked.

The image of him sprawled across her mattress had stayed with her all day. With one arm thrown over his head and one leg bent to the side, all six foot three inches of him were a sight to behold. But it was the nine inches laying heavy across his lower abs that had her wanting to crawl back into bed. She would have given anything to draw the curtains, turn off the phones, and spend the entire day showing her new husband just how much she craved him. But instead she merely pressed a soft kiss to his forehead as she was about to head out the door.

He'd blinked up at her, his gorgeous blue eyes cloudy with sleep. "Come back to bed," he'd drawled.

"I need to head to work so the dynamic duo out front will leave their post."

"What time is it?"

"Almost seven. I wanted to clear out so you'd have time to stop at the penthouse before your first meeting."

A slow, sexy smile had formed on his lips. "Which isn't until nine." He'd reached for her but Allie held her ground, knowing if she indulged in even a moment, she'd have been there for the day. He'd reluctantly agreed when she reminded him that he needed to add a meeting with Max to his morning agenda, but made her promise they'd find a way to spend at least part of the evening together. The naughty words he'd growled on her way out the door had her counting the hours, and when the clock finally read six, she was more than ready for a secret rendezvous.

The phone on her desk rang as she was packing up her things. After the third ring she called out to Colin, but when he didn't reply, she picked up the line.

"Alessandra Sinclair," she said, her own name suddenly sounding all wrong. It had only been a little over a week since she'd married Hudson, and even though no one else knew, she already thought of herself as Alessandra Chase. Allie Chase, if truth be told. Hudson had told her he wouldn't argue if she wanted to hyphenate, but taking his name suited her just fine. As soon as they went public with the news, she planned on changing it.

"We need to meet." The sound of Julian's raspy voice sent a chill down her spine.

"Fine," she agreed. As much as she hated the idea of seeing Julian, she had been wondering what excuse she was going to give him for meeting. He was too clever to ever implicate himself in her parents' murder over the phone. The fact that Julian was requesting a meeting meant there was one less piece of the puzzle that needed to fall into place. She cradled the phone between her ear and shoulder and opened the calendar on her laptop. "When?"

"Now."

"Now?"

"I spoke English, Alessandra. Surely you understood."

"I just thought—"

"I don't need you to think," he interrupted. "I need you to do as you're told. There is a car in front of the building. Don't keep me waiting or I may use the time to renegotiate our terms."

The line went dead. Allie's mind raced. She and Hudson had agreed Max would orchestrate the meet with Julian, and she'd promised to follow his instructions to the letter. But she hadn't expected Julian to contact her again so soon, and his less than subtle threats didn't really leave her much choice in the matter. She had to meet with him. There was no guarantee they'd have another chance to speak privately.

Allie drew a deep breath through her nose and tried to focus. She needed to be ready in case Julian implicated himself. Her phone had the ability to record audio, but the last time he "requested" her presence, his goons had confiscated it. In all likelihood they'd do the same thing again. She needed another option.

A thought occurred to her as she gathered her belongings and headed for the door. When she reached the reception area, Colin was back at his desk.

"Everything okay, Boss Lady?"

"Yes, I just have a late appointment and I'm in a bit of a rush."

He frowned at his computer screen. "I don't have anything on your calendar."

"Yeah, sorry, forgot to mention it." Allie shrugged into her coat. "Don't know where my head is these days. Hey, do you have your digital recorder handy?"

"Sure." Colin slid his desk drawer open and pulled out the device. It was even smaller and thinner than she remembered. *Perfect.*

"Oh, and a pair of scissors?"

He grabbed them before closing the drawer. Curiosity was written all over his face as he handed her both items.

"Thank you," she called over her shoulder while hurrying down the hall. If she'd lingered any longer he would have asked questions she neither had the time nor ability to answer.

In the elevator she fired off a quick text to Hudson, cringing when she pressed send. There was no doubt he was going to be livid. But there wasn't time for him to set a plan in motion, and she didn't even know where the car was taking her. She would have preferred calling him, to have heard his voice and reassured him with hers, but she had to stash the burner phone before she reached the lobby.

She used the scissors to make a small slit at the bottom of her purse, concealing the burner phone beneath the lining and piling her wallet and makeup on top. She slid her other phone into her coat pocket, keeping it easily accessible should the driver ask for it.

Her eyes darted frantically at the dial above the elevator doors. Only five more floors. She quickly switched the recorder to voice-activated mode and tucked it inside her bra, leaving the top two buttons of her blouse undone in the hopes the fabric wouldn't obstruct the sound.

God, I hope this works. Her makeshift plan was far from professional and, truth be told, based largely on movies she'd seen over the years. There was no guarantee she'd be able to steer the conversation in the direction she needed, let alone that the device would pick up a clean recording. But on the outside chance Julian said something incriminating, she had to be ready.

The car Julian sent was waiting at the curb. Allie recognized the driver immediately. It was the same hired thug from the château, the one who had held her captive in the library while Julian saw to "pressing matters." He climbed out of the black

Lexus as Allie spun through the revolving doors, holding out his leather gloved hand as she approached.

"Protocol," he said with a smirk.

Allie handed over her smartphone and watched as he powered it off. "Where are we going?" she asked when he yanked open the rear door.

"Home." His patronizing tone sent a wave of unease through her.

Home? What the hell did that mean? Julian kept a suite at The Peninsula whenever he was in town. As she settled into the leather seat she began to wonder if the arrogant bastard had actually purchased a home for the two of them to live in as husband and wife. It wouldn't have surprised her. Seeing as how he thought of her as nothing more than an accessory, selecting their home without consulting her would be par for the course. But the further they drove, the more clear their destination became. The car was headed to Lake Forest.

Julian was literally having her meet him at the scene of his crime.

Adrenaline coursed through Allie's veins as the car veered onto the small lane that ran parallel with the lake. One by one they passed historic homes that dotted the north shore, and before long she could see the stone wall that surrounded her family's waterfront estate.

"Home sweet home," the driver said as he pulled through the iron gates of Mayflower Place.

Allie glared at him in the rearview mirror. "Give me a minute." Her stomach rolled at the thought of being in that house again, and for a moment she felt as though she might be sick. She took a deep breath and climbed out of the car on shaking legs. In front of her stood the brick and stone mansion that had once been her home. Now it was nothing more than a crime scene. Her worst nightmare brought back to life.

Julian was waiting for her in the living room, just beyond the marble floored foyer. "Good evening, Alessandra. How was your commute? Not too much traffic, I hope."

Allie frowned. He was making small talk with her as if he were just an ordinary man at the end of an ordinary work day. Not a man who'd summoned the woman he was blackmailing to the home where he'd had her parents slaughtered.

"Care for a drink?"

"Why are we here, Julian?" The quiver in her voice betrayed the appearance of outward calm she was trying so desperately to maintain.

He strolled over to a set of decanters arranged on a silver tray. The fingerprint dust that had covered them the last time she was there had been wiped away, and the facets of the crystal caught the flickering light of the fireplace. "I'm the king of the castle," he said, filling a glass with a generous pour of vodka. Allie noticed he didn't even bother adding ice. "Might as well live in it."

Of all the sadistic plans Julian had for her, this was by far the worst. Living at Mayflower Place had nothing to do with the esteemed address and everything to do with their future residence serving as a constant reminder of exactly what he was capable of doing.

"That horrible room will have to go," he said, nodding toward the dining room. Without thinking, Allie followed his gaze. The markings from the crime scene investigators were long gone, but it was far from the room she remembered. At one point beveled mirrors covered every inch of the walls, but now one section stood bare. Bullets had shattered the panel that hung there, and in its place remained nothing but streaks of blood.

"Honestly, did your mother really think she could pull off her own Versailles?" He let out a derisive snort. "Of course it would need to be redecorated either way. All that blood and brain matter." He clicked his tongue. "Shame the rug had to be taken as evidence. It was the one acceptable piece in the room."

Allie closed her eyes against the onslaught of images that

flooded her mind. When she opened them, she noticed for the first time that the table was set for an elegant meal. White linen, fresh flowers, and her mother's favorite china were arranged in what would have looked like a romantic dinner for two if it weren't for the bloodstains on the wall. Candles had even been lit. "What's all this?"

"A celebration." Lifting the tumbler to his lips, he took a hefty sip. "You've done well, Alessandra. With the stock transfer underway, I thought we should toast our impending nuptials." He smirked. "No time for an engagement party, after all."

"Are you sure you want to rush this, Julian? I mean, I thought you wanted a lavish affair that was covered by all the media outlets?" she asked, echoing the sentiments he'd previously expressed in an effort to buy herself more time.

"I assure you, our wedding will be everything your mother ever dreamed it would be. Pity she won't be able to see it." There wasn't a hint of remorse in his tone. "The arrangements have all been made, although none of the vendors know the identity of the bride and groom. Once you have secured the shares, we can announce our engagement." He reached for the decanter and topped off his glass. "We'll wed on Valentine's Day, as previously discussed, and when we return from our honeymoon, you will tell the board you've had a change of heart and no longer wish to serve in any capacity at Ingram. That's when you'll use your considerable stock percentage to vote your new husband into your vacated position."

"Seems you've thought of everything." Maybe if she could stroke his ego she could get him talking about his plans. While he'd revealed himself to be a callous, male-chauvinist asshole, he'd yet to say anything incriminating.

"I'm very thorough, Alessandra. And I always get what I want. You'll do well to remember that. But as for the details of our arrangement, no need to worry about keeping up. It's all spelled out in the prenuptial agreement."

"You expect me to sign a prenup?"

"The details of the very generous wedding gift you'll bestow on me."

Damn him. Especially when taken out of context, none of his words amounted to admission of a crime.

He drained his glass and set it down on the coffee table as he made his way across the room. "In fact, let's get the paperwork out of the way before dinner, shall we?"

As if he was giving her a choice. With his hand cupping her elbow, Julian guided Allie toward her father's office. Her throat tightened as she remembered the last time she'd strode down that hallway, so confident in her mission. She'd planned to take control of her life that night. But instead it had shattered into a million pieces.

Julian pushed open the door to the office and all at once she was back there . . . her father was slumped over his desk, blood seeping from beneath his chest, and the phone was cradled in his lifeless hand. The police determined her mother had been shot first, surprised by the gunman as he made his way in through the kitchen. Had her father heard the shots? Had he been trying to dial 911? It broke her heart to imagine him during those last horrific moments, and yet it was a scenario she'd replayed in her head a thousand times.

"Alessandra, it would facilitate matters if you would pay attention when I'm speaking to you."

Allie turned to find Julian standing in front of a wall safe concealed in one of the bookcases. For a split second she wondered how the hell Julian knew the combination. But then she remembered he'd been her father's right-hand man for months; his heir apparent. Of course he knew the combination. Her father had trusted Julian implicitly. In return, he'd betrayed him by taking his life.

"You killed him," she whispered, tearing her eyes from the

dark crimson stain on the desk. "He trusted you to take care of not only his company, but his child, and you killed him."

With a final spin of the dial the lock disengaged. "Well, to be fair, I merely paid a man to shoot your parents in cold blood." He smirked as he swung open the small iron door. "It's not as though I actually pulled the trigger."

The fucking bastard. This was all just some twisted game to him. But she had him. All she had to do now was pray to God the recorder had captured what he'd just said. That, and get the hell away from him.

"I'm not feeling so well all of a sudden," she said, offering the only excuse she could think of for a hasty exit.

"No need to feign a headache, ma cherie. I'm entertaining a guest later, so Philippe will drive you back to the city after dinner." A salacious grin curved his lips. "Unless, of course, you'd like to join us. Amber does have a fondness for blondes."

Julian turned and Allie's breath caught. In one hand he held the prenuptial agreement, and in the other hand he held a gun. "Why do you have a gun?" Her mouth was so dry she could hardly get the words out.

He walked toward her, oozing arrogance. Allie's heart rate spiked as he drew closer.

"Never hurts to have incentive," he said, coming to a halt in front of her and setting the paperwork on the desk. "After all, you're of no use to me if you don't sign." The pleasure he took from her fear was obvious in his tone. He stroked her blonde hair, curling a strand around one of his fingertips. "So be a good girl and don't make me kill the golden goose."

"Just tell me what you want me to do."

"Hmm." A leering grin curved the corner of his mouth. "That's what I like to hear." Releasing the lock of her hair, he ran his index finger down her throat, tracing the wildly throbbing vein in her neck. "Perhaps this arrangement won't be so intolerable after all." His tongue darted out to lick his lips as his finger

233

trailed to the deep V of her blouse. Allie tensed beneath his touch. If he went much lower . . .

Julian's fingertip slipped inside her blouse and his hand stilled. His nostrils flared and his face contorted with rage. "What the fuck is this?"

27

*I*t was pitch-black as Hudson brought the DB9 to a stop at the perimeter of the Lake Forest estate. He'd killed the headlights about fifty yards back and stayed deep enough in the shadows so as not to be spotted. From what he could see, there was only one car parked in the driveway, a piece of shit we'll- pick-you-up Lexus rental. He'd half expected to be greeted by a welcoming committee of Julian's thugs, but so far all he'd been met with was silence. It was quiet, too quiet; just the hissing and ticking of the car's engine cooling.

He'd been in the bowels of the garage beneath his building when he got Allie's text. The damn thing had rebounded him into pissed-off territory and left him feeling frustrated and powerless. The only advantage he had in this impromptu recovery mission was the burner phone that had allowed him to track her. But what the fuck was she doing meeting with that asshole alone? Her safety was Hudson's top priority, and this move was a direct contravention of the proposed and agreed upon plan.

Goddamnit.

He ran a hand through his hair, then checked his watch. Where the hell was Max? Needing to do something besides cool his jets, Hudson pulled out his cell and punched the speed dial. Max picked up on the first ring.

"ETA?" Hudson's voice was low but still razor sharp.

"Twenty out."

Too fucking long. Hudson ended the call with a curse. His gut twisted at the thought of Allie in such close proximity to that sociopath, and the oxygen he was sucking down burned his already dry throat. Christ, the depravity Julian was capable of was limitless, and he had no remorse over its execution.

As if on cue, lights flared in a room at the far end of the house. Hudson knew from the crime scene photos that it was the study where Allie's father had been shot. Anxiety jacked the rate of his heart until he felt like the thing was going to explode out of his chest. He had to do something. He couldn't just sit there and wait, not while Julian was doing God knows what to his wife.

Hudson yanked on the door handle and made a quick lunge to get out of the car. At a mission- critical pace, his long strides took him in the direction of the brick mansion and toward the pair of French doors flanking the study. He dodged a bird bath that was dry as a bone and hopped over a row of low-lying bushes. Damn, there was a lot of glass. But the outside garden area was an unlit sanctuary of low-hanging branches, affording him the perfect cover.

He lined himself up flat against the house and listened. There was no sound of anyone approaching from the sides or the back. Inside, the sharp inflection of a French accent fired up Hudson's temper. He shifted, and what he saw was someone writing his own obituary. Julian was standing only inches from Allie, who was backed up to a massive desk. Her face was frozen in a mask concealing what he knew was a replay of the gruesome scene she'd walked in on not long ago.

Impulse told him to storm in there and assume control of the situation. But as much as it killed him to admit it, he had to wait.

Still, the urge was damn near overwhelming, and the feeling only intensified as he watched the scene play out in front of him.

Julian pivoted and crossed the room to a safe concealed in the bookcases. Hudson's eyes refocused, his gaze tightening on the iron box as Julian spun the dial—right, left, then right again. He swung the door open, and when he turned back around, Hudson's blood went ice cold. It wasn't the papers in Julian's left hand that did the deed, but the glock gripped in his right.

Hell no. Hell motherfucking no.

Allie's chest rose and fell with each breath, and her body trembled. Julian was even closer now, direct-contact close, and the rank joy on his face was a kick to the head. The prick looked like he was in the throes of some orgasmic rush.

Hudson shifted his weight, bracing his feet in the patches of snow that clung to the earth. His spine straightened, his stance widened, and his glare narrowed on the guy who stood precariously close to the edge of his own death.

One fucking move . . .

Then he was touching her. Julian's fingers twisted in Allie's hair before trailing down her neck. Abruptly his expression changed and his face contorted with rage. Allie flinched as he ripped down the front of her blouse with a sharp jerk, leaving the delicate garment in tatters and exposing the recording device tucked inside her lace bra.

Fueled by hatred and protective instinct, Hudson surged forward at a dead run. His shoulder slammed into the door, smashing it back against the wall and shattering the glass into a million pieces. Julian's head shot up at the unexpected interruption, with the business end of the gun following his line of sight. With that hardware in his hand, Hudson knew Julian was a man with a purpose. But so was he. And anyone who got in his way was putting themselves in front of a speeding fucking train.

On a crash course, Hudson launched himself at Julian with brutal force. The two men collided, and using the full weight of his body, Hudson shoved Julian hard against the mantel. Picture frames clattered to the floor and a crystal vase took a dive. One hand wrapped around Julian's throat while the other caught his wrist. The veins in Julian's neck bulged and Hudson tightened his grip, hoping like hell the fucker would go hypoxic on him. But the son of a bitch wasn't going down without a fight. He locked eyes with Hudson and twisted the gun between their bodies.

Allie's world stopped spinning at the sound of the gunshot. The thundering noise echoed in her ears, and the smell of gunpowder burned her nostrils. For several agonizing seconds she stood frozen, watching the two men locked in a violent embrace with a gun lodged between them. Then a scream was ripped from somewhere deep within her as Hudson fell to the floor, blood soaking through his shirt in an ever expanding circle.

She dropped to her knees beside him. His eyes were closed and his body was so still. "Hudson . . . stay with me." The words lodged in her throat as she tried to choke them out. "Please. Don't leave me." Tears blurred her vision as she placed both hands over the wound, trying to stem the flow of blood. Beneath her palms she felt no heartbeat, no rise and fall of his chest, only a wet pool of crimson.

Julian grabbed her arm. His fingers dug into her flesh as he tried to pull her away.

"No." Allie struggled against his hold. "Let go of me."

"Get up," he snarled, yanking her to her feet and shoving the barrel of the gun beneath her ribs.

"We can't just leave him like that." Tears flowed hot and steady down her cheeks as he dragged her down the hall. "We need to call an ambulance."

Julian ignored her, but she could see the panic in his eyes. Sweat had formed on his brow and upper lip, and his breath came in short, shallow pants. If she could reason with him, even offer him a way out, maybe it wouldn't be too late.

"Please," she cried, sobs racking her entire frame. "Don't do this. He might still be alive. Let me call for help." Her words tumbled out in a desperate plea. "You can leave with Philippe. I swear, I won't tell anyone you were here. I'll say someone broke in, or that it was an accident, just please . . ."

"Shut up," Julian shouted. Lashing out, he backhanded Allie across the face. The force of the blow spun her toward the table, and she landed with a crash atop a place setting of china. "And stop crying, for fuck's sake. I need to think."

In the reflection of the cracked mirror Allie watched as Julian reached into the breast pocket of his jacket and pulled out his cell phone. He jabbed the screen with his thumb and almost immediately began barking orders. "Bring the car around back . . . No, in the garage. There's a situation I need you to clean up."

Allie pushed to her feet. Everywhere she looked she saw blood. Her mother's, streaked across the wall in front of her; her own, dripping from the cut on her face; and Hudson's, smeared across the white linen where her hands had tried to break her fall. Down the hall her husband lay dying, or maybe he was already dead. She needed to be by his side. Julian had taken her parents from her. There was no way she was letting him take the only man she'd ever loved.

Julian ended the call and strode to where she stood, her arms braced against the table. She drew a shaky breath as he reached for her, and when his fingers curled in her hair, hers curled around the knife resting alongside the cracked plate.

"Let's go," he growled. He yanked Allie up by the roots of her hair. She turned, ignoring the look of terror that registered in Julian's eyes as she plunged the knife into his heart.

28

*A*llie rode with Hudson in the ambulance. At first they'd tried to tell her she had to follow in a different car, but after a few quietly spoken words from Max, she'd been ushered to a seat in the corner of the rig and told to stay back and allow them to work. She had no idea what he'd said to them, or to the police for that matter, but he'd made it possible for her to stay with her husband, and for that she would always be grateful.

Max had arrived shortly after she'd called 911 and immediately took control of the situation. His confident and calm demeanor was her lifeline amidst the bedlam that erupted after what had seemed liked hours but in reality had only been a matter of minutes. Paramedics and police, loud sirens and flashing lights. Allie blocked them all out and kept her focus on the man Hudson trusted most in the world, relying on him to see her through the darkest moment of her life.

The ride to the hospital was a blur. Allie sat in the corner as instructed, wearing the jacket Max had given her to cover her torn blouse, and offering silent prayers. A team met them when they arrived, and she watched in fascinated horror as the scene before her played out like one of Dick Wolf's television shows.

Words that had no meaning to her were barked by men and women wearing hospital scrubs or white coats. There were a million questions she wanted to ask them, but before she had time to form even one, Hudson was being whisked through a set of double doors.

She followed his gurney down a wide hallway and into a large trauma room. Once inside the room, the team moved at a pace that could only be described as organized chaos. To her it looked like total confusion, everyone moving in different directions and all talking at once, but to them it was a series of well-choreographed maneuvers. And at the center of the storm was Hudson. She could barely see him through the mass of bodies, but at one point she caught a glimpse of his left hand. It lay unmoving at his side, unadorned of the platinum band she'd slid on his finger only nine days before.

"You can't be in here," someone called out.

Allie didn't move. She didn't even breathe.

"Ma'am, you need to wait outside," a man said from beside her.

"There's so much blood," she murmured. The room shifted beneath her feet and she swayed.

Hands gripped her shoulders. "Let them do their job. And come sit down. You don't want them to have to stop because you've passed out, now do you?" the man said, gently coaxing Allie back out into the hall. "Here, have a seat. Someone will be out to update you as soon as we know more."

She took a seat on a padded vinyl chair at the nurse's station, but kept her eyes trained on the closed trauma room door. No one came in or out, yet she knew that despite the room's calm exterior, inside the team of professionals was still working hard to keep the man she loved alive. Or maybe it was over. Maybe they had lost him, and instead of an update someone was going to come out of that room at any minute to tell her she was a widow. Tears brimmed her eyes as she rocked back and forth in her seat, willing them not to fail. *Please . . . please save him . . .*

Behind her the automatic doors swung open on a sharp buzz.

"Allie!" Nick jogged toward her. His hand was linked with Harper's, and even from where she sat Allie could see his white-knuckle grip. "What's going on? Max's message said to meet you at the ER, but he didn't tell me what the fuck happened."

She stood and took a deep breath, trying to find the strength to say the words out loud. "Hudson was shot," was all she managed to squeeze past the lump in her throat.

The blood drained from Nick's face. "How bad is it?"

Allie blinked away her tears. She had to be strong for Nick. No matter what the outcome in the room behind them, Nick was her family. And just like Hudson, she would do anything for him. "I don't know yet," she said, trying her best to keep her voice level. "They're still working on him."

Nick ran a hand back through his hair. "How the fuck did this happen?" The nurse at the station looked up from her computer monitor and Nick lowered his voice. "My brother doesn't live in a world where people get fucking shot." His head snapped up, and Allie saw realization dawn. Guilt flashed in Nick's eyes. He swallowed hard, and when he spoke his voice was barely a whisper. "Is this because of me?"

"No." Allie shook her head emphatically. "It's my fault. Your brother is lying in there because of me." A commotion at the end of the hall stopped her from explaining any further. The door to the trauma room opened and a young doctor in blood-splattered hospital scrubs approached.

"I'm Doctor Weber," he said, glancing between Allie and Nick. "Is one of you Mr. Chase's next of kin?"

Allie took as step forward. "I'm his wife." Behind her she heard an audible gasp escape Harper's lips and a mumbled *Fuck* from under Nick's breath.

"Your husband lost a lot of blood," the doctor said. That

much she knew already. What she didn't know was if he was going to be all right. The man standing before her had the ability to give her hope or bring her world crashing down around her. Time ground to a halt as she waited for him to tell her if the man she loved was still alive. "The bullet missed the hilum of the lung, which is a good thing."

Allie nodded as though she understood. But in reality all she clung to was the word "good."

"However, a pulmonary injury of this nature can still be very serious. The chest tube we put in is filling with a lot of blood, but we won't know the extent of the injuries until they get him into the OR."

"He needs surgery?" she asked.

"Yes. They're taking him up now."

As if on cue the double doors swung open. Several people rushed alongside the gurney as they wheeled Hudson down the hall. He was so still, too still, and covered with tubes that at the moment were the only things keeping him alive. Allie's hand flew to her mouth as they passed by, holding in the sob that silently racked her small frame. If she let it out, she didn't think she would ever be able to stop.

"We'll know more once they can see the damage." The doctor continued talking, explaining how the lungs were extremely vascular and how they were essentially sponges filled with gas. Allie listened, trying to take in the complicated medical jargon he was translating into layman's terms. But all she could think about was Hudson, in a room somewhere above them, being prepped for surgery by a team who quite literally held his life in their hands.

"But they can fix him, right?" Nick's heartfelt words broke through the fog of fear that clogged her mind. His question was simple and straight to the point, and really the only one that mattered.

"Doctor Katz is doing the surgery. She's one of the best in the world."

Allie wondered briefly if it was a coincidence that a world-renowned surgeon just happened to be on hand. "How long before we'll know anything?" she asked.

"Surgeries like these can take anywhere from four to six hours, depending on how extensive the repair. There's a waiting room for families on the same floor as the OR. The surgeon will come out to update you as soon as Mr. Chase is taken to recovery."

"Alessandra."

Allie turned to find Ben Weiss standing behind her. The sight of him nearly took her breath away. He looked so much like her father, easily passing for a real uncle and not just the kind you called by that name because he was such a close family friend. It was too much. This time, when her eyes brimmed with tears, she could do nothing to hold them back.

"I had the Ingram helicopter pick up Elena Katz," he said. "They landed on the hospital's helipad a few minutes ago."

"Thank you," she said, hugging the man who had been a constant source of quiet strength the past few months. "I don't know what I'd do without you."

"You're welcome." His eyes crinkled in a weak smile. "And did I hear congratulations are in order, Mrs. Chase?"

"We planned to tell everyone. But with everything that's been going on, it was . . . complicated."

"Obviously." A deep crease formed between his brow. "Max bought you some time with the police, but they're going to want to interview you as soon as possible. I won't be able to hold them off for very long. And the press coverage is twice what it was after . . ." He stopped talking and drew a deep breath. "I'm going to need you to tell me everything, Alessandra."

Nick pushed away from the wall where he'd stood slumped in a quiet conversation with Harper. "That goes for me too. Starting with who the hell shot my brother and ending with when you two got hitched."

Her gaze shifted to Harper. Under any other circumstance she would have been all over Allie, pumping her for details after complaining about being denied the opportunity to meet hot groomsmen. But instead she stood quietly next to Nick, fear and worry written all over her face. Her uncharacteristic silence was an unnerving reminder of the gravity of the situation.

"It's a long story," Allie said.

Nick slung his arm around her shoulder. "Well, according to that doc, we've got a few hours to spend with our asses parked on plastic chairs. Let's head on up and you can start from the beginning."

Allie tried her best to answer Nick's questions. She took him through the past few weeks step by step, carefully avoiding any mention of the footage Julian was using as leverage. The fact that Hudson had exposed himself to blackmail the night he helped Nick cover up his dealer's accidental death was only one part of a very complicated story. But Allie knew it would be the only part Nick would cling to, and in doing so would blame himself for everything that had transpired since. There was no way Allie would let him live with that guilt. Protecting Nick would be the approach Hudson would take if he were there. Following what she knew would be his wishes was the least she could do for him.

"So did you get the bastard on tape?" Nick asked when she was done.

Allie pulled the recording device out of her pocket. It was splattered with blood, but whether it was Julian's or Hudson's, she couldn't say. Either way, the sight of the dark red streaks caused her stomach to roll. "The device was on, but I don't know if it picked up the conversation or not. I haven't had a chance to play it."

"Would you like me to listen to it?" Ben offered

She nodded. "Yes, please." Hearing Julian gloat about murdering her parents in cold blood had been bad enough the first time. She certainly didn't need to hear him taunt her again from beyond the grave.

Ben had no sooner left when Harper moved to take the seat he'd vacated next to her. "So my best friend got married and I didn't even get a piece of cake?" she asked. She tried to keep her tone playful but Allie saw right through her attempt to lighten the mood.

Nick spun on his heel, shooting her a look from the spot where he'd begun pacing. "Yeah, what the fuck is that about?"

"Nick!" Harper said.

"Sorry, I didn't mean it that way," he said, looking remorseful and suddenly shy. "You know I'm crazy about you, Allie, and goddamn, you're the best thing that ever happened to my brother." He sat in the chair on her other side. "But the mighty Hudson Chase with a ball and chain is not something I ever thought I'd see."

In spite of everything, Allie smiled. She reached for each of their hands and held them tight. "I'm sorry we didn't tell you. We both really wanted you to be there. And we plan on doing it again if . . ."

"When," Harper corrected. "You'll get married again *when* Hudson recovers. And I don't care what he says, I'm throwing you a bachelorette party. There's no way I'm missing out on Chippendale action just because you're already married."

Nick perked up. "Does that mean I can hire a—"

"No." Harper cut him off before he'd even had a chance to get the word "stripper" out of his mouth.

Nick gave a small laugh. "S'okay. Mr. Uptight probably wouldn't go for it anyway."

The door opened and Ben walked back into the room. "Alessandra," he said, his voice low. "Detective Green is here. She would like to take your statement. I told her this wasn't a good time, but . . ."

"Did you listen to the recording?"

He nodded. "It's all there." His eyes clouded and she knew he was reliving the loss of his best friend all over again. "With any luck we can put this to rest quickly."

Detective Green was waiting for them at the nurse's station. She offered a brief hello, asking if there had been any update on Hudson's condition before leading them to a small room at the end of the corridor. Inside the confined space was a chair and loveseat, and on the table between them rested a box of tissues. It was the room where family members were given bad news, and a quiet moment to grieve. Just being there made Allie's skin mist with a cold sweat.

"Please, have a seat, Miss Sinclair," she said, lowering into the armchair.

"It's Mrs. Chase, actually," Allie murmured. She and Ben Weiss sat side by side on the small sofa.

The detective stilled momentarily before continuing to unpack her notepad and pen from a worn leather satchel. Somewhere in the back of Allie's mind it registered that this was a woman who was not often caught off guard. "Congratulations. I wasn't aware you and Mr. Chase had married."

"It's a very recent development," Ben answered on her behalf. "And one they chose not to share with the press at this time. I'm sure you can understand, given the media scrutiny Miss . . . Mrs. Chase has been under since her parents' passing."

"Not to mention Mr. Laurent's reaction," Green added. Allie's gaze flicked up from the scratch on the wood coffee table that had become her focal point and met the detective's steady gaze. "I spoke to Max Knight at the scene," she said, and for not the first time Allie wondered if that was really his last name. "He explained that Mr. Laurent had been threatening you."

Ben shifted forward in his seat. "If you've already taken his statement, I don't see why this can't wait given the current situation."

The look on the female detective's face made it clear their meeting wasn't up for debate. "Which is why we're speaking here rather than at the station." She turned to Allie. "I need you to tell me your version of the events that lead up to the incident tonight at Mayflower Place."

Allie took a deep breath. She knew full well Max would have never revealed what Julian had been holding over their heads. Without a doubt his statement would have been brief and to the point, focusing on Julian's crimes, not Hudson's. "Julian contacted me when we were in Europe over New Year's. He wanted me to return his ring, but when I brought it to him, he was livid that I had ended our engagement. In his mind I had backed out on a business deal and he was to be compensated."

The detective didn't write a single word on the notebook she held in her hands. Instead, she kept her eyes trained on Allie. The scrutiny left her painfully aware of not only the words she spoke, but every movement or gesture she made. She folded her hands in her lap in an effort to keep her trembling fingers from betraying her nerves.

"He wanted me to break up with Hudson, then offer to take him back only if he signed over his interest in Ingram Media. Once that was accomplished, Julian wanted me to marry him with a prenup in place that gave him full reign over the company he felt he rightfully deserved."

"What did you tell him?"

Allie let out a disgusted huff. "That he was crazy and that there was no way I would ever agree. That's when he told me he killed my parents." Her voice cracked and her gaze dropped to her hands. After a beat passed, she cleared her throat. "He murdered them, Detective, same as if he'd been the one to pull the trigger." Allie met her shrewd stare. "And he was threatening to harm Hudson if I didn't do exactly as he instructed."

"Did it ever occur to you to contact to the police?" Green asked, scribbling a few words on the notepad that Allie couldn't make out.

"Of course it did. But the investigation wasn't yielding any results, and I didn't have any proof. It was my word against his. Until now. I had a digital recorder tucked inside my blouse tonight. Julian discovered it just before Hudson arrived." She swallowed hard. "It was what set him off."

"He admitted his involvement?"

Allie nodded. "Everything."

Ben reached for the device inside his suit jacket. It was wrapped in the handkerchief that usually peeked from the front pocket in an immaculate square. "It's all on here."

Green pulled a plastic bag marked EVIDENCE out of her leather satchel and sealed the recorder inside.

"Julian Laurent killed my parents, and right now all I can do is sit in that waiting room praying he hasn't taken my husband as well. Julian might be dead, but the damage he's done is irreversible. For that he will never fully be out of my life, but the sooner I can start trying to put him behind me, the better."

"If what's on this device corroborates your story, I don't anticipate any further issues." Her eyes softened. "I'm not an especially religious woman, Mrs. Chase, not with what I see on a daily basis. But I'll be praying for your husband's recovery. If anyone deserves a happy ending, it's the two of you."

"Thank you, Detective." Out of the corner of her eye Allie caught a flash of blue. She turned her head just in time to see a woman in hospital scrubs entering the family waiting room. "If you'll excuse me," she said, not even bothering to wait for a reply before hurrying down the hall.

"Is he okay?" Allie blurted out the moment she yanked open the door.

The woman in scrubs was standing in front of Nick, who was seated in one of the molded plastic chairs. His foot was tapping at a frantic pace, making his entire leg shake, and his face seemed to have aged well beyond his twenty-two years.

"He's still in surgery," Nick said. His voice was so quiet and flat, Allie hardly recognized it.

"These are Mr. Chase's personal effects," the woman said, holding out a large manila envelope. "I'm sorry I don't have any news for you. Hopefully someone will be out with an update soon."

"Thank you." Allie sat in one of the chairs on the opposite wall and reached into the envelope. Hudson's smartphone and wallet were inside, but there was no sign of the burner. Surely he'd had it; how else would he have gotten her text and known she was with Julian? But where the hell was it? *Max*, she thought. Of course he would have taken care of any loose ends before the police arrived. Unlike the unregistered phone Hudson had used for their covert conversations, the phone Allie held in her hand was for business. The four inches of technology that was his constant link to an ever-expanding conglomerate. Allie felt confident the only entries would be work-related, but on the outside chance there was anything even slightly incriminating . . .

She powered on his cell phone. The fact that his pass code was her birthday made her smile, but when the home screen popped up, her smile faded and tears sprang to her eyes. Staring back at her from the device Hudson looked at all day while he ruled his empire was their wedding day selfie. She drank in every detail of the photo, from the way she snuggled so close to her new husband to the way his hand curled possessively around her shoulder. But it was the look in their eyes that jumped off the screen to pierce her heart. A look that said simply, "I am home."

Curious if the shot of the two of them sharing a kiss after

sampling wedding cake was also on the phone, Allie tapped the album icon. When she did, she found not only the photo she was looking for, but dozens of others. All candid shots, and all of her. Browsing the rolls of wrapping paper at the Christkindlmarket; sharing a laugh in front of the fire with Harper; reading a book, wrapped in a cashmere throw in Hudson's library. Picture after picture taken during unguarded moments of happiness. The fact that Hudson had not only captured them, but kept them stored on his phone, was just another example of the romantic nature he so vehemently denied having. She smiled to herself. When he woke up, she was going to give him hell for this.

When he woke up . . .

If he woke up . . .

No. She shook her head to clear it. Thinking that way wouldn't help anyone. She had to stay positive. If not for her, then for Nick. With the few exceptions when Harper had corralled him into a chair, Nick had been pacing the room nonstop. The panic and fear in his eyes the few times he'd glanced her way had caused the ache in Allie's chest to tighten to an excruciating level. It was clear his emotions, and quite possibly his sobriety, were hanging in the balance. Seeing Allie break down would only test his tenuous hold. The last thing she wanted to do was make this any harder on him.

So instead of lingering on photos that conjured memories so happy they were sad, Allie turned her attention back to the manila envelope. She reached inside to retrieve his wallet, but when she did, her fingers encountered something else: his wedding ring. She held the platinum band up, and for the first time realized there was an inscription. She hadn't noticed the words when she'd slipped the band on his finger. The barn had been lit in dim candlelight, and her gaze had been focused on the man she loved, not his ring. But in a hospital waiting room, under harsh fluorescent light, the words etched inside were impossible to miss.

Hers Forever 1/17/15

It was too much. Allie clutched the ring in her hand and held it to her chest. Hudson was her love, her life. She couldn't imagine a world without him in it. Tears fell in heavy streams down her cheeks and her body shook with sobs.

"Mrs. Chase?" Allie looked up to find a woman in pale blue hospital scrubs standing just inside the door. Her delicate features were drawn with exhaustion. "I'm Doctor Katz. Why don't we find some place private where we can talk?"

*H*udson woke, and his first instinct was to sit up. Shit, not a good fucking idea. His side let out a scream that hit him with a shot of pain so intense, he had to draw in a shallow breath. Because anything deeper was going to feel like a nail gun between the ribs.

Gun . . . Julian . . . Allie . . .

What had that fucker done to her? He fought the urge to go full throttle out of . . . where the hell was he? The place had about as much warmth as a meat locker and looked like a cross between a flower shop and a funeral home. Christ, was he dead? No, the pain shooting through his whole body was a reminder that he was very much alive. His head and chest ached and his lids were heavy, but he was alive. So fucking alive.

He needed to get to his wife.

Instead of making another attempt to sit up, Hudson turned his head. The face of an angel rested on the hospital grade blanket, her blond hair fanned out, her lips slightly parted. His gaze shifted to a delicate hand encompassing his, and his fingers squeezed with what little strength he had.

"Allie . . ." he rasped. His throat felt raw.

She lifted her head and blinked. "Hudson . . ." As awareness seeped in, tears brimmed her eyes. "Oh, thank God."

"Where am I?"

"Northwestern. You're in the ICU."

"How long have I been out of it?"

"A day." She started to pull away, but his grip tightened.

"No. Stay." His hoarse voice sounded louder than he'd have thought possible.

"Shh, it's okay." She gave him a reassuring smile. "I'm here. I'm not going anywhere. But I need to let them know you're awake. They'll want to check your vitals, and from the looks of it, you could use another dose of morphine."

"No, don't. I want to be lucid for this. Tell me what happened."

"How much do you remember?" she asked.

"I remember seeing the two of you through the window." The image of Julian with his hands all over his wife caused an ache in Hudson's chest worse than anything he'd felt since he came to. "And I remember struggling for the gun. After that, it's a blank."

"The gun went off between you." She paused for a beat, and Hudson knew she was fighting to control her emotions. It killed him to think about what she'd been through in the last twenty-four hours. If the situation had been reversed, he would have gone out of his mind.

"Did they arrest Julian?" Hudson winced as a sharp pain stabbed him, then receded.

"He's dead." The color drained from Allie's face. "You were bleeding to death on the floor and he was making me leave you there. If I hadn't stopped him . . ." Her voice trailed off, but then she cleared her throat. When she spoke again, it was with an unquestionable resolve. "I'd do it again if it meant saving your life."

He reached for her. "Come here." Allie leaned down, and with a shaky hand he pulled her closer. "You're so brave. You amaze me," he said, pressing a tender kiss to her lips. "Thank you." The sense of relief he felt over Julian being out of the picture was short-lived as reality bombarded him from every direction.

"Fuck," he said. "What about Nick? Did they find out about him? The video?" He made a move to get out of bed. "Where's my phone?"

"Oh no, you don't." Allie pressed a gentle hand against his shoulder. "No moving. Doctor's orders."

"Fine." Hudson lowered his head. As if he was going anywhere hooked up to miles of tubing and a goddamn catheter anyway. "Now answer me."

"Your phone is with me." Before he could speak, she added, "And you don't need it. Darren is taking care of everything at the office. As for Nick." She lowered her voice. "Max arrived shortly after I called 911. I don't know the details, nor do I think we should discuss it here, but he assured me the threat no longer exists."

"Have the police been here?"

"Detective Green came by yesterday. She took my statement and I gave her the recording."

"You got him to admit what he did?"

Allie nodded. "Everything. From the sound of it, wrapping up the case is just a matter of a few formalities now. Although I believe you still have some explaining to do."

"Explaining? I was fucking shot, what's there to explain?"

"Not to the detective, to your brother. He's rather pissed."

Hudson lifted a brow. "And why's that?"

"In the chaos he *may* have heard me blurt out that I was your next of kin."

"Is that so?

ANN MARIE WALKER & AMY K. ROGERS

The smile she'd been fighting curved her lips. "Mmmhmm. And he may be a little pissed there wasn't a bachelor party."

"Shit." Hudson rubbed the stubble on his chin. No doubt Nick would have tried to recreate the Playboy club right in the middle of Hudson's penthouse. Yeah, not a chance in hell.

"He's out in the waiting room with Harper. Neither of them would go home."

A vague memory flashed through Hudson's mind, and he shot her an amused look. "Was I hallucinating on painkillers or did you pull the do-you-know-who-I-am card?"

She blushed. "I did, shamelessly. But there was no way they were keeping me out of that recovery room, no matter how scary that nurse was."

He laughed, then winced as his chest erupted in pain.

Allie frowned. "Are you sure you don't want me to call for meds?"

"Not yet. I'm not ready to go back to sleep. But water would be good. My throat feels like fire."

"That's from the intubation. They said it would feel better in a couple days." Allie poured water into a plastic cup and held the bent straw to his lips.

"What about the rest of me?"

"A few weeks. And before you say another word, it will be spent resting."

"With you as my nurse?"

"If you promise to behave."

"Not a fucking chance."

She grinned. "I was hoping you'd say that."

"I love you."

"I was hoping you'd say that even more." Allie leaned down to kiss him again. "I love you, too."

"How about you get up here with me?"

"Oh no." Allie let out a throaty laugh. "Save it for when you're all better."

"I assure you we won't be waiting that long, Mrs. Chase. But how about a honeymoon when I'm better?"

"Sounds perfect."

Hudson's hand stroked Allie's hair. "Where would you like to go?"

She placed another kiss on his lips. "Anywhere but Paris."

*A*llie peeked up through the canopy of the elliptical chaise. The month of April was said to be one of the most desirable times to visit the Maldives, and so far it had lived up to its reputation. In fact, after a solid week of blue skies and sunshine, she and Hudson were seriously considering moving their corporate headquarters to the remote island chain. At least for the winter months.

She popped her earbuds in and settled back against a cluster of white pillows. With its thick cushion, the dark wicker lounger was more of a pod-shaped daybed than a chaise per se, making it the perfect choice for two people on their honeymoon. Sunbathing side by side with their fingers entwined had become a daily ritual, as had stargazing at night. Although to be fair, that usually involved a lot more than holding hands.

With a swipe of her thumb, Allie pulled up the playlist she'd created especially for the trip. Ed Sheeran began to sing and she closed her eyes, picturing the dances she and Hudson had shared not only when they eloped in January, but at the small reception they'd had with family and friends the night before their trip. Originally they'd discussed having a big society event, something befitting the union of a billionaire tycoon and his heiress bride. But in the end that wasn't the type of celebration either of them really wanted. So instead of a ballroom full of five hundred people they cared little to nothing about, Hudson and Allie renewed their wedding vows in an intimate ceremony attended by the people who mattered most to them.

The first song rolled into the second, and Sinatra crooned about summer winds. Allie pressed the center button on her phone and stole a glance at the lock screen photo. It was a picture of Hudson she'd taken when they first arrived on the island. They'd been sitting on the deck that ran the length of their over-water bungalow, enjoying a fruity cocktail, the kind served in a coconut shell with a tiny umbrella. The panoramic view was right out of a travel brochure, but it wasn't the breathtaking views of the Indian Ocean or even the pod of curious dolphins that inspired Allie to take the first snapshot of the trip. It was Hudson, flashing a grin she'd come to know quite well over the three months they'd been married; the one that said "you're about to be naked." His eyes were the same blue as the turquoise lagoon, and the tropical breeze was playing in his hair, giving it that sexy, unruly look she found so irresistible. "Freshly fucked" was the style Hudson sported most days, whether in the boardroom or the bedroom, but recently, at least, it had lived up to the name. It seemed her new husband had spent the entire first week of their honeymoon buried deep inside her.

When the second week began she'd insisted they see something besides the inside of their bungalow. Hudson had finally agreed, but only to one day. He jammed it full of everything the resort's concierge suggested. They'd spent the previous morning exploring the remote island hideaway and visited the Marine Discovery Center where Hudson made a generous donation to the sea turtle fund in his new bride's name. After lunch they went snorkeling with manta rays and strolled hand in hand along the pristine white sand that stretched the length of the atoll. Allie even gave paddle boarding a try, but she drew the line at shark feeding, stating she'd had enough danger to last her a lifetime. When they finally made it back to the room, she was hardly through the door before Hudson tackled her to the oversize canopy bed. They'd fallen asleep sometime just before dawn and she'd barely dragged herself to the chaise by noon. Honestly, the man was insatiable.

Instinctively, her gaze shifted to the sex god himself. He was sitting on the edge of their private infinity pool, staring out across the lagoon wearing nothing but a pair of black swim trunks. Shielding her eyes from the sun, she took a moment to appreciate her husband, drinking in every detail, from the hard planes of his tanned chest to the rippling muscles of his abs to the super sexy V of his hips. The only imperfection on his otherwise flawless body was the small scar where a bullet had pierced his lung. The sight of it should have brought a pang of sorrow, triggering the memories of that horrible night. Instead it centered her and gave her a sense of calm. Because as much as she hated to be reminded of the night she almost lost her husband, that scar was also a reminder that he'd survived.

His emotional scars were healing as well. Hudson had been more open with her since the conversation on the couch the night before their wedding. He was still hesitant to talk about his past, but little by little he was sharing details of his childhood, both the happy and the sad. Nick had even been able to convince him to give a few sessions of therapy a try. Hudson grumbled about having his head shrunk, but Allie could already tell the burden he carried had lessened. Of course some of that had to do with how Nick was doing. Six months of sobriety had done wonders for him. Not only was he holding down his job at the coffee shop, but he was even being considered for a management position. Hudson had asked him numerous times to join him at Chase Industries, but Nick insisted he had to take responsibility for his own life. Allie imagined the two brothers would eventually end up in the same building, but she respected the fact that Nick wanted to do it on his own terms. When the time came, he would no doubt insist on starting at the bottom, and she would no doubt have to convince Hudson to go along with the idea, but in the end they would be just fine.

Allie wondered if Nick's presence would be enough incentive to persuade Harper to join her at Ingram headquarters as well. While Allie continued to work closely with the foundation, she missed day-to-day contact with her best friend. Now that Allie was married and Harper was spending nearly every night with Nick, their girl time was far less frequent. Her best friend and her brother-in-law had become fairly serious over the past three months, and even though their relationship thrilled Allie to no end, she still missed their chats over cocktails at Tavern or a salad at her desk. These days Harper was a homebody, opting for a quiet night of Netflix with Nick and Harley over a night out with just about anyone else.

Allie closed her eyes again and a smile stretched across her face at the thought of her canine "niece." Little Harley had not only been a welcome addition to the family, she'd taken quite a liking to her Uncle Hudson. Despite his best efforts to keep the Yorkie at arm's length, Harley always managed to find her way onto Hudson's lap. He would roll his eyes and pet her as though she were hazardous material, but deep down Allie knew Hudson not only liked the effect the tiny dog had on Nick, but that he'd grown fond of her as well. He might refer to her as a barking squirrel or curse about a chewed up shoe, but no amount of protesting could offset the secret stash of doggy treats she had discovered in his desk drawer.

A shadow crossed Allie's face and water dripped onto her bare stomach. She opened her eyes to see Hudson looming over her, his body glistening in the late afternoon sun, and her smile widened.

He plucked the tiny headphones from her ears. "That's quite a satisfied grin, Mrs. Chase."

The thick cushion dipped as he climbed onto the daybed. He pressed his lips to her stomach, licking a bead of water that rolled across her skin, and then a heartbeat later sealed his mouth over hers, kissing her passionately. As if he had to. As if the fifteen minutes without touching her had been excruciating. And as if he hadn't had her in every way possible the night before.

Allie moaned, and when her lips parted, his tongue thrust into her mouth, stroking hers with lush, velvety strokes. She craved her husband constantly, but when he was like this, his lust for her so raw and untamed, it made every cell in her body come alive.

"So what caused that look on your face?" he asked when he finally broke their kiss.

"Huh?" she asked, her senses momentarily stunned. "Oh, um, just thinking about Harley."

His lips brushed across her cheek. The stubble on his jaw brought with it a reminder of how it felt between her thighs, and a jolt of pleasure shot through her core.

"Your nearly naked husband is kissing you and your mind is on a barking squirrel? I see."

"Not now, before." She giggled as his lips found her neck. "And more the way my nearly naked husband is with said squirrel. I see right through you, Chase. You enjoy having her around."

He made a noise that was more grunt than agreement as his mouth moved across her collarbone. "She's good for Nick, who I'm sure has let her have the run of the penthouse while we're gone."

Nick and Harper made good use of the third floor when she and Hudson were out of town. Despite their best efforts to train and clean up after Harley, there always seemed to be one puppy puddle left behind. One that Hudson would undoubtedly discover with his bare foot.

"Tell the redhead to hurry up and house break the damn thing." He chuckled against Allie's skin. "And while you're at it, tell her to do the same for Nick."

Allie rolled her eyes, though she knew he couldn't see. "Say what you want, but you're very sweet with Harley." Her voice grew serious. "You'll make a great father."

Hudson stilled. After a beat he lifted his head, and when his eyes met hers they conveyed a look that was a mixture of loving concern and sheer panic. "Are you . . ." He swallowed hard.

"Oh God, no," she said, realizing she had inadvertently given him the impression she was pregnant.

Hudson rolled onto to his back and exhaled. She hadn't meant to scare him, and she could certainly understand his relief from a timing perspective. They hadn't been together that long and most of that time had been spent dealing with situations far beyond those any normal couple would face. Wanting time to enjoy each other was understandable; desirable even.

But then again, they weren't teenagers anymore. And they were married. Would it really have been so bad if she had been pregnant? The image of a little boy with Hudson's blue eyes and dark wavy hair filled her mind, and a warm sensation washed over her before settling right in her belly. She hadn't thought even for a moment that she might be pregnant, nor was she ready to be a mother just yet, but she couldn't deny the twinge of disappointment she felt over not carrying Hudson's baby. More than that, she couldn't deny the concern she felt over the contrast in their reactions.

She gazed across the chaise at her husband, his arm resting across his eyes, and her heart sank. They hadn't really discussed the topic of children before they got married. Hell, they hadn't discussed *marriage* before they got married.

Allie shifted to her side and propped herself up on one elbow. "Sorry, I didn't mean to scare you."

He scrubbed his hand over his face. "Just took me by surprise. Hadn't really considered the possibility."

"Well, there's always the possibility, even when you're taking precautions." She gave a small laugh. "And we do tend to practice quite often." Her lame joke earned no reaction, causing her even greater concern. She took a deep breath, and when she spoke, her voice was small. "I know we married in a rush, Hudson. And not under the best circumstances." Her throat tightened. "If you're having second thoughts about . . ." She stopped talking, unwilling or unable to finish the sentence.

Hudson lifted his arm. In one swift move he rolled her beneath him. "Don't ever say that again. Don't even think it." He bore his weight on his elbows so he could look into her eyes. The intensity she saw there was rivaled only by the emphatic tone of his voice. "You're my fucking world, Allie. The air I breathe. You are the love of my life. You were ten years ago, you are now, and you always will be. Forever."

"But you were so relieved—"

He shook his head. "You caught me off guard, that's all. Of course I want children with you. Do you have any idea what it does to me to think of my child growing inside you?" He reached between them and his fingers brushed her stomach, sending goose bumps racing across her skin. "Christ Allie, I want that. But I'm a selfish bastard and I'm not ready to share you yet."

"I was afraid maybe now that the dust had settled—" This time it was Hudson's raised eyebrow that kept Allie from finishing her thought. His gaze was dark and playful all at once, and if it was any other topic she would have pushed the envelope a bit to see how the scenario played out. But their future wasn't a joking matter. So even though her body was already responding to the thought of whatever delicious torture he might punish her with, she let the naughty fantasy go. "Fine," she said, blushing under the heat of his stare. "I won't say it."

Hudson grinned down at her. "Progress." He reached for her hand and brought their entwined fingers to his lips, pressing a kiss to her wedding band. "You're stuck with me. I would have thought the vows, not to mention these rings, would have proven that point." A crease formed briefly between his brows, then a knowing smile curved his lips. "Don't move," he said, dropping a quick kiss to her mouth before climbing out of the daybed.

Allie rolled onto her stomach and watched him through the glass walls of their villa. He was on the far side of the room, partially obscured by the gauzy white fabric that hung in billowy curtains around the bed. She couldn't quite make out what he was looking for, but whatever it was had something to do with his suitcase. She flipped over when he turned back toward the glass, but not fast enough. *Busted.*

"Do you ever do as you're told?" he asked. His voice was meant to convey disappointment but amusement lit his eyes.

"What?" Allie asked in feigned innocence. "I didn't move." She grinned. "Much."

Hudson smiled and shook his head. "I had these drawn up before we left." In his hand he held a thick document, folded into thirds and tied with a white satin ribbon. Without opening it, she knew it was a legal document, but what she didn't know was what kind. It wasn't a prenup, that was for sure. They'd married not only once without one, but twice. Ben had urged her to allow him to draft something that would protect her family assets, but she'd assured him no such paperwork was necessary. She planned to be married to Hudson for the rest of her life. If their relationship ended, losing half of the assets she acquired during the course of their marriage would be the least of her concerns. Besides, with Hudson's net worth topping into the billions, he was the party with more on the line. Which is why she'd asked him if he wanted *her* to sign a prenuptial agreement. That conversation had lasted approximately ten seconds. Just long enough for Hudson to say the words "No fucking way."

"Consider this a belated wedding gift," he said, passing her the document then stretching out alongside her on the chaise.

"What is it?"

"A stock transfer."

"Hudson, I don't want your shares of Ingram. How they were acquired is irrelevant now. And I rather like being Mr. and Mrs. CEO. I want us to remain partners." She fixed him with a teasing grin. "Assuming of course you can handle it when I dominate the boardroom."

Something dark flashed in his eyes. "Bring it on. Just be prepared for a rough night in the bedroom."

Her breath caught. While Hudson loved to go toe-to-toe with her in the boardroom, he made no apologies for his caveman tendencies once he had her alone in their bed. Or bent over her desk. Or chained to the ceiling. And truth be told, she fucking loved it. "If that was supposed to be a deterrent—"

"It's wasn't."

She cocked her head to one side. "Then what's all this about?"

"Open it," he mouthed.

Allie tugged the ribbon free and unfolded the pages. What she saw stopped her cold. As promised, it was indeed a document authorizing a transfer of stock to Allie's name. But the company in question wasn't Ingram Media. It was Chase Industries. Her eyes were wide when she met his steady gaze. "I can't accept this."

"You can and you will," he said matter-of-factly. As if he was offering her a mai tai and not fifty percent of a multibillion dollar empire.

"You built Chase Industries from the ground up. I can't let you sign half of it over to me."

"The company wouldn't exist if I hadn't met you," he said. "The first time I saw you, my world shifted on its axis. Quite simply, you made me want to be a better man. For you." The breeze kicked up, rustling the thatch roof above their heads and blowing a loose curl across Allie's face. Hudson tucked it behind her ear, letting his knuckles brush across her cheek after he did. "And besides, that's your name on the building too, Mrs. Chase." He leaned closer so his mouth hovered mere inches from hers. You're my wife, my lover, and my partner. Not just at Ingram or Chase. In everything," he whispered just before their lips met.

The word *partner* echoed in Allie's heart and mind as Hudson deepened their kiss. He was right: No matter what obstacles or hardships they faced, they had each other, and they always would.

Forever.

Keep reading for an excerpt from the last book in the Chasing Fire series

EXCERPT: EMBRACE ME

"*L*ook at the size of that cock!"

Allie turned to find her best friend's bright red lips pursed around the head of an enormous penis. Actually, it was a straw in the shape of a penis that she was using to slurp down a hefty portion of her third strawberry daiquiri, but still. Harper's wide eyes were glued to the stage, prompting Allie to wonder if she'd been referring to the oversize drinking utensil or the well-endowed man dancing directly in front of her. Of course they had front-row seats. "Not worth going if you aren't in the splash zone," Harper had said. Allie hadn't bothered to ask what in the world she meant by "splash zone," and something told her she didn't want to know.

Around her the crowd of women buzzed with excitement, not to mention hormones, as they waved fistfuls of cash in the air in an attempt to attract the attention of one of the performers. And there was certainly no shortage of takers. Allie had never seen so much naked flesh in her life. The stage was literally covered with gorgeous men gyrating to the beat of "Pony." It was as if she'd walked out of her office and straight into a scene from *Magic Mike*.

Harper had originally wanted a more traditional bachelorette party, complete with party games that would have no doubt proved embarrassing and a stripper who would have no doubt arrived dressed as a policeman ready to conduct a strip search, handcuffs and all—in other words, Allie's worst nightmare. But Harper was nothing if not persistent, and in the end Allie had agreed to a hen night under the condition that it be just the two of them. In a weak moment she'd even told Harper the rest was up to her, which was how she'd ended up sitting in front of a dozen oily bodies wearing a white sash that read BRIDE-TO-BE.

Allie tucked a loose blond curl behind her ear, then nonchalantly brushed her fingers across her shoulder in an effort to help the satin material slip out of place. With any luck it would only take a few well-timed shifts to send it discreetly to the floor.

"Oh no," Harper said, not missing a beat as she restored the sash to its original position. "You wouldn't wear the crown, but the sash stays on."

Allie cringed. As if she would have walked into the bar sporting a tiara and veil? But since she suspected Harper had envisioned this as a night of trashy gag gifts and drunken rounds of "Never Have I Ever," she thought the least she could do was humor her by wearing the sash. Harper had one, too. Over her black-and-white polka-dot dress she proudly wore a hot pink sash that read MAID OF HONOR. It was a role she'd clearly been born to play, but still, all the fuss seemed ridiculous given the situation. "You know I'm not technically a bachelorette?" she said. "In case you've forgotten, Hudson and I have been married for almost three months."

"As if I could forget. My best friend runs off to elope in what I'm sure was the world's most romantic ceremony and I don't even get so much as a lousy piece of cake." Harper shook her head in feigned disgust. "I still haven't forgiven you." She plucked the strawberry garnish from the rim of her glass, popped it into her mouth, and smiled. "But this is a good first step."

Colored lights dimmed, then flared, as a new song began. A curtain rose at the rear of the stage and a new group of men made their way to the catwalk. They weren't in place for more than a few minutes before they tore their pants away in a simultaneous maneuver that sent the entire club into a near frenzy.

"Fine," Allie said when the crowd calmed. "But can we call it a night after this round and eat Chinese takeout in our flannel pajamas?"

Harper rolled her eyes. "I'd ask if being a married woman has turned you into my grandma, but you were like this before Hudson slipped that rock on your finger, so I can't really blame him."

Allie snorted to herself before taking another sip of her lemon-drop martini. Blame Hudson? Hardly. If anything, her husband had brought out a side of her she'd never experienced before. With Hudson she wasn't the shy, reserved debutante her mother had tried to raise. With him she felt wanton and sexy and free of all her inhibitions. Allie hid her smile behind her glass as thoughts from the previous night filled her mind. The black leather cuffs had made an appearance but this time there were two sets, and when Hudson had explained how he intended to use them . . . well, she dared say even Harper would have blushed. And when he—

"Is there a dick on my head?" A woman at the table next to theirs shrieked, pulling Allie from her very private thoughts and right back into her very public reality. Women whooped and hollered as the red-faced girl attempted to hold completely still while a nearly naked dancer gyrated behind her.

Allie reached for her purse. "On second thought, maybe we should just leave now."

"Can't leave yet," Harper said, never taking her eyes off the spectacle taking place beside them. "You haven't had your turn."

An uneasy feeling began to stir in the pit of Allie's stomach. "My turn?"

Harper's grin was more than mischievous; it was downright wicked. "You didn't think we'd leave before the bride had a lap dance, did you?"

Allie's mouth dropped open. "You're not serious?"

"Indeed I am. So unless you're reaching into that purse for more singles, you can just put it back down"—she nodded to the cowboy weaving between the tables as he made his way toward Allie— "because you're next."

"Jesus fucking Christ." Hudson leaned forward and planted his elbows on his knees as he watched the Chicago Bulls turn the ball over to the Cleveland Cavaliers for the third time in as many minutes. The Bulls had a passionate fan base with a love-to-hate for LeBron James, but the team was trailing in what was sizing up to be more of a massacre than a loss. The season was all but shot if they didn't turn this shit around, and then the courtside seats Chase Industries had shelled out a fortune for might as well be flushed down the ever-loving toilet. Forget about impressing important clients, Hudson wouldn't be able to give the tickets away at this rate.

As if agreeing with him, LeBron sunk a basket from behind the three-point line.

For fuck's sake.

The Bulls couldn't seem to catch a break despite doing their best to recapture the glory days of their nineties dynasty. They'd fired their coach—bringing in a former player to turn things around—and had spent a fortune on point guard Derrick Rose, a local kid who grew up a hard-core Bulls fan and Michael Jordan disciple. Hell, he'd probably cheered them on from the nosebleed seats while sporting Air Jordan 7's. But the kid with a lot of promise had been benched more seasons than he'd played, out with one injury after another. Ninety-four million dollars down the shitter along with his season tickets.

Then, on a powerful drive, Olympic hopeful Jimmy Butler brought the fans in the United Center to their feet when he scored on a crowd-pleasing alley-oop. Thank fuck. Hudson had money riding on the game.

"Ya know," Nick said, once they'd settled back in their chairs, "for the guy whose penthouse is in the old Playboy Club, this has got to be the lamest bachelor party in the history of the world." He took a loud slurp from his blue raspberry ICEE.

Hudson whipped his head to the right and shot his brother a look, but he couldn't knock the smile off his face. Nick's lips were blue from the frigid concoction. "You asked me what I wanted to do. This is what I wanted to do," Hudson said. He glanced down at his watch. Tonight was going to feel like an eternity, and not because the game had gone to hell, but because Allie was out with that redhead doing god knows what. Harper had been tight-lipped about the festivities, which he doubted were taking place around tiny tables set with teacups and canapés.

"Dude, we're supposed to be surrounded by a harem of strippers worshipping us while we go broke stuffing bills into their bras and panties and licking body shots off them. I mean, I don't drink so it would have to be Shirley Temples for me. Maybe a cherry out of the navel." Nick shrugged. "But it's cool. At least I have the Lovabulls, umm, performance to look forward to at halftime."

Hudson cocked a brow at his brother, who'd turned his attention to the Bulls' scantily clad cheerleaders as they attempted to rev up the crowd by shooting T-shirts into the stands with air guns. "And what would Ms. Hayes think about that?"

"She'd be cool." Nick took another long pull from his straw. "Ah, fuck . . . brain . . . freeze." He pinched the bridge of his nose and squeezed his eyes shut. "Oh, shit."

Hudson kicked his head back and laughed as Nick dropped

his fist into the armrest, trying to shake off a headache that must have felt like he'd snorted a line of ice through his nose.

"Laughing at me, bro? Not okay."

"With you, Nicky, not at you." Hudson scrubbed the mop on top of his brother's head. "You need a haircut."

"You just can't resist getting in a shot about my hair, can ya? If it's not that it's my clothes, which you—"

"Advised against." Hudson's gaze followed the players as they sprinted up and down the length of the court. A sharp whistle blew, calling a Cavalier foul. Seemed the refs were finally starting to pay attention to the game.

"I was going to say paid for," Nick chuckled. "Floating your good ol' double C my way wasn't much of a protest."

"I pick my battles wisely. And if you prefer to present yourself to the public looking like . . ." Hudson waved his hand in the air. The outfit Nick had chosen for the evening, while newly purchased, still looked like he'd pulled it out of the hamper. For the life of him Hudson couldn't wrap his head around the concept of buying clothes that were already torn. But hey, at least they were clean. Progress.

"Like . . . ?" Nick taunted.

"Presentation, Nicky."

Nick looked down at his T-shirt and cargo jacket, then over to Hudson, who had opted for a pair of charcoal-gray pants and a cashmere sweater for the evening. "Well, my presentation is fucking wicked while yours is boring and old—"

Loud cheers erupted, cutting Nick off, and Journey's "Don't Stop Believin'" echoed through the stadium. Bulls fans, "stop believin'"? Yeah, not in this lifetime.

Hudson's cell shot off, rivaling Steve Perry's pitch-perfect serenade. He started to dig into his pocket for his phone.

"Do you ever shut that fucking thing off, bro?"

"No. A fact you're aware of from your previous late-night pontifications." Hudson's mouth lifted into a humorous grin.

There was a time when he couldn't make it two nights in a row without a rambling, drunken late-night call from his little brother. The fact that they could joke about it now was nothing short of a miracle.

"Pontifications? More like words of wisdom, my dear brother, wisdom. Pure verbal—"

"Diarrhea?" Hudson said, finishing his sentence for him. While crude, it was apt and on the level of his brother's humor.

"Har-har. Seriously dude, it's your bachelor party," Nick said, using his fingers as air quotes to accentuate the words "bachelor party." "Take a night off."

"My work never takes a night off."

Nick rolled his eyes. "Yeah, you're right. Better get that. It could be Pepper Potts alerting you to Iron Man up."

"At least you chose the appropriate Marvel superhero—dashing, brilliant, and—"

"Cocky as hell?"

"Rules with an iron fists." Hudson chuckled as he lifted his phone to his right ear and plugged a finger into his left. His brows furrowed as he listened to the head of his security team on the other end of the call. It only took a few words from Max for him to know he'd heard enough. "Text me the address," he said before ending the call with a jab of his thumb. He rose to his feet in a rush, the phone gripped tight in his hand. "We're leaving."

"What? The game's not over. Hell, it's not even halftime."

"I mean it, Nick. Let's go."

"Fine." Nick shoved his half empty cup into the holder on the armrest. "What's the big emergency? Is Captain America moving in on your territory? Or did the Incredible Hulk bust out?" he asked, following Hudson as he made a beeline for the exit.

"Something like that," he said, never breaking stride.

ACKNOWLEDGMENTS

Our acknowledgments always begin with a nod to our agent, Pamela Harty, and this book is no exception. We thank our lucky stars to have an agent who not only offers continuous support and encouragement, but who loves our characters almost as much as we do. Pamela, the Chasing Fire series wouldn't exist without you and the fact that you teared up when we told you how it ends made the journey seem all the more complete.

Huge thanks to our editor Leis Pederson and her assistant Bethany Blair. We could talk about Hudson Chase with you ladies until the restaurant closes around us . . . oh wait, we did! To Erin Galloway and Ryanne Probst, thank you for helping us spread the word about our sexy CEO. And to Lisa Filipe, you are the Queen of Blog Tours. You not only came through for us when we needed it the most, but you always go the extra mile. Not to mention coining the hashtag #HudsonChaser, which in case we haven't told you is flipping amazing!

Each book in the series has been dedicated to David Gandy, our inspiration for Hudson Chase, but we would be remiss if we didn't also thank his assistant, Laura Terhune, and the people who make up the Gandy Nation. Thank you for the chance to fan girl along with you on a daily basis. Laura, it was an honor and a privilege to have you as our guest at our first official signing. So glad to call you friend!

To the bloggers and readers who astound us with their support: whether Tweeting, posting on Facebook or just telling your friends and family, your endorsements and kind words mean so much to us. To those who maintain the Chasing Fire fan sites and to the role players who devote their time and talents to making the series interactive, thank you for your creativity and dedication. We will never forget the day we got an e-mail that said, "Hudson Chase is now following you on Twitter."

ABOUT THE AUTHORS

Ann Marie Walker writes steamy books about sexy boys. She's a fan of fancy cocktails, anything chocolate, and 80s rom-coms and her super power is connecting any situation to an episode of *Friends*. If it's December she can be found watching *Love Actually* but the rest of the year you can find her at AnnMarie-Walker.com. Ann Marie attended the University of Notre Dame and currently lives in Chicago.

Amy K. Rogers writes contemporary romance about sexy, alpha men. She loves good wine, cheese of any variety and finding hidden speakeasies. On a rare quiet night she can be found watching old James Bond films. After living in San Francisco for 20 years followed by a short stint in Oregon, Amy recently relocated back to the beaches of Los Angeles.

Made in the USA
Columbia, SC
06 July 2022

62814342R00174